Please check all items for damages
before leaving the Library.
Thereafter you will be held
responsible for all injuries
to items beyond reasonable wear.

Helen M. Plum Memorial Library

Lombard, Illinois

A daily fine will be charged for
overdue materials.

FEB   2015

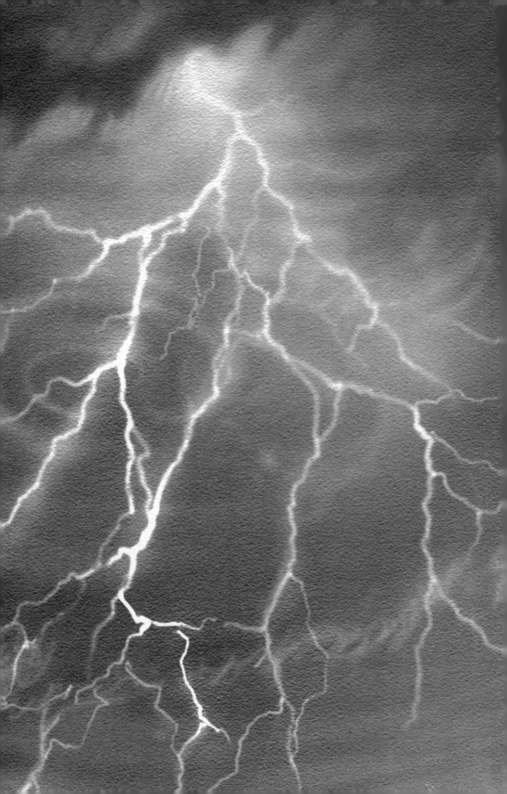

THE BOOK OF STORMS

Ruth Hatfield

Henry Holt and Company
New York

FICTION
HATFIELD

Henry Holt and Company, LLC
Publishers since 1866
175 Fifth Avenue
New York, New York 10010
mackids.com

Henry Holt® is a registered trademark of Henry Holt and Company, LLC.
Text copyright © 2014 by Ruth Hatfield
Illustrations copyright © 2015 by Greg Call
All rights reserved.

Published in the United Kingdom in 2014 by Hot Key Books.
Published in the United States of America in 2015 by Henry Holt and Company, LLC.

Library of Congress Cataloging-in-Publication Data
Hatfield, Ruth.
The Book of Storms / Ruth Hatfield. — First edition.
pages   cm
Summary: When his parents disappear after a fierce storm, eleven-year-old Danny,
unaccustomed to acts of bravery, comes to their rescue after finding a valuable shard of
wood that enables him to talk to plants and animals and battle terrifyingly powerful enemies,
including the demonic Sammael.
    ISBN 978-0-8050-9998-0 (hardback) — ISBN 978-0-8050-9999-7 (e-book)
[1. Adventure and adventurers—Fiction.   2. Storms—Fiction.   3. Missing persons—
Fiction.   4. Supernatural—Fiction.   5. Human-animal communication—Fiction.]
I. Title.
PZ7.1.H38Bo 2015   [Fic]—dc23   2014029352

Henry Holt books may be purchased for business or promotional use. For information on
bulk purchases, please contact the Macmillan Corporate and Premium Sales Department at
(800) 221-7945 ×5442 or by e-mail at specialmarkets@macmillan.com.

First American edition—2015

Printed in the United States of America by R. R. Donnelley & Sons Company, Harrisonburg,
Virginia

10 9 8 7 6 5 4 3 2 1

To L & L

~ CONTENTS ~

The house is falling in.

The house is falling and Danny is falling, knees and elbows crumpling onto the floor, and an earsplitting crash is tearing through the air—that's surely the roof, breaking in two, about to come pelting down on top of him.

His bedroom is flashing with the screams of rain and thunder bolts poured out by a storm in full, raging flow. Outside, the wind is flinging itself against buildings, howling into chimneys, twisting trees round benches, and leaping in spiteful glee as bicycles crash into cars and roof tiles fly through windows. The sky is singing with thunder, and an iron avalanche of hail is pounding onto the glistening roads.

Danny listens for a moment. As his bedroom curtains blaze with lightning, he curls his fingers tightly around the duvet, wanting to pull it over his head and hide in the soft darkness. But even that won't save him when the house breaks apart. He'll be crushed inside it. Trapped under fallen roof beams, he'll struggle for air. Once the last breath has been squeezed out of him, he'll die.

He shivers, watching flash after flash through the crack in the curtains. More than anything, he wants to creep into his parents' bedroom, even though he knows he's too old now for that sort of nonsense. And anyway, his parents aren't home. Always, at the first sign of a storm, they run outside, pile into the car, and drive away to the nearest high point. They go to watch how storms behave, they say.

And he has to stay in his bed. But they've told him what to do.

Don't go to the window. Don't look outside. Hide under the duvet, cover your face, and everything will be fine. It's only a storm: only rain and wind, thunder and lightning. Close your eyes and go back to sleep. Just tell yourself: it's only a storm.

The skin of his scalp prickles, as if a horde of ants is burrowing into his hair. He clambers back up into bed and tries to force himself to sleep.

The night around him begins to burn with lightning; he closes his eyes and buries them in the crook of his arm. Everything will be all right in the morning. Everything is always all right in the morning. His parents come back, and he eats breakfast with them and laughs about how silly it is to be so scared by a thunderstorm. However long the night and thick the darkness, however loud the roaring storm, the morning always comes.

CHAPTER I

THE SYCAMORE

Danny O'Neill rubbed his eyes against the sunlight and wandered into his parents' bedroom to find some clean socks from the washing pile. The double bed was empty, the crumpled bedclothes thrown back. Normally they made their bed as soon as they were up.

Danny put his hand on his short brown hair and tried to press it down to his scalp.

"Mum?" he called. "Mum? Dad?"

The house echoed with silence.

"Dad?" he tried again.

Again there was no answer.

Perhaps they were outside doing something in the garden. It was a bit early, but parents did strange things sometimes, for odd reasons of their own.

Downstairs in the hallway he found the front door ajar and the carpet soaked with rainwater. The phone table had blown against the bookcase and overturned, spreading scraps of wet paper all over the walls. Two framed pictures had fallen off their hooks and smashed against the baseboard. They were both of baby Emma, who'd died before Danny was born, and they'd hung there his whole life, fading a little more every time the sun broke through into the hall. Now that the glass was broken, raindrops had splashed over Emma's cheeks, giving her a red rash that looked like chicken pox.

Where were his parents? They always came home. They were always there in the morning, no matter what happened at night.

He picked up the phone and tried to call their mobiles, but both numbers put him through to a recorded voice. Dead.

A thin breeze pierced his cotton pajamas, puckering his skin into goose bumps. As the prickling sensation crawled up over his neck, he wasn't sure that it was all due to the cold.

The house was entirely still.

He padded through the kitchen to the back door, his feet leaving wet prints on the tiles, and pressed his nose against the glass panel. Twigs, leaves, and pieces of broken fence littered the lawn, but it wasn't until Danny stepped outside that he saw what had woken him in the middle of the night. The old sycamore tree had been struck by a huge bolt of lightning and had split, right down its trunk, almost to the smoking earth.

It stood blackened and dead. A swing once tied to a low branch hung melted on its chains, and a few wisps of mist clung around the ground where the trunk was whole.

The lightning had struck only yards from his house. Only yards from the bedroom where he'd lain, trembling under his covers.

For a second Danny forgot his parents and gazed at the twisted wood. He wanted to reach out and touch the charcoal branches. Would they feel solid, or somehow light? Would they crumble away into dust under his fingers? A patch of ashy debris lay around the trunk: gray-black lumps of sycamore and charred stems of undergrowth. He stooped down, wondering if it was still warm, and his eye stopped, noticing something brown against the black cinders. A stick the color of the old, living tree.

He picked it up. Although the stick was as thin as a pencil, it didn't crumble but stayed hard, refusing to break under the pressure of his fingers. For a second he frowned, wondering at its strange heaviness.

A low moaning sound crept into his ear.

"The last . . . the most precious piece of me. . . . Oh . . ."

Danny instantly knew it was the tree that had spoken, although he had no idea how he'd known. It hadn't moved a single twig.

"Hello?" he said, unsure of how to address a dying tree.

"Oh . . . don't bother . . . with the niceties. . . ." The tree was gasping a little now. "No time . . . It had to be . . . Step into the light. I can hardly see you. . . ."

Danny was standing in bright sunlight. "I'm in the light," he said.

"Oh . . . oh . . . there's light. . . . Then this must be the darkness . . . and there's no time . . . not for anything. . . . No time left . . ."

The tree fell silent. Danny cast his eyes around for something to make it talk again. What had it said? The most precious piece of it? The last? He looked down at the stick in his hand. Maybe if he returned the last good piece to the tree, it would have some energy left to speak.

He stepped forward and wedged the stick into the cleft trunk. As soon as his hand let go, the world seemed to fall silent. Birds sang and traffic rumbled along in the distance, but a frozen hush hung about the air.

The tree shook. Danny thought it looked more like a shiver of anger than one of death, but then, what did he know about the body language of trees? Either way, returning the stick didn't seem to have helped.

With a last spasm, the stick fell to the ground and Danny bent to pick it up again. As soon as his fingers touched it, he heard the tree's voice, much fainter this time.

"Idiot boy . . . I can't . . . You'll have to . . . work it out . . . but . . . why is . . . Where is it? Why not . . . come . . . back . . ."

"Work out what?" asked Danny. "What d'you want to get back?"

The tree was losing the last breath of its speech, and the words that followed were said carefully, as if it knew it had no time to think of more impressive ones.

"It's . . . Sammael. . . . He wants . . . He'll use sand . . . put dreams . . . in your mind. . . . Be careful . . . who you ask. . . . Most important . . . most . . ."

The last sigh drained from the sycamore tree, and the earth under Danny's feet seemed to swell in one final clench before settling back down into scorched lawn. He looked at the stick in his hand, then put it down and picked it up again. Each time his fingers let go of it, the same hush seemed to fall.

He tried clutching it tightly and saying "hello!" in as

clear a voice as he could muster. To which he could have sworn he heard a faint, echoing gasp that rippled for a moment around his feet like the wind swaying through a cornfield. But nothing more.

Danny decided that he'd better tell his dad, who knew about trees. Swinging around, he stopped with one foot half in the air as he remembered. His parents weren't there. And they weren't here, either.

What could have happened? Maybe when they'd gone to look at the storm, they'd been trapped somewhere and couldn't get out.

Maybe they were dead.

No. He shook his head to clear it of the thought. They couldn't be dead. Someone must know where they were.

Perhaps if he told someone else—but he didn't quite like the idea of that, either. Last Christmas, up at Aunt Kathleen's farm, he'd said something about being outside in a storm and there'd been a furious row—Mum going off-her-head ballistic at Aunt Kathleen, and Aunt Kathleen yelling about obsession, and Dad screaming about how she'd get Social Services sniffing round them again, as if last time wasn't bad enough.

Even though Danny's parents sometimes ignored him for so long that he reckoned he could walk halfway to France before they noticed he'd gone, there was something about the idea of Social Services that made him nervous. Sure, Mum was always on the computer, and Dad mostly hung around outside staring at the clouds, and sometimes dinner didn't happen until he was so sleepy that he nearly fell asleep facedown in mashed potato, but at least the things around him were his own. And his parents might be scatty, but they did make sure he had a nice home and clean clothes, so even when dinner *was* late, at least he didn't have to go to school the next day in the same potato-crusted shirt.

But Social Services would look at his family and see what they didn't do, not what they did, and he had a pretty good idea that they wouldn't like what they saw.

What else could he do? Monday mornings meant going to school. Danny always quite enjoyed them, because they had double art and there wasn't a proper art teacher anymore, so he got to keep his head down and draw whatever he liked while the rest of the class made their phones bark like dogs and tried to climb out the window, then come back in through the door without the substitute teacher noticing. Art was the only class where nobody looked at the clock.

He felt a strong urge to be there, sitting at the quiet table by the window, trying to draw something complicated. He never thought about anything when he was drawing, apart from lines and shadows.

Well, why not? Maybe his parents were just delayed

somewhere. They'd probably driven farther than they'd meant to, that was all. They would definitely be back when he came home.

Danny stepped back inside, put the stick on the table, and got himself a bowl of cornflakes. He sat down, but he couldn't manage more than a couple of mouthfuls of cereal before he started to feel sick.

What was that stick? Sitting next to his bowl on the table, it just looked like an ordinary piece of stick. His fingers wanted to reach out and pick it up again, but he was suddenly scared of what else might happen. Would he hear other strange voices, breaking through the silence of the house?

No, of course not. His mind was playing tricks on him. Or someone else was. Yeah, that must be it—his parents liked trying to catch each other out with silly tricks, and they'd just played one on him. That's all it was. A silly trick.

He got dressed and picked up his schoolbag. Some trick. Whatever his parents were doing, it wasn't very funny.

"Bye!" he shouted backwards as he left the house, so that if they were around, they'd know he hadn't been fooled. And as he walked down the path to the garden gate he listened hard for sounds in the house behind him.

But when he turned his head around for a last look, there was still nobody there.

CHAPTER 2

KALIA

The gray lurcher put her head between her front paws and waited. Sometimes there was nothing else to do. The room was dark, her coat did little to protect her from the biting cold, and the air stank of ripe decay.

She'd have watched the clock, but her master didn't hold with clocks. What was the point of time to someone like him?

The crackling of breaking twigs stirred the dog into raising her head. A heavy tread—he had brought someone back with him, then. These days he normally did. And even though he could have kept his journey short and neat, could have spun back into this bitter room with a flick of his wrist, he still preferred walking as much as possible. He said it gave him time to see what life was up to.

The lurcher was ready and standing by the time he ducked through the doorway.

"Another one gone, Kalia," he said, and slung the corpse onto the floor in front of her.

Kalia sniffed at it and wrinkled her muzzle. She was well used to corpses by now, but this one was a young girl, smooth skinned and frail with a stretched face as though she'd struggled in the last minutes of her life.

"Don't turn your nose up, mutt," said Sammael, taking off his long coat.

As he turned to hang it on a peg, the lurcher glanced up at him. When he wore the coat, he could get away with walking among humans—he almost looked like one, if a little too tall and thin, with eyes a fraction too black. But now that he'd taken it off, she could see that his arms were narrow as broomsticks, his shoulders as sharp as wings, and his skin paler than ice.

"And don't stare at me," said Sammael, turning back to the corpse.

"I'm not staring," said the dog. "It's what my eyes look like when they're looking. Oh, but you've been gone so long, I missed you. Why wouldn't you let me come?"

"Some things aren't for dogs," said Sammael. "I had a bit of business to sort out. Your presence wasn't necessary."

"What sort of business?"

Sammael didn't reply. Instead, he rolled up his shirt-sleeves and bent over the young girl's corpse, placing his bony palm against her shoulder. For a moment nothing happened, then the girl began silently to disintegrate. Her skin puckered and shriveled, twisting into knotty lumps. The features on her face crawled toward each other and screwed themselves up into twists. Her eyes shrank into raisins, her lips into a tiny walnut.

After a few seconds, she seemed to be weeping through the pores of her skin, but it wasn't water that oozed out. Grains of sand were pushing themselves between the stitches of her clothes and forming little mounds, spreading in a mass over the smooth stone floor.

It took less time than usual. She must have been very small.

Sammael picked up the pile of clothes, shook them out carefully so that each clinging grain was returned to the floor, then chucked them into a corner. He surveyed the sand. A pathetic amount. Hardly worth the effort.

"I should have given her more time," he muttered. "But she didn't think to ask for any. All this one wanted was to be able to slide down a rainbow. Can you believe it?"

"Only that?" asked Kalia. "She didn't ask for anything else at all?"

"Only that," said Sammael. "She could have demanded hundreds of years in exchange for her soul—she'd no idea what it was worth. But she sold it to me in exchange for the power to slide down a rainbow. And then she got to the bottom of the rainbow and fell straight into the middle of the sea. Drowned in minutes."

He looked at the lurcher. Her tail wagged.

"You didn't sell yourself so short, did you?" he said. "You've gotten all you wanted out of me. You could have all the rainbows you like, without giving up a second of your life for them. Here you go."

He stooped down, picked up a couple of grains of the sand, and cast them into the air. A rainbow blazed up along their path, filling the room with light of every color. It hung for a few seconds, caressing the faces of dog and master, then swooped into a corner and exploded into a shrieking fire of emerald green. Sammael watched the fire as it gradually died.

The dog pattered forward and pressed herself against his leg. Fingers like icicles brushed her head.

"Old mutt," he said. "Come on, let's get this lot stored away with the rest. There's enough sand there now to put dreams into the heads of a million creatures."

As Kalia gazed up at his shuttered face she saw a flicker of muscles across his cheeks, pulling his mouth into something that could possibly have passed for a human smile.

"What things they could have done," he said softly. "What dreams I could have given them."

Then the smile vanished completely. "But it's too late now. They should have thanked me while they had the chance. It's too late for them all now."

And he turned away to fetch his brush.

The strange brush was made of some kind of hair, although the strands were so fine that Kalia's own hairs seemed like fat dreadlocks beside them. It swept up every single grain of sand, so that nothing escaped or was wasted, but she'd never dared ask whose hairs it was made from. Instead she watched as he methodically cleared the floor until the stone slabs were spotless again.

When he'd swept the last of the girl's sand into a box and balanced the box on top of a neat stack, he put his coat back on. The coat smelled of earth, rain, and age.

"Right," he said. "Let's go and see what that storm left behind."

Kalia trotted after him. She had to press herself to his legs while they stepped through the doorway, so that he remembered to reach down a hand and take hold of her wiry hair. Sometimes he went too fast and she didn't get to him in time, then she had to travel alone through places that no mortal creature should ever see, between the solid world of the earth and the high, thin air. They did odd things to a dog, those places. The last time she'd been separated from her master, she'd ended up with purple feet and ivy growing out of her toes and curling up around her legs.

Sammael had laughed and cut off the ivy, but he'd left the purple hair growing on her feet.

"Teach you to meddle, mutt," he'd said. "Teach you to sell yourself into things you've no idea about. Although I suppose the purple does add a certain point of interest to your otherwise dull legs."

She'd tried licking her feet. The purple hadn't budged. Sometimes she looked down at it and thought it might be spreading up her legs, but it was hard to be sure.

No more mistakes, though. She leaned close up to his legs this time. Stretching tall out of scuffed old boots, they were as hard as lampposts.

By the time they'd walked the entire path of the storm, all the way from the hills where it had gathered to the island where the last raindrops had been squeezed from its clouds, Kalia's purple feet were sore and stuck with thorns. She flopped down in the shade of a bush and began gnawing at her pads.

The bright June sunshine shone above them. They had stopped on a shingle beach, which fell flat and gray back toward the sea. A couple of terns sat dozing over their nests, but nothing else stirred along the beach, apart from the dry wind.

Sammael frowned. He fished out a notebook from his trouser pocket and flicked through it. Its pages were thinner than spider's-web silk.

"The storm should have left another taro behind," he said.

"A taro?" asked the lurcher. "Haven't you picked it up yet? There've been loads of sticks and acorns and things—I thought it was always one of them. . . ." Her voice trailed off for a moment, and then, before she could sigh, she said very faintly, "Does that mean we have to go back again and look for it, all that way?"

"Of course not, you fool!" snapped Sammael. "I would have found it if it'd been there!" He ran a finger down the page of writing. "But I suppose one can't always be sure with storms. What a waste of time. Except I did sort out those idiots."

"Idiots? Oh . . . you mean those two humans in the cold-smelling house. What did they do?"

"They were dabbling in storms, trying to find out how to 'control' them. Control them! Hah! I thought I'd show them a little bit of what they were up against."

His mouth twisted into a scornful smile. Kalia was about to ask what he'd done with the humans when an urgent twinge across her well-kicked ribs reminded her that he disliked too many questions.

Then Sammael's head went up and his jaw clenched. Kalia hadn't heard anything, although that wasn't unusual. Sammael's ears were sharper than those of any earthly creature. He listened for a while, the sunlight prodding at his thick black hair. When finally he relaxed again, Kalia stole another long gaze at him.

"It's that flying ant," he said. "I knew something was wrong."

The flying ant had come a long way from home to deliver its news. Although its tiny wings were exhausted, it shifted anxiously and tried to give over its message as quickly as possible.

". . . The boy picked up a stick and spoke, right out loud, spoke so's I could hear . . . and the grass went very still and the tree shook, so something must've gone on with them, too. Humans talking! How would that happen? It's never happened before, not that I know of. . . ."

"A human talking? Indeed. And you heard him?" Sammael watched the ant on the back of his hand, treading at his pale skin.

The ant was too worried about leaving to give more than a glance back at him.

"I did. He said 'hello.' Just 'hello,' and a couple of other things that didn't really make sense. But it must be because of something *you've* done, mustn't it? I thought that when I was halfway here. I thought, I don't know why I'm going off to tell Sammael—it must be something he's done, anyway, given this human the power to talk in exchange for his soul. You're the only creature who could do something like that. You made me able to fly farther than any other ant in the world—no one else could have done that, could they?"

"Hmm," said Sammael. "A stick, you said. You're sure he picked up a stick?"

"Just before he spoke, yes. A stick from the tree that had been struck by lightning."

Sammael thought, for longer than the ant could bear. Visions of being grabbed by sentry ants and dragged before the queen began to screen through its mind—of being accused of that most heinous of ant crimes: Desertion of Duty. Its feet twitched. "But if it's a problem, you can just take his powers off him again, can't you?" it twittered. "I mean, like I said, I don't know why I thought I should come and tell you about it, only I suppose it did seem so strange at the time. . . . Look, I really have to go. . . ."

"Scared of your little ant friends, are you?" Sammael raised an eyebrow. "But you can fly forever. Why don't you just fly away from them?"

"I'm an ant," said the ant. "I can't live without other ants. Please . . . please, I have to . . ."

"Go." Sammael waved his hand, and the ant flew through the air. As soon as it landed, it spun on its hind legs and scrabbled at the ground, then hurtled away.

Sammael didn't bother to watch it go—it was just an ant. Instead he stared at his hands and faced a couple of unpleasant facts. There *had* been a taro. And somehow, although it was the kind of thing that ought never to have happened, it had been found by a human. Was it as the ant had said? Was the human beginning to uncover the taro's power?

There was really only one thing for him to do. And it had to be done quickly, before mere uncovering turned into full understanding.

Sammael clicked his fingers to Kalia. "Get up," he said. "We've work to do."

Kalia wasn't sure she'd followed all the stuff about the stick and the talking and the lightning, but she'd managed to remove the final thorns from her paws. Her pads still stung. Standing up would be painful, especially on the sharp stones of the beach.

"My feet do hurt an awful lot. . . ." she whimpered.

"Fine," snapped Sammael, turning his back on her. "Find your own way home."

Kalia scrambled up and leapt after him. He'd already taken three giant strides toward the sea's edge by the time she caught up. "Wait! I can't go back without you! You know what happened last time!"

"Bah! You can turn into an entire forest full of purple ivy for all the difference it makes to me."

Sammael's face was motionless, his eyes tight and hard. As he strode over the shingle toward the sea, Kalia raced to stay with him. Once he started walking, unless he was kind to her, she could never keep up—he could walk faster than the wind if he chose to. Or he could just go back through the strange lands into the room and come out again wherever he pleased. Mostly he avoided doing that when she was with him, but Kalia hadn't seen him this angry since he'd used the sand to put an idea for making a telephone into the head of a man called Bell. And then Bell had taken all the credit of course, and Sammael had been driven even wilder than usual; the lurcher suspected it might have been an idea he was particularly proud of.

There was nothing proud about him now. He reached a hand out to grab the back of Kalia's neck so she could stay with him, but he didn't look at her and he didn't speak anymore.

As they swept together into the whispering sea, her bruised pads and bony knuckles scraped over the pebbles and knocked against sharp rocks hidden just under the surface of the water. Sammael didn't swim. When he crossed the sea, each foot touched the top of a wave and stayed firm against its crest. But Kalia had been born a dog, just like any other, and the waves wanted to swallow her up. Especially now, when Sammael was paying no attention to her.

She gasped for breath as the waves smashed over her nose. Sammael's hand tightened on the hair at the scruff of her neck.

"How can some numskull blundering human have got his hands on *that*?" He yanked at Kalia's neck as a large wave rose up, curling in front of them. She choked but was saved from the stinging spray.

"Does it—urgh!—does it matter?" She struggled for more air as his grip tightened so much that her own neck skin nearly throttled her.

"Of course it does!"

She should have saved her breath. He never got angry without good reason.

"But what could a *human* do with it?"

With relief she spotted the mainland thickening the horizon ahead. They'd be there in seconds. Kalia didn't suppose for a moment that Sammael would answer her last question, but talking at least stopped her from thinking about the leagues of sea below.

However, once he'd dragged her up onto the next beach and begun walking over firm ground again, he let his pace slacken a little and, after a long silence, began to speak.

"A human could do all sorts of things with that stick," he said.

The sand dunes whizzing by beneath them turned into scrubby seaside fields. Sammael vaulted over hedges and gates, as weightless as a paper bag on the wind. But Kalia wasn't sure about the way his chin had sunk down into the collar of his coat. This was usually a sign of evil rage, the lasting kind.

She glanced nervously up at his face. A dark flame had begun to dance in the pupils of his eyes, and his skin flickered with shadow.

A cloud rolled over the sun. Kalia shivered as the breeze

cut through her shaggy coat. She longed to sit on his feet and prevent him from going back to wherever this lightning was supposed to have fallen. Nothing could go well when Sammael gave himself up to white-hot fury.

"I'll kill him," said Sammael. "That brat is a walking barbecue already."

"Couldn't you just take the taro off him?" Kalia ventured, shuffling a little closer to his boots.

He landed a kick on her ribs, sending her flying sideways. She scrabbled to stand upright, shaking earth out of her ear.

"You forget yourself, Kalia," said Sammael. "Do you think I need a dog to suggest ideas to me? The taro's his now. If I yanked it from his dead fingers, it'd still be his. But at least if he were dead, he couldn't use it."

"I was only asking," Kalia whimpered, licking her bedraggled fur where his boot had stuck wet mud to it.

Sammael continued walking toward some distant hills, leaving the lurcher no time to explore her bruises. She raced to keep up with him, ignoring the pain in her ribs. He was muttering to himself; it wasn't until she'd sprinted right up close again that she heard what he was saying.

"Merry Old England." The words, full of scorn and venom, barely reached Kalia's ears before they were swept away on the breeze from the distant sea. "I'll turn those gray clouds of yours jet black, as soon as I've dealt with him. That's a promise."

And Kalia the lurcher, who had been born in Shropshire and learned to love the wide-open green of the hills that she'd raced over as a young dog, had to close her eyes for the briefest of seconds against a sharp stab at her heart.

I'm his dog, she told herself. His dog. And I'll always stand by him, no matter what.

"Good," said Sammael, looking down at her with a nasty grin on his thin lips. "You know your place, dog. And now I'll teach this human exactly where he belongs too."

CHAPTER 3

THE NOTEBOOK

At three o'clock, Danny ran the entire mile from the schoolyard to his own house. When he arrived at the front gate, panting hard, he didn't look at the house, because houses always looked still from the outside. However silent it seemed at first, there'd be people inside, he knew it.

Next door's cat, a long-haired tabby with a white front and a tail as bushy as a feather duster, was lying along the fence that separated the gardens, basking in the sun. She blinked at Danny as he went past.

He put out a hand to stroke her plushy side, getting his breath back. Even though he'd run home so fast, a small part of him wanted to put off going inside for a few more seconds. Just in case.

"Hey, Mitz."

The cat was called Mitten, which had only suited her when she'd been about the size of one. Under his fingers, her fur was warm and familiar. She pushed her head against him, wanting a scratch behind her ears.

"Are they there, Mitz?" he whispered. Of course she didn't answer.

"Right." He forced his feet to the front door, unlocked it, and stepped inside. "Mum?" he called. "Mum?"

Nothing stirred. Danny went through to the kitchen and his stomach went cold. The bowl of pale orange mush with the spoon beside it lay on the table. There was no use pretending any longer. No one had been in the house all day.

And there was the stick. That piece of twig, the size and shape of a pencil, waiting for him. What would happen if he picked it up? Probably something odd, like before. Oddness and aloneness weren't easy to deal with together.

If baby Emma had stayed alive and grown up to be his sister, the two of them could have been jumping on the beds by then, throwing stuff down the stairs, dragging food out of the cupboards, making dens out of the furniture in the front room, and waging war through the house. They could have done whatever they liked, with no parents around to tell them to keep quiet or tidy up. But what would be the point on his own?

Or maybe, if Emma had been alive, she'd have just gone out and found them already. She wouldn't have been scared and stupid and run off to school.

Danny stood by the table, looking at the stick. He could feel its contours under his palm, as vividly as if he were already holding it. It would be warm, like the cat's fur. It would fit him somehow.

So he picked it up and listened.

At first there was silence again. Then a thin whine wheedled out from somewhere to his left, over by the window.

"... It just isn't *right*, all of this. Staying in the same place every day, staring out there at all that. . . . What *is* all that?"

Then another voice, slightly rougher in tone. "It's grass, innit? But out there's a battleground. You don't wanna be out there. . . ."

"We should be fighting! We should be fighting the good fight, standing up for ourselves, striving against all that horrible, bitty, stringy stuff! Who will fight if we don't? And then there'll be none of us left, and the world will be covered in those . . . those *strands*. Except we'll still be here, looking out at it, powerless to help our brethren."

" 'Xactly," said the other voice. "We're better off in here."

It was the two potted plants on the windowsill. Danny could even understand which one was which—the furry-leaved geranium was the first voice, while the spiky aloe that his mum squeezed goo from to heal burns was the second, quieter one.

"How can you say that?!" the geranium shrieked. "What would the world come to if we were all like you? We should be marching! We should be shouting! We should be squashing that . . . that grass with our leaves until it goes white and rots in the soil! We should be *murdering* it as it sleeps! The world belongs to the *plants*, and we're sitting here just staring!"

Danny opened his fingers sharply and dropped the stick back onto the table. It rattled against the cereal bowl and lay still. Potted plants, shouting at each other? Talking about murder? It was . . . it was just *weird*.

He stared at the stick. If the sycamore tree could talk and the plants could talk . . . there must be other things that could too. Things that might have seen his parents leave. There could be a whole trail of them, along the garden path and the street outside and the roads leading out of town. He could just ask them all, one by one by one, and follow his parents like that. Except that the tree had been crazy and the plants were crazy and this whole *thing* was crazy. There weren't sticks that made you hear things talk—they didn't *exist*, and he must be still dreaming, in his bed.

But this was far too long to be a dream.

And then he thought, Mitz the cat, sitting outside on the fence. She stayed out all night, didn't she? Last night she'd probably been sheltering from the storm, crouching underneath the bushes close to the houses and trying to keep her fur dry. What if she could talk too? Mitz didn't seem like an angry sort of cat, so she might not start yelling loads of scary stuff about murder. And at least hearing animals talk might be a bit less strange than plants.

Mitz was still languishing on the fence, her fur spilling over both sides. Danny approached her, holding the stick in front of him like a sword. She watched, her great yellow eyes unblinking.

Perhaps she ought not to know about the stick. The tree had told him to be careful, after all. He put it in his pocket, keeping hold of it.

"Mitz?" he said, tentatively. "Mitz, can you hear me?"

The cat's eyes stayed very still, fixed on his face. She said nothing.

So it didn't work, then. The other voices must just have been a trick. Danny turned away, not knowing whether to be relieved or angry.

"Was that you?" the cat asked.

He turned back to her. She didn't move her mouth or make any cat sounds when she spoke, but he heard her thin voice, as soft as milk.

"Was that *you*?" he echoed.

Mitz blinked and stretched out a paw in his direction. It didn't alter her balance in the slightest.

"That was me," she said. "But was it you?"

Danny nodded. Did cats nod? Would she even understand what a nod was? "Yes," he said.

"Odd," said the cat. "I would have sworn you weren't a cat. But you're talking to me. I thought only cats could talk."

"Cats . . . and me," said Danny. Perhaps if he didn't try to explain anything, she might not even think to ask.

Mitz pulled back her paw, tucked it underneath her body again, and regarded him with the same unmoving stare.

"Strange," she said. "Very strange."

Danny resisted the hysterical laugh that wanted to burst

out of his lungs. What was so funny, anyway? He shouldn't want to laugh, not right now.

"Were you out in the storm last night?" he asked. "Did you see my parents? They're not here anymore, and I don't know where they've gone."

"I did see them," said the cat. "Urgh, what a night! I was crouching under the privet by the gate, and even that didn't stop the rain getting through. And all that horrible dirt, splashed up by the raindrops! I was surprised they came outside in it, to be honest."

She gave her white bib a couple of licks, whether in memory or to dislodge actual dirt Danny couldn't be sure. His heart began to quicken.

"Where did they go?"

"They got into the car and drove off," said Mitz. "That way." She flicked her tail and turned her gaze toward the end of the street that went out of town.

What more would a cat know? They'd driven away and hadn't come back.

"That's it?" asked Danny. "They didn't say anything?"

"I wouldn't know if they had, would I?" said Mitz. "*They* didn't appear to be able to talk. Though I must say, I've always wondered how you humans communicated with each other. You don't have tails or ears, and you don't seem to smell things much. It must be difficult."

"Not really," said Danny. "We do talk. Actually . . . *we* think that only *we* can. But . . . this is just too weird. I've got to find my parents, that's all."

He looked at the front hedge. If it could see like the potted plants, it must have seen the car leave. He could try asking it . . . but what if the plants outside were even angrier than the plants inside?

Surely there must be some more normal, human way of trying to find his parents. Danny took a couple of steps back toward the house, forgetting that his hand was still in his pocket, holding the odd little stick.

"Hold on!" called Mitz, pushing herself up onto her furry white paws and arching her striped back. "You can't just talk to me and run away! I've never talked to a human, not *ever*! The way you're going about it, anyone would think you've been chatting away to cats all your life. You haven't, have you?"

She dropped from the fence onto the ground by Danny's feet. Cats were such silent creatures. They walked, sprinted, prowled, and washed, all without making a sound. Hearing a long stream of words pouring out from one, even though it looked exactly the same as normal, made the mysterious seem a little mundane.

"No," said Danny. "No, I haven't ever spoken to a cat before."

"Then why now? *How* now?"

Danny fingered the stick, trying not to shake his head in disbelief. "I just can," he said. "Some people can."

Quickly, before Mitz could speak again, he stumbled into the house. The cat followed him, trotting neatly at his ankles.

He tried phoning Aunt Kathleen. She never answered her home phone during the day, because she was a dairy farmer and was almost always somewhere around the cattle yards or fields, tending to cow wounds or disease infestations. Most of the time, she didn't answer her mobile either, because cows needed to be attended to with one hand and held tightly with the other, but this time she must have had Danny's cousin Tom with her, because a man's voice answered her phone.

"Yup?"

Not that Tom was a man—he was only sixteen. But he spent so much of his life working, feeding cows and driving a tractor and talking about important things like the thickness of baler twine, that he was a world away from the other boys Danny knew.

"Tom? It's Danny."

"Hi, Danny, what's up?"

Tom sounded busy and short of time. An outraged moo-ing in the background suggested he was probably doing something to a cow that it didn't like.

"I'm . . . I'm . . . um . . ."

He was what? Alone in his house without his parents? Tom wouldn't think being alone was anything to get scared about. He'd just tell Danny to stop being a wuss and have some fun.

Danny's eye caught the picture of Emma spotted with raindrops. He could have raided the fridge by now, watched all the DVDs he wasn't allowed to, and invited his friends round to play *Grand Motorized Death Squad* on his Xbox, safe in the knowledge that no one would appear and tell him to turn it off. His parents were bound not to be away long—he should have made the most of them being gone.

Instead he was bleating on the phone to his cousin.

"Oh . . . I'm sure it's just something stupid," he tried, expecting that Tom would ask him exactly what.

"Oh, okay," said Tom. "Right you are."

"Er . . ." said Danny.

"I'm a bit tied up at the moment!" Tom yelped. A loud crunching sound rattled through the earpiece, as if the phone were being chewed by large teeth. "Can it wait?"

"Er . . . sure," said Danny. "Bye . . ."

"Bye!"

Another bellow wailed up in the earpiece as Tom cut the connection.

Danny stared at the phone in his hand, then replaced it slowly. He could feel Mitz's eyes fixed on him. She'd climbed the stairs and arranged herself neatly on a step just above the level of his head. He'd always wondered why cats did that.

He put his hand in his pocket and took hold of the stick.

"Why do cats always sit in high places?" he asked her.

"So we can look down on the world, of course," she said. "Why else? So come on, what's this about your parents?"

Danny's eyes fell to the carpet at his feet.

"Oh, nothing," he said. "They've gone away, that's all. I'm going to have a great time without them."

"Clearly you're not," said Mitz. "You've got a face like a Siamese cat eating tripe."

"What do you know about expressions?" asked Danny. "Cats don't have expressions. They just stare."

"Bah!" said Mitz, standing up and stretching out her back legs. She began jumping down the stairs, making for the front door.

Danny panicked. "Don't go!" he said, his fist clenching around the stick. "You're right, I've got to find them. Will you help me?"

"I don't see what I can do," said Mitz stiffly. "Besides, I have a very time-consuming grooming routine. And I become a complete ogre if I don't get my beauty sleep. I've told you which way they went. Isn't that enough?"

Danny looked hard at his shoes, which interrupted the pattern of blue and green swirls on the carpet. He always cleaned his school shoes on a Sunday night. Only yesterday he'd sat down on the kitchen floor, spread out a newspaper, and rubbed polish into them while his mum had chopped potatoes for dinner.

"I don't want to be by myself," he said. It was barely a whisper, but the cat heard it.

"Why ever not?" She arrived at his feet and spread her plumy tail out along the swirls.

Danny gritted his teeth. He really must pull himself together—he was eleven, not five. But still. "I just don't," he said. "I've got to find them, and I don't want to do it on my own."

"Well, where are you going first?"

He didn't know. Out the gate, down the street, out of town—and then where?

"Can't you just follow their scent?" The cat stalked toward the phone table, jumped up onto the pile of papers, and sat, tucking her tail around her paws. "Or the scent of their car?"

"People don't leave scent," said Danny.

"Of course they do," said Mitz. "Everything smells of something."

"Yeah, I'm sure it does, but people can't follow scent like that. We don't have those kinds of noses."

"You can't *smell*? But how do you tell each other where you've been? Or where you're going?"

"Just . . . leave a note, I guess, if they aren't around. . . ."

A note! He could have kicked himself. What if there was a note? Where would they have left it? Not in the kitchen: he'd been there already. Upstairs, maybe? In their bedroom?

"Yeah," he said. "There must be something like that. They'd have left something in case of emergencies—a note, or a list of the places they usually go—I'm sure they would. Why didn't I think of that?"

And he raced up to his parents' room again, taking the stairs two at a time.

There wasn't a note there, either. The more he thought about it, if they'd left him a note, they would have left it somewhere he'd have been likely to find it first thing in the morning—under his bedroom door, say, or on top of the boxes of cereal, or balanced on his schoolbag. Of course there wasn't a note.

Danny stood in the middle of their room, looking

around for ideas. There had to be *something* that suggested where they'd gone. Maybe a map of some kind? Some photographs?

He opened the computer, but, as always, it asked him for the password that he'd never been able to guess. He searched in the drawers, in the blanket chest, and in the boxes under the bed, pulling each box out and tipping its contents onto the floor. Piles of his schoolwork, bundles of cloth, bags of ribbon and old Christmas cards: that's all there was. Nothing unexpected, nothing new.

Mitz lay curled in a ball on the bed, her eyes narrowed into watchful slits. Whenever he looked up at her, she feigned sleep.

The last of the drawers yielded only socks and handkerchiefs. Danny emptied it onto the floor, then stood still for a moment, looking at the empty inside. A nerve bit inside his shoulders, and tiny claws began to pinch at the sides of his eyes. He dropped the drawer, sat down on the bed, and clenched his fists. What had they *done*? What happened inside the brains of people who decided to get up, run out of their house, and not come back?

Lying back on his dad's pillow, he stared at the ceiling. When he moved to put his hands behind his head, something jabbed him in the neck. Twisting, he saw the corner of a thick spiral-bound notebook with a dark blue cover, almost the same color as his parents' duvet.

He'd never seen it before, which was odd. When you'd been the only child in a house for eleven years, you got to know most of the things around the place pretty well. Danny had spent hundreds of rainy days trawling through drawers, finding all sorts of bits and pieces to play with: fake-fur hats, bags of feathers, albums full of colorless photographs. But never this notebook. And he'd hardly ever seen his parents writing anything down apart from shopping lists, but the notebook was nearly full. Almost every page was covered in writing.

He flicked through the pages, then turned back to the beginning. It was laid out like a sort of diary, and the first date was a couple of years before he'd been born. The letters were neat and round: his mum's handwriting, then.

The notebook of Anna and John O'Neill. Jan 1, it read. *Today we begin a new chapter in our lives. It has to be this way, because we can't keep going if we try to stay the same people that we were. We have to make our lives new again, make ourselves again, turn ourselves into people who haven't been through what we've been through. We can't be Emma's parents always. Not just her parents. We can't live our lives waiting for her to*

come back. Because she died in that storm, under that
tree that no one ever thought would blow over, and she's
not coming back, not ever.

The writing became a little shaky at this point, but still
carefully, deliberately penned.

So we've taken a decision together. We'll put our baby
girl to bed and wish her sweet dreams, and we'll find
out all we can about the storms that blew down that
tree and killed her. And maybe one day we'll know
enough about storms to be able to say, this one will do
such and such, at such a time, in such a place, and no-
body will be caught in a freak storm again, and nobody
will die. Our little tiger won't return. But other people
will live long lives and be all the things they're supposed
to be, and then we might feel we've let her live a little,
in a small way, and that's all we can ever do.

Danny let the notebook rest on his knees. Mitz's fur
brushed his bare arm as she breathed.

His parents never spoke about Emma. He'd tried asking, a few times, but all they'd ever said was that Emma
had died, and that was that. Emma was the photographs
in the hall, not even a person, no matter how much he

ever tried to think about her. But his parents were obsessed with storms, and that was the reason: Emma had died in one. He thought of the lightning and the sycamore and a tiny child a bit like himself standing lost beneath its black branches, and he saw for the first time something wild and screaming, impossible to frame and hang on a wall.

What kind of person had she been? Had she liked computer games and green beans and hated melted cheese? Had she even been old enough to know that she liked or didn't like anything?

"Emma." He tried it out for size, but it had never sounded like a part of his family, and it didn't now. "Emma O'Neill."

Why did they never talk about her? Were they worried he'd think he was some kind of replacement? But he was, wasn't he? That's why they'd had him and then stuck her silent photos on the wall, to remind him every time he went into the hallway.

He went back to the book. Tell me about Emma, he urged it. Tell me about my sister.

The entry for January 1 was finished. There wasn't another entry until April 12 of the same year.

Great Butford and surrounding area. Time of storm: 8:20 p.m. until 3:30 a.m.

That was one big storm.

Behavior: Oppressive day. Clouds began to gather in the skies above Great Butford at approximately 5:30 p.m. At 8:20 p.m., the first roll of thunder was heard. We were fortunate to be staying in Great Butford at the time and saw the first flash of lightning at 8:49 p.m. The lightning increased in frequency until roughly four flashes per minute were occurring.

Danny turned the page. The description of the storm continued in minute detail, so he skipped to the end and read what else had been written about Great Butford.

Questioning the local residents of Great Butford revealed that in the previous two weeks they could think of little out of the ordinary that had happened. Mrs. Simmonds, who runs the post office, had broken her arm as she fell over the hairdresser's step when returning from having her highlights done. Some children had killed a duck when they threw a suitcase they had stolen from the railway station into the village pond. The weather had been generally normal. Yet, questioning of residents in villages as close by as Little Butford and Stony Hamlington, both just under three miles

away, revealed that there had been no storms in these
places. Also that many of the inhabitants of these
places were of the opinion that Great Butford was a
"funny place" they would have avoided had they not
been obliged to send their children to school there.

Well, thought Danny, it was a local storm. There was
a last bit about Great Butford.

In conclusion, we cannot rule out the possibility that the
storm was responding to something it did not like (a
human or nonhuman factor???) in Great Butford. Al-
though nothing immediately puts itself forward to us
as a cause, we fully anticipate that in time we will be
able to look back at these notes and understand what
happened in Great Butford, at which time a postscript
will be added.

There was no postscript. More of the same followed.
Page after page of tiny detail, storm forecasts, graphs of iso-
bars cut out from the newspaper, pictures of lightning.
When had they written all this stuff? Now they were into
the year that he'd been born. On his birthday, June 21, his
father had scribbled in a frantic scrawl across the page, his
words defying the lines meant to keep them neat.

Today our son was born! Daniel Adrian O'Neill. Such a strange thought, that five years ago we thought our family was complete, and three years ago we thought it was destroyed, and now there is this new life, a small boy, entirely himself. We should never compare our children, but he was late and arrived quickly, then just lay there looking around with huge blue eyes. When Emma came she was early, not ready, and she cried as soon as she saw the world, full of strong anger. I think Daniel might be a thoughtful sort of a person, the kind who sees a lot more than he says. And all I wish is that he should live and breathe and be happy, and never have to enter those dark places into which we have followed our beloved daughter.

Danny turned the page quickly. It felt wrong, reading stuff about himself that he wasn't meant to see. But it was okay—they'd gone back to talking about storms, and only storms.

More storms, more years, passed by. Then he came across another entry, dated from the previous summer. They'd gone to a village fete. Actually, he remembered it well: he'd eaten five ice creams, because each time he asked his parents for more money, they'd given it to him without question. They'd been too busy talking to an old man whose beard was long, white, and separated into pointy tufts like hairy icicles.

August 8. Today we met an old Polish man, Abel Kor-sakof, at the Hopfield village fete. We'd stopped to ex-change a few pleasantries about the weather—he was the father of one of Anna's friends from her Women's Insti-tute group. As we chatted, we noticed (and he noticed too, both at the same time, I think!) that we were all referring to last week's storm in terms that you'd use about people ("he," "they," etc.). Anna and I tend to do this between ourselves, but we try to avoid it with other people, as it probably makes us sound strange. But be-cause this Abel Korsakof was doing it too, we just didn't think anything of it at first. Anyway, after a while he started to drop in references to something he called "the Book."

"The Book says that bird populations are a big fac-tor," he said when we were discussing the path of the storm. "The Book says there are various methods of tracking but you have to watch out for the secondary pieces of storm that join up on the way—they can alter the trajectory a great deal," was another thing he said.

We asked him, "What book?"

"The Book of Storms," he said.

Neither of us had ever heard of it. We asked if it was some kind of encyclopedia.

"No," he said, shaking his head. "The Book of Storms is no mere encyclopedia."

He told us it was a book of so many pages that you couldn't even count them. Each time he read it, he learned something new. It taught him how to watch storms, how to listen to them, how to pull himself into them and start to absorb their knowledge. It taught him, he said, how to "plunge through the maelstrom and seek refuge in the becalmed eye" so he could look at a storm from deep inside its heart.

"The Book of Storms!" he said with a sigh, in the same way that someone might talk about someone they loved. "Had I known of its existence only a few years earlier, what things I might have done. . . ."

We asked instantly where we could buy a copy.

And then he laughed, a dry, old kind of laugh. He told us no one on earth could buy another copy of the Book of Storms. There was only one copy, and that was his own.

We asked if we might see it.

"Well, he gave it to me, of course," he said. "I'm not at liberty to show it to others. I should not even refer to it, really, but then I think, what more can I lose than I have already lost?"

At this point he wished us good day, very abruptly, and left. We didn't even get his address, though we presume he lives near Hopfield—his daughter said she grew up there.

But what is the Book of Storms? It sounds like a treasure trove of information of a kind undreamed of by scientists. Birds? Other pieces of storm? We must get hold of that book. It will revolutionize the way we think. What could birds have to do with storms? It's nonsensical, but the idea is . . . right.

They hadn't got hold of the Book of Storms, though. Instead they'd recorded in minute detail the contents of rain gauges, the wind speeds, the number of lightning flashes counted per minute in various storms, and they'd entered every scrap of information that they could find into their blue notebook.

And then, once more, a few months later, again in his dad's handwriting:

We've found his address. He lives (where else?) at Storm Cottage, Puddleton Lane End, Hopfield. He used to write the Weatherwatch column for the Hopfield Parish magazine, but he doesn't do anything now, it seems, apart from study the behavior of storms.

What can we do? He told us he wouldn't show the book to anyone. Perhaps we could steal it? But we've never done anything like that. How would we explain it to the police if we were caught?

We'll have to find a way, though. They tell you that grief lessens with time, but for me it seems to be the other way around. Each day, I realize a little more what we lost when Emma was taken. Each day, I wake up and see her slip away out of the corner of my eye, and no matter how fast I run, I can't catch up with her.

I must do all I can to make sure no one else suffers the same fate.

The Book of Storms wasn't mentioned again. Danny scoured every entry, all the way to the last, which was followed by a handful of blank pages and then the inside cover of the notebook. They were tidy people, and they'd kept a tidy journal. Nothing was stuck to the back or hidden away under glued-on strips of paper.

His parents talked about storms like you'd talk about people. Was that normal? Actually, it clearly wasn't—they'd said so themselves. Danny had never noticed them talking like that, but then all this—the extent of it, the reason for it—had been purposefully hidden from him.

He hated the thought. Of course, there were loads of

thing that his parents tried to hide, like when they had an argument or they were sad or there wasn't quite enough money for something and they thought that if they didn't say anything about it, then Danny wouldn't notice they were twitchy and distracted and full of tight little sighs. He never told them that he knew about these things, but they were obvious. Yet somehow they'd managed to keep this notebook entirely secret from him.

His chest felt hollow as he stared at the dark blue cover. Could they have gone to find the Book of Storms? In the middle of the night?

There was only one way to find out. "We're going to see an old guy called Abe . . . Abel Kors . . . Korsakof," he said, taking hold of the stick so that Mitz could hear him. "Some weird name. He's got a book that might help me find them, if he'll let me see it. And if he won't, then . . . then I don't know, I'll think of something."

"Something?" asked Mitz, blinking innocently.

"I'll steal it," said Danny. "I don't care if it's bad. I'll steal it."

He got up and made for the door, trampling on purpose over the mess still strewn across the floor. Mitz dropped down from the bed and stalked after him, her fluffy britches carrying her lightly over the mountains of chaos.

"Stealing isn't bad," said Mitz. "Everybody steals.

Everybody that I know, anyway. But, then, I suppose we *are* all cats."

Danny remembered what it had felt like, last night, when he'd woken up and thought the roof was falling in. He remembered the bright gold of the night sky as the lightning set fire to the clouds.

"Not everybody," he said, "steals the Book of Storms."

Downstairs, he opened the drawer where his dad kept his wallet and took all the money out of it, then emptied his schoolbag and chucked the single spiral-bound notebook into it. Somehow he doubted that school was going to see him tomorrow, and maybe not even the day after that.

Forgetting even to change out of his school uniform, he let himself out into the late-afternoon sunshine and pulled the door closed after Mitz had trotted briskly through.

This time there was no point in looking back.

CHAPTER 4

A VISIT

The only thing in the garden that didn't feel slightly colder was the sycamore tree, because the sycamore tree was dead. Even the grass shivered, although sunlight still warmed its blades. Roses curled their petals inward, returning half-opened blooms into buds, and bushes tightened their roots in the soil. Birds and mice pulled their heads down into their necks, puffing up feathers and fur. Spiders hung motionless in their webs, and even a trapped fly gave up its struggle against the sticky threads.

Sammael had walked into the garden. His appearance never changed; his dry, sweatless skin stayed cool, his short black curls unruffled. Things didn't stick to him if they could avoid it—there were better ways to travel for even the smallest thorn or burr than stuck to his long black coat. Journeys didn't tire or alter him, no matter how long they took or how fast he traveled.

The lurcher at his side was a wreck. She staggered to the patio outside the house, swayed for a couple of seconds, then toppled sideways and lay flat on her side, her legs stretched out. Her rib cage pushed up through gray matted curls, each bone distinct from the next like the sleepers of a railway line.

Sammael ignored her and went straight to the sycamore tree, resting a hand on it. The dead wood stayed mute under his fingers.

"This is the tree, then," he said, taking his hand away. "You'd think the lightning could have picked a better specimen."

The grass under his feet trembled as the blades reached out to each other. He felt it wriggling and kicked at it.

"Did you see the human?" he asked.

The grass was silent.

"Grass," he said. "I'm talking to you."

A few of the grasses whispered among themselves, trying to keep their voices down.

"Don't irritate me," said Sammael. "Just answer. You,

the meadow grass. Trueflax, that's your name, isn't it? Tell me what you heard."

The grass was small and thin, only a young shoot. "The human boy came into the garden," it said, trying to sound bold. Inside, the sap that kept its stem firm had turned into bubbling soup.

"Yes. And?" Sammael knew there was just a chance that the ant might have got it wrong. Ants were notorious for being focused on their work and only ever had a maximum of half an eye on anything else, which did sometimes make them unreliable witnesses.

"He went over to the tree, stood—well, just where you are. He stood on top of me as well. . . ." Trueflax tried to keep his breathing steady. The bubbles inside him were turning into rattling chips of ice.

"Get on with it!" snapped Sammael. "I'm not asking you to retell *The Odyssey*!"

"He picked up the stick and stood for ages, then started to say some stuff—it didn't make much sense. He said, 'hello,' and 'I'm in the light,' and . . . what else? Oh, yes, he said, 'Work out what?' That was it, I think . . . oh, yes, he said 'hello,' again. And he put the stick on the tree, then picked it up again, and we heard him speak after that . . . but why he should suddenly have learned to talk, none of us can tell. We never thought humans could talk, not in that way, though we do hear them make strange sounds sometimes, but you can never be sure that they're really sentient, can you? It seems so unlikely. . . ."

Trueflax gave a gasp and his leaves wilted, unable to keep up with the effort of speech. Sammael thought about flicking him back into life just to terrorize the other grasses, but there were more important things to be done.

Clearly the boy had found the taro—that was beyond doubt now. Clearly, too, he had no idea what it was or how to use it. He'd be easy to track. He was probably running around somewhere close by, making more noise than a herd of stampeding wildebeest as he tried to discover all the things that could speak, and what each and every one of them had to say.

Sammael looked about him. No sign of the boy here.

He stamped on the grass to revive it. "Where did he go?"

"D-d-don't know . . ." tried Trueflax. The other grasses were all too petrified to help him out.

"Wrong answer!" Sammael crushed his heel into the ground. Trueflax yelped, although any pain he was feeling must have been imaginary. It was amazing what imagination could do.

"M-maybe . . . maybe he went into the house, then out the other side, then maybe he came back . . . and went again . . . somewhere else. . . ."

"Where else? Come on, don't pretend to me you don't know. Grass sees everything! It tells each other everything! You could track down a beetle in Outer Mongolia!"

"B-but that's because Mongolia's full of gr-gr-grass!" stuttered Trueflax. "The boy went onto the road, and no grass knows what goes on there, until the cracks start to appear and we can grow through them."

"Cretin!" Sammael stamped again, and Trueflax the grass lost his stoutness, fainting from fear. "Kalia!" Sammael bellowed. The lurcher raised her nostrils from the ground but couldn't lift her head. Even pricking an ear required more energy than she had left. "Kalia!" Sammael said again, snapping his fingers.

In the end he hooked an arm under her rib cage and carried her in the crook of his elbow round to the front of the house. Her limp legs knocked against each other as they swung in the air.

The boy wasn't anywhere to be seen. Sammael dabbed a finger into some grains of sand at the bottom of his pocket and pressed it against the lock.

"Open!" he commanded, and the lock turned.

He deposited Kalia in a heap on the hall carpet. It was the sort of color that could only have been produced by a hippopotamus throwing up all over the hallway after eating too many iced cupcakes.

And then he stopped. In his fury over the missing taro, he hadn't observed the path he was traveling quite as carefully as he normally would have.

"Damn!" he said to the comatose dog. "I *know* this house."

"When have you been here before?" Kalia's voice was so tiny that he barely heard it, but he was already staring through into the kitchen, examining a picture in his mind.

"Those storm-chasing idiots! This is *their* house!"

For a second he floundered, but Kalia was too tired to notice, and he forced his voice quickly back to its usual acidity, knowing that such mistakes could never be admitted to.

"So he must be their son," he muttered to himself. "He'll be looking for them, of course. Where would I go if I were a small human of extremely limited imagination looking for people who were looking for storms?"

Every creature in the house heard his quiet voice. Every fly, every mite, every last wood louse and woodworm and silverfish. Not all of them could answer him; some had slumbered on all day, unaware that anything peculiar was happening. But upstairs, underneath the bed, the dust mites were stirring. They had been scurrying around when Danny had put his hand to the stick and talked to Mitz the cat. They had heard him speak.

Through the silence, a small voice muttered a single word, and then a second and a third joined in.

"Korsakof!" they whispered. The first time, it was a haze of broken sounds, single syllables following half-begun words. The letter *K* echoed through the house like the rattle of a machine gun.

And then, the second time, they said it all together.

"Korsakof!"

Sammael smiled, bending down to hoist up his dog again. As the evening sun began to dip in the sky, a ray broke through the glass in the back door, streaking the kitchen doorway with orange.

"Got you now, boy," he said, tucking Kalia under his arm, apparently unaware of her weight. "Got you, well and truly. It's all very well running away and throwing yourself on the mercy of strangers, but you can't always tell who's been there before you."

And as he began to walk, his feet picked up so much speed that even to the fastest cheetah on the planet they would have seemed little more than a blur.

Abel Korsakof was small and ratty looking, with a beard that would have fallen almost to his waist if it hadn't been tangled and frizzy and sticking out at all angles in yellowing prongs. As a young man he'd been clean shaven, but these days he spent a lot of time muttering to himself, and he'd realized quite quickly that beards were useful for muttering into. None of his family liked his beard, but he told them he didn't care what they said: he had important things to mutter about, and if *they* weren't going to listen to him, then the beard would have to.

He had cared about his family a long time ago, but something much bigger and better than mere humans had come along and gradually eaten him, bite by bite, until he belonged inside the belly of an obsession so strong that he could hardly breathe unless he was thinking about it. And this obsession was the study of storms.

Because it was sunny and calm over England, with hardly enough wind to tickle a fly's wings, that evening saw Abel Korsakof at work in his shed, a huge piece of paper spread over the floor. The paper stretched to all four walls, so Abel had to sit right on top of his work, which gave him a grand feeling. As if somehow he might one day be able to sit in a similar position in the sky itself, watching the real storms gather below.

Still, for now this was just a dream, for several reasons unlikely to become reality. One of which was framed in the doorway of his shed, blocking out the evening sun.

"You're not still going at this, old man, are you? Of all the pointless things . . ."

Abel looked up, and his heart dropped like a stone into his knees.

"What are you doing here?" he asked, his old voice shaking.

"I've got a little job for you," said Sammael.

Although Sammael was only standing and watching him, Abel Korsakof could never quite relax while those black points were boring into his own weepy blue eyes. He shifted from knee to knee and then latched his bony knuckles around the table leg to pull himself upright.

"Not in here," he said. It was bad enough when he remembered where all the work in this room had come from and what he owed it to, without having the room further polluted by the actual shades of the creature itself.

"Suit yourself," said Sammael. "You useless old bag of rickets."

He raised an eyebrow and stood back to let Korsakof out. The old man tried not to brush against Sammael's coat as he passed, expecting that it would chill him to the marrow, but when he touched it by accident he found it surprisingly warm and soft.

Korsakof's garden was bursting with flowers. They'd all escaped from their original flower beds and grew now wherever they chose, leaping to waist and neck height, clinging on to their neighbors and climbing toward the sky. Neither Sammael nor Korsakof looked at their bright colors, though: Sammael's eyes were on the old man, and Korsakof's were fixed on a garden bench that he'd always hated. It was some fancy of Mrs. Korsakof's, a twisted affair covered in mangled iron daffodils. Abel never normally sat on it, and he certainly would never sit on it again after it had felt the cold figure of Sammael resting on its squashed flowers.

"What were you doing in there, anyway?" Sammael leaned back against the bench and nodded his head toward the shed. "What's with all the paper?"

Abel noticed a huge dog lying on one of the flower beds, flattening a squat display of pansies. It was a gray lurcher, thin and woolly, and it looked dead. He cleared his throat. "A map."

"A map? Of what?"

Korsakof shrugged. "Of storms."

Sammael laughed, his face scornful. "A map of storms? And do you think it's correct? Have you checked it with one of your 'satellite pictures'?"

"Not that kind of map. A chart of how they work. What they do. I have watched their behavior for a long time. I have observed their reactions. I have noticed some patterns in their process of formation. I have seen, over the years, how they are becoming more and more fre-quent." He broke off, unwilling to look into Sammael's eyes, wanting strongly to ask a question that had been playing on his mind for some years.

"Oh yes?"

"I have wanted . . . I have wanted to know, is this a natural phenomenon? Or something . . ."

"Or 'something' what?"

Korsakof swallowed. "Or something . . . controlled . . . dictated . . . persuaded . . . by other, er, influences . . ."

"Such as?"

"Well, er, yes, quite. Other influences. So I have made a map, to see if there is a logical answer. . . ."

"Such as myself," said Sammael. "You want to know if I am controlling storms, and you don't have the guts to ask. That's right, isn't it?"

A fear paralyzed Korsakof's throat, and he looked away at the garden. There was no reason to be so terrified. They had made a bargain years ago, and Sammael never went back on his word. But how could anyone trust such a black-eyed, inside-out creature? His thin, dark shape sat just inside the periphery of Korsakof's vision, as still as a vulture.

The old man could see his wife through the kitchen window, her head and shoulders swaying. She must be making bread. He wondered what would happen to her once his years were up. Strange that he'd never thought of it before. "What are you here for, anyway?" he asked.

"You're to kill someone," said Sammael.

"No," said Korsakof immediately with a staunchness he didn't feel.

". . . Isn't a word you can say to me, not anymore." Sammael stretched his legs out. "Remember, the fifty years I gave you when we made our bargain—the time *you* agreed on—are nearly up. Your soul's mine to do what I like with after that."

"You can't make me kill someone," said the old man. "I would never do that. And you told me yourself, you can't kill people. Death won't take them if you try to."

"*I* can't. But if *you* decide to, who knows what Death will think? If she's having a busy day, she might overlook it."

"No," said Korsakof again. "No matter who it was, I wouldn't do it. I couldn't."

"All right." Sammael got to his feet and pulled his coat straight. It was a shame the lurcher was still so exhausted; being able to click his fingers and have Kalia come running up always made the threat of departure look so much more impressive.

Korsakof should have stayed silent and let him go. He

knew he should. But the only thing worse than knowing what Sammael was going to do was *not* knowing what he was going to do.

"Is that it?" he asked.

"You've refused. Next month, your fifty years will be up. You'll die on the first second after that. I'll take your sand, as we agreed." Sammael paused.

Korsakof watched his face. The skin had a translucence about it that shimmered, as though it wasn't quite at ease in the ruddy sunlight.

"And I'll take everything else as well," Sammael went on. "Every memory of you. Every paper you've ever written on. Every word you've ever said to anybody else. I can, you know. It's in the nature of things—all that you've ever created is a part of you, and I can remove any of it that I want to. The world will carry on just as if you'd *never been born.*"

"But my studies," said Korsakof. "You couldn't take that knowledge out of the world. The things I discovered, the papers I've written—they exist, whether I'm here or not."

"Interesting that you didn't say your children," said Sammael, his smile slicing the air again. "Who will still exist, although they won't know a thing about you. But your studies? Easy! Gone like that!"

He snapped his fingers in front of his mouth, cutting

off his own words. Kalia, gradually coming back to life in the bed of pansies, raised a sleepy head. Seeing that he didn't want her, she let it sink gratefully down again.

Korsakof looked at his own hands, his wrinkled, blotchy old hands with the calluses on the first and second fingers of the right one from holding a pen. The thousands of words that he'd written, all to be gone in an instant. To know that his entire life would be obliterated in one second, that nobody at all would remember him, or be able to use the results of the study he'd devoted his life to— would he be able to go peacefully to his death, knowing that?

He closed his eyes. And in a voice that he'd never heard before, he said, "Who do you want me to kill?"

Sammael didn't smile. Triumph didn't seem to mean a great deal to him.

"A boy who's coming to see you."

"A boy? As in, a child?" Korsakof's blood fled from his face, leaving behind two scarlet eyes on his cheeks. "I couldn't kill a child."

"You did a whole lot worse when you sold your soul to me. You've no idea what I'm going to use it for."

The biggest creature Korsakof had ever killed had been a sheep, back on his parents' farm in Poland. Even that had made his hands shake. His brothers had mocked him.

"Hold the knife steady!" they'd laughed. "Better for the sheep! You'll hurt it twice as much as we do, with your shaky-woman hands!"

But sticking a knife into a child? Hitting him round the head? Strangling him?

Korsakof shuddered. If Sammael wanted a stout-hearted assassin, he'd picked the wrong old man.

"Why do you need him killed?" he asked, his voice creaking.

"He's taken something that he shouldn't have. In his hands it's dangerous. I must get it back."

"Why not just take it off him? If he is only a boy?"

Sammael gave a bitter laugh. "If that were possible, do you think I'd be here?"

Korsakof frowned and looked at the tall figure. In the stories that he knew, this creature was eternal. Sammael ruled the underworld, without beginning or end. How could he need an old man's help to do anything?

But apparently he did. The threat must be serious. And he was the rock upon which Korsakof had built his own life. If Sammael was being threatened, where would that leave the people who had given their souls to him?

"Well? Does that answer your question? The boy must die, and Death won't let me do it myself, so you'll have to do it for me. Try and make it look like an accident and Death might not ask too many questions. Agreed?"

"I would want something in return," said Korsakof. "More life. Another fifty years, like before."

"So you could read the Book of Storms a hundred more times and still not understand any of it?" said Sammael.

"I understand it very well," said Korsakof. "I admit, at first I did not know how to use the book. But now—now I understand more every day, of the Book's true nature, and how it is to be used. Each time I read it, I see further. With fifty more years, I would see into the very *soul* of a storm, perhaps even before that soul knew what it would become."

Sammael didn't blink. He had his own views on exactly how far Korsakof would be able to see. "Sure. The years are yours."

"And I want to be able to leave my work to someone," continued Korsakof. "An apprentice or something. I want that guaranteed."

"Unorthodox, but accepted," said Sammmael.

"Give me some proof," demanded the old man.

Sammael shook his head. "No proof," he said. "I keep my bargains down to the last letter. That's all the proof you get."

Korsakof knew he wouldn't get any more out of Sammael. You could tell it, when he stood there before you, his hands as rigid as wax. Whatever he knew, no mere human had ever made him explain anything he didn't choose to. He had his own reasons.

But he also had Korsakof's soul. Which meant that in a way, he was Korsakof's master, although the old man had never once, in the last fifty years, been made to feel like a slave. In fact, the first four decades of his life, before he'd found Sammael and gotten hold of the Book of Storms, had been the time that he now counted as slavery, when he'd had to spend his days working instead of pursuing his obsession with storms. Now, for the very first time, he was being asked by Sammael to do something he didn't want to do.

I shall have to stand up and be counted, he told himself. Each person faces these times of crisis. I shall face mine like the man that I am—it is surely a fair return for all these years of wonder he has given me.

"I suppose," he said slowly, "with extra knowledge, I could even begin to save some of the lives of humans who die in storms. Perhaps hundreds of lives . . . perhaps this one small life, weighed against all of those, is not so important. . . ."

Sammael raised an eyebrow and waited.

Korsakof shrugged. "Okay," he said. "It is a deal. I will do it. Who is he?"

"Good of you to ask," said Sammael. "You've met him before, actually. Or at least, you've met his parents. They were obsessed with storms, like yourself, to the point where I got really quite irritated with them. However, I think I may have comprehensively cured them of their little hobby. Now it's your turn."

Then Sammael called softly to Kalia. This time, the lurcher got to her feet unassisted and padded after him, her purple toes bright against the green of Korsakof's lawn.

By the way Sammael walked, slow and swinging, he was in a good mood again. He reached out and caressed the ridges of the dog's skull.

"Panic over, mutt," he said. "Just took a little persuasion, that's all. I reckon we'll get away with it, if no one blabs to Death about it. But Death looks horrendous these days—I don't think she's seen a hairbrush in centuries. No one talks to her who doesn't have to."

Kalia pressed her head up to his fingers. He always knew where she liked to be scratched.

"Panic over," repeated Sammael. "Dead boy, all quiet. Back to the task. Back to the storms."

He tickled the base of the lurcher's ears and picked away a long piece of straw that had become tangled in her wiry coat.

Korsakof stared after him for a long time as he walked away. The old man could picture every stitch of that long, worn coat in his mind, could almost feel what it would be like to slip his aching old arms into its sleeves. He thought of the years of work he'd put into his map. He thought of a boy who he didn't really care about, and he thought of his wife in the kitchen making bread. She made excellent bread; it was one of the things Abel loved most in his entire life. Although she hadn't even put it in the oven yet, he was sure he could smell the sweet crispness wafting out to him.

It wasn't any good. Abel Korsakof had spent his life chasing one thing. Everything he knew was down on his map. Sammael never made an idle threat.

He stumbled back to his shed, longing once more to be kneeling on that precious paper, sinking down at last as if it were a carpet of thick velvet beneath him. He ran his hands over it, knowing without looking every single word that passed under his fingertips.

And as he stood up once more, feeling his way blindly to the doorway, he tried desperately not to remember the scent of freshly baked bread.

CHAPTER 5

BEHIND THE HEDGE

Working out a way to get to Hopfield was easy. Danny just walked to the railway station and found the timetables stuck to the wall. He hadn't traveled much on his own before, but he did walk to school by himself—there was no reason why he shouldn't walk onto a train and get off again at the other end. It's exciting, he told himself, trying to push away the little voice in his ear that was muttering about strangers and kidnapping and murder.

He sat down on a bench to wait for the train while Mitz slunk away to investigate the mouse situation on the platform. His stomach grumbled, reminding him of missed breakfast and forgotten lunch. Even in the early June sunshine, he was cold; the wind seemed to be wriggling through the fabric of his navy sweatshirt and creeping over his bare skin.

Mum never bought food at railway stations. She said it was too expensive and he could wait until they got wherever they were going. But she wasn't here and he had money in his pocket. There was a kiosk along the platform selling hot pasties. The more he thought about it, the more the smell seemed to waft straight up his nostrils, filling them with the scent of baked pastry and stewed meat.

Danny bought two, ate them in less time than it normally took him to brush his teeth, and sat back down on the bench, feeling a bit like he'd just wolfed down a load of cardboard. His stomach was painfully stretched.

But he'd have his parents back soon. This Abel Korsakof might even help him find them. He was probably some kindly old foreign man who would talk in broken English and give Danny stale biscuits to eat, or tea to drink, which Danny didn't really like unless it had a lot of sugar in it. But that was what old people did. Before she'd died, Gran had always given him milky tea and proper chocolate biscuits with layers of white cream in the middle.

Abel Korsakof might have those kinds of biscuits. He might even make hot chocolate instead of tea, and then go out and find Danny's parents and bring them back again while Danny sat in his house eating biscuits.

That might be the best kind of adventure, thought Danny. He liked adventure stories, but actually it was pretty horrible sitting on a railway platform all alone, feeling a bit sick. At least he wasn't cold anymore. But he had a vague sort of prickling feeling that something might be watching him, from somewhere he couldn't see.

Of course I'll be okay, he tried to tell himself. I'll just shout as loud as I can if anyone tries to grab hold of me. I'll shout so loudly that their eardrums will burst.

The train pulled up. As he stepped up into the carriage he brushed the tips of his fingers against the stick in his pocket to reassure himself that it was still there. He needed it to talk to Mitz, he told himself. No trees, no plants. Just Mitz.

Hopfield wasn't far. Out the window, the streets and warehouses quickly ended, replaced by vast green fields and hills. When Danny visited his aunt's farm, he and his parents drove out along the main road most of the way, and the view from there wasn't that good, hidden away behind hedges. Here, the countryside opened out before him, huge and empty, rolling up toward the sky.

Normally the sight of the hills made him feel small and alone, but for the first time he found himself watching the trees and hedgerows with narrowed eyes. Were they really all chattering away to each other? If he were walking over those fields instead of sitting on a train, would the bushes and grasses be watching him, following his every move?

It didn't matter, he told himself. It was just countryside, that was all. Even if it could think or speak or scream with anger, it still couldn't rise up and come after him.

He forced himself to think about something else. Perhaps Abel Korsakof might give him cake, as well as biscuits? Old people ate cake on days other than birthdays. Danny's friend Paul did too—it must be good to be someone like that who could eat as much cake as they liked. Why hadn't he bought cake back on the platform, when he'd had the chance?

And Danny was still cursing himself for being a slow-witted idiot when the train rolled up at Hopfield.

Danny and Mitz stepped off onto the deserted platform. The station clock said half past five, which was a little worrying. Things should be nearly over for the day by now— Danny should be watching *The Simpsons*, hearing his mum beginning to cook dinner, and keeping himself very quiet so she wouldn't hear him moving, be reminded of his presence, and ask him to help. Instead he was in an unknown railway station, with only a cat for company.

Looking around for somebody to ask the way to Puddleton Lane End, he saw that no one else had gotten off the train at Hopfield. In fact, he couldn't see anybody else around at all. There was no hum from passing traffic, no murmuring from the voices of pedestrians up on the road, only quiet birdsong and the occasional bark of a distant dog.

The station buildings were closed and the cars outside were parked, empty. Danny waited for five minutes, but nobody came. He went up to the road to look for a shop, only to discover that its blinds were drawn, the orange sign hanging in the window turned firmly to CLOSED.

Mitz, who had been stalking in his footsteps, sat down and gave a few irritated licks at her white ruff. "Where are we going, exactly?" she asked.

Danny hadn't realized he was turning the stick over in his pocket. It had quickly become an unconscious habit— too quickly, he thought. It shouldn't have become a part of him so easily.

But if Mitz didn't know where they were going, and he himself didn't know, and there were no people around to ask, what could he do? He was going to have to use it. There were plenty of plants around—cow parsley, sticky weed, and dandelions crowding above the grass in the verges. But their leaves and petals were sharp and pointed, and their white and yellow flowers clashed starkly with the glossy greens below. As he looked at them, they seemed to bristle with spite.

He couldn't bring himself to go up to them. Maybe he could ask a tree? The sycamore hadn't seemed that bad, had it? If other trees were like that, perhaps it would be okay. Well, he would have to try it. There was no other way.

Danny tried to relax against the rising tightness in his blood and forced himself to sidle up to the nearest tree. Gripping the stick, he took a deep breath and whispered, "I'm sorry, do you know the way to Puddleton Lane End?"

There followed a longish pause.

"I beg your pardon?" said the beech, in a tone of mild surprise.

"Puddleton Lane End," whispered Danny again. "I'm trying to get there. Do you know where it is?"

Another pause, but shorter this time.

"Yes, I do."

Danny missed the suspicious note in the tree's voice.

"Well, where is it? How do I get there?" He let himself breathe a little. Perhaps this wasn't going to be so bad after all.

"I beg your pardon," said the tree. "Have you noticed that I'm a copper beech tree? I know it must be easy for something as short as yourself to make mistakes . . . but . . . a copper beech tree! *You* can't ask *me* for . . . for *street* directions!"

"Oh . . . sorry," said Danny. "I didn't know you were . . . one of those. Can I ask one of the other trees, then?"

The copper beech was silent for a good few minutes, until Danny had almost given up. Finally, it spoke again.

"I . . . don't wish to fraternize with a . . . with *you*. Please be so good as to remove yourself from under my leaves."

Danny stepped back gladly. At least the tree hadn't started shouting about anything. Maybe cats were the only other creatures worth talking to.

"D'you reckon there are any more cats around here?" he asked Mitz. "We could ask one for directions."

Mitz was peering into a hedge. "Sssh!" she said. "Oh, it's gone."

"What's gone?"

"Bah! The mouse. How do you humans ever get any food? You're so noisy all the time."

"Same way you do," Danny pointed out. "We open tins. Doesn't matter how noisy you are, the tins still open."

"Oh, but there's nothing like a fresh, juicy mouse," said Mitz. "Crunching its little bones between your teeth. . . . Mmm . . . beats any of that mushy stuff the servants feed me. . . ."

She darted away. Danny went after her, not trusting that she'd come back to him again if she got on the trail of a mouse. She hared through a small churchyard and came to a pouncing stop just by the opposite gate, which led out onto a different road. And there it was—a sign tucked away in a hedge. Puddleton Lane.

"Great!" said Danny. "This is it. Puddleton Lane— we've found it."

"Lost that weasel, though," said Mitz, looking sulky. "A weasel! What a prize that'd have been!"

"You're bloodthirsty," said Danny, but he quite liked it. If there was a fight, at least Mitz would get stuck right in, fluff-ball tail and all. Although she'd probably have to spend a week cleaning herself up afterward.

"I," said Mitz, "am a good cat. One of the best. Although generally there are very few inferior cats."

Fluffing up her tail again, she flounced off toward Puddleton Lane.

✦ ✦ ✦

Puddleton Lane End was a narrow path leading off to the south, about 200 yards outside the village. Danny nearly missed it; it was so overgrown that he had to search in a thicket for the road sign. And walking down it, he became unsure again. It was flanked on both sides by high hedges. There didn't seem to be any houses at all; if there were, then the hedges were growing over their front gates, because there were no gaps that Danny could see.

He would have missed Storm Cottage completely had he not heard a sudden loud cacophony of squawking and seen a great cloud of crows launch themselves into the air from the boughs of an oak tree. Dangling from one of the branches was a nameplate, tiny and almost invisible between the leaves. The shine of varnished wood flashed once as it caught the sunlight, and Danny read the name with relief.

Storm Cottage was small and white behind a jungle of climbing roses and ivy; purple wisteria hung in giant garlands over the front door. The gate was overgrown with creepers and set on hinges rusted as red as autumn leaves, so he climbed over. If there had ever been a garden path, it had long since been reclaimed by grass and nettles, so he had to fight his way up to the door through the crowding greenery, swishing it aside with a stick.

He knocked at the door and a woman opened it. She was about Danny's height and had gray hair in a neat bun. She peered at him with a ready smile on her face.

"Yes?"

"Um . . . I'm looking for Abel Korsakof. Does he live here?"

"Yes, of course. Come in, dear, come in. He's in his den at the moment."

The old woman stood aside to welcome Danny into the cottage. He stepped in cautiously, noticing that the walls were covered with paintings: stormy skies, clouds rolling over bleak moorlands, ships being tossed at sea, rain lashing against horses struggling to pull their carts along sodden roads. The kitchen smelled of baking and his stomach rumbled as he thought of dinner.

"You'll have to go out and find him, dear. He never hears me shout when he's in his den. Go on, just out the back door and go left across the lawn. Off you trot. I'm just making a pot of tea; tell him I'll bring it over in a few minutes."

She indicated the French windows across the room that were open and led out onto a tangled green lawn. Danny crossed the garden and knocked hesitantly on the door of the small shed that stood on the other side.

"Yes?"

He opened the door. Abel Korsakof was crouched on the floor, holding down an enormous sheet of paper with both legs and one hand. With the other hand he was putting detail into what looked like a complicated flow diagram tracing hundreds of pathways over the paper, most of which seemed to originate from a spot hidden underneath his knees.

Abel Korsakof was about the oldest man Danny had ever seen, with a straggling white beard that hung from his chin and folded into a small pile where it fell on the paper. What was visible of his face was wrinkled like a walnut, but his eyes were hard and bright.

"Mr. Korsakof?" Danny relaxed. This man was so old, he couldn't be scary. It would probably take him half an hour just to stand up.

"Yes, yes! Come in, come in!"

Danny stepped into the shed. The wooden planks creaked underneath his feet. Abel Korsakof's flinty eyes were staring at him with an intensity that made him wonder if he'd got gravy drying on his chin or had suddenly sprouted a third nostril.

"Sit down, sit down!" said Abel Korsakof.

Why did he repeat everything twice? And why didn't he ask Danny who he was?

"I'm Danny," said Danny, to make it a bit less weird. "I think, um, I think you know my parents?"

"Do I? Do I? I do not know if I do. I do not know many people . . ." said Abel Korsakof.

What was wrong with him? Didn't he know it was rude to stare? His gaze was so hard that Danny could almost feel it scraping at his face with its teeth.

"Um . . . yes, I think you do know them. . . ."

Danny was about to tell him their names when he remembered the bit in the notebook about how the old man had refused to give them the book. It had been a while ago, but you could never be sure what people might remember. Perhaps it wouldn't be such a good place to start.

He tried again. "Um . . . I think you've got something I need. . . ."

Where were the biscuits? Where was the cup of tea? Danny glanced over his shoulder, but there was nobody there to help him. Don't be stupid, he told himself. Just ask.

"I need the Book of Storms," he said. "You've got it, haven't you?"

Abel Korsakof rose to his feet. It took him so long that Danny had almost lost his nerve again by the time the old man was upright. The ancient face had taken on a look of panic, but the eyes were still staring.

"What for?" he demanded.

He didn't even ask how I know about it, thought Danny. It's like he saw me coming a mile off. It's like he'd *known* I was coming, although he couldn't have.

But at least he hadn't said no.

"To find my parents," Danny said. "I think they went to see a storm, or something, and got lost. I need to find out how . . . and where . . ."

"I see," said Abel Korsakof. Then he cleared his throat. "In that case, you must certainly have the book. Sit down. Let me find it for you."

He indicated the single chair, and Danny perched on the edge of it, taking a closer look at the papers on the floor.

"What's that?" he asked.

Abel Korsakof went over to the bookshelves behind Danny and started to turn books over, looking for the one he wanted. "A map," he said. "The work of my life. A map of the various processes of storm formation." He turned over another couple of books, examining the spines.

Danny peered at the words on the map. Most of them were at least fifteen letters long. There were a few drawings—bad drawings: he could have done better himself—but they didn't help to explain any of the words. Was it storm language? How did storms even speak? Would he, Danny, have to try talking to one? He tried to memorize a couple of the words just in case they came in useful someday, then realized they were probably just a normal foreign language. Hadn't the notebook mentioned something about the old man being Polish?

"It looks complicated," he said, to try and sort of praise Abel Korsakof so he might remember about biscuits. The pasties seemed a long time ago.

"It *is* complicated!" the old man snapped, and then hurriedly added, "but I am sure a clever boy like you could learn about it, if you wanted to."

Well, that's stupid, thought Danny. For a start, he doesn't know if I'm clever or not. He doesn't know anything about me.

For a moment he was tempted to open his mouth and say that actually he wasn't very clever but that he could do some much better drawings of all those flashes of lightning and mountaintops that were dotted around the paper, if the old man wanted him to. But there was definitely something a bit missing about Abel Korsakof, like he didn't really know much about what was going on around him. He was probably just thinking about something else. Well, that was fine. As long as he handed over the Book of Storms. What would it be like? Big and leather bound, with gold lettering? Or small and darkly mysterious?

So Danny kept quiet and waited.

✦ ✦ ✦

Abel Korsakof found what he was looking for. He opened the book and ran his fingers inside the cut-away pages.

It was his elder brother's army knife. Thick handled, with a wide, short blade—perfect for slicing or stabbing. It had been hidden in the book of Polish fairy tales ever since Abel had stolen it, seventy years ago. His elder brother had hated fairy tales.

All he had to do was lean around the boy and drag the blade across his throat. There would be blood, but Sammael was sure to deal with all that. Or would he? If Korsakof had only fifty years more to live, he didn't want to spend half of them in prison. Sammael did look after his own, but maybe he'd better do it a cleaner way, just to be sure.

Stab him in the neck, then. Or in the back. No—that was too difficult. He might hit a rib. The neck it was.

The old man looked at the boy's neck. Danny's head was bent over the map, reading its symbols. He seemed to be offering up that patch of exposed skin to Korsakof's knife.

He wants me to kill him, thought Korsakof. Else why walk in here, asking for the Book of Storms? He must know whose it is. He's probably trying to outwit Sammael in some way. It is my duty to help Sammael, in return for all he has given and promises yet to give me. It is my duty to kill this boy.

He gripped the knife as he closed the hollowed-out book and replaced it on the shelf. Then he took a single step, which brought him close to Danny, and raised his hand. Let it be quick, he prayed. Let him not say anything to me when he knows he is about to die.

Korsakof closed his eyes and swung the knife.

The cat appeared as if fired from a crossbow and flung itself against the old man's arm, sending him jerking backwards. Danny swung round and scrambled to his feet. Korsakof's arm flailed in the air, reaching out toward him, trying to grab him. Fingers touched his shoulder, and the knife swooped down again, catching a glint of the evening sun as it fell.

Danny ducked and threw himself sideways, but the shed wall was too close and he couldn't get far enough away. The knife sliced toward him again, and he crashed against the small table.

The table! He could use it as a shield! He scrambled underneath it and heard the knife rattle against its top, inches from his head.

"Stop!" he yelled. "Stop it! Don't!"

His ears buzzed. The old man's feet shuffled toward him. He was wearing leather sandals and brown slacks.

Without thinking, Danny reached up and gripped the edge of the table, then shoved it toward the brown slacks. It caught them just above the knees, sending Abel Korsakof tumbling to the floor. The table fell over on top of the old man and he wriggled, struggling to free himself with a moaning cry.

But he couldn't do it one-handed. He had to drop the knife for a moment. He was very old, older than most people ever got, and he hadn't much more strength than even twig-armed Danny.

So Danny leaned hard on the table, pressing it down into Korsakof's stomach. The old man cried out in pain.

"Oh! Do not! Do not crush! Let me up!"

Danny didn't care. An angry flush sprang onto his face. He wanted to push the table again, to pin Abel Korsakof down until he was begging for mercy.

"You tried to kill me!" he gasped. "You'll only do it again if I let you go!"

"No . . ." moaned Korsakof, "no, I promise . . . I will not. Please."

Danny stuck out a foot and dragged the knife toward him, keeping his eyes on the old man in case he tried to grab it on the way.

Once he had the knife safely in his hand, Danny looked at Abel Korsakof's face again. This time he saw the wrinkles and the straggly beard. Korsakof wasn't staring at him anymore. His eyes were half closed.

Danny curled his fingers around the solid handle of the knife. Standing back, he tipped the table up and freed the old man.

"Don't do anything," Danny said, holding the knife before him. "You can get up, but don't do anything."

It took Korsakof even longer than before to get up. He had to have a break halfway, when he was on his knees. Seeing him kneeling, wheezing, and trembling, his shuddery old arms shaking as though he'd been working a pneumatic drill, Danny wanted to help him. He'd helped his Gran when she'd fallen over a couple of times. It was a kind thing to do. But there was no way he was going near this old man, not any nearer than he had to.

Korsakof finally made it upright. His feet wouldn't hold him; his bandy legs crept farther and farther apart, and he reached for the chair. The knife handle grew clammy, but Danny didn't relax his grip.

Finally, Abel Korsakof put his face in his hands and pressed his bony fingertips against his skull. He was silent for a long, measured breath, then he dropped his hands down, looking at Danny in an almost normal way for the first time.

"I am sorry," he said. "I will not try to hurt you again."

"You couldn't," said Danny. "I've got this." He was still holding the knife braced in front of him, ready to slash at the first sign of another attack.

"Yes," said Abel. "Keep it. But you will not need to use it again. Not on me, for certain."

"I want the Book of Storms," said Danny. "Don't move. Tell me where it is and I'll get it."

"It is not here," said the old man. "I cannot keep it here. It is not the kind of thing you wish to have around you for very long."

"Tell me where it is, then."

Korsakof shook his head. "I cannot betray him," he said. "He may be terrible in many ways, but he is always honest, and it is his book."

"What?" said Danny. "What are you talking about? Whose book?"

"Sammael, of course. I take it that is why you want it— you think it has some secret in it that will help you destroy him. He said you had found a way to discover it. There is nothing in the Book of Storms about him, though. I can tell you that for certain."

Danny's stomach scrunched itself into a knot. Sammael. That was the name the dying sycamore had gasped out, with its warning about being careful, and something about dreams. But surely that couldn't help him find his parents? No—it was just this horrible old man trying to make him scared.

He pushed away the thought, as sharply as he could. "I've got no idea what you're on about," he said. "I told you, I want the book to help me find my parents. They've disappeared and I want to find them—that's all I want. And then you try to kill me! And I just thought you'd give me biscuits!"

They stared at each other. Abel swallowed and rested a frail hand on one of his worn-out knees.

"Let us start again," he said. "I did not want to kill you. Sammael told me you were coming and that I had to. And you know what he is like. He has ways."

"I don't know what he's like," said Danny. "I don't know anything about his 'ways.' I've only ever heard his name once before. And that was from a—" He stopped himself quickly, not wanting to say "tree." Why did *he* have to know things that nobody else would ever believe?

"But . . . you are looking for your parents, are you not? And you know they are alive, because you know Sammael has done something to them. Is that not right?"

Danny ground his teeth. "No! Stop trying to confuse things! I didn't say anything like that. They went off in a storm. It was nothing to do with Sammael."

"But of course it was. Sammael can control the storms—you must already know that? He has done something with a storm, taken them away, or some such thing. That is why they cannot get back to you. Quite clearly he was aggravated by what they are trying to do and wanted to deter them somehow."

From confusing to horribly simple. Danny swallowed hard and couldn't breathe for a few seconds. But he forced himself to speak.

"So . . . so you think he's . . . *killed* them?"

Abel Korsakof took a small step backwards. "Of course not! He cannot kill anyone himself. Of course he cannot. He is forbidden to take life with his own hands."

Danny tried to calm the rising panic in his chest. Sammael couldn't kill them. Then they must be alive. They must be somewhere. "But . . . but if it's them he was after, then how does he know anything about me?"

The old man shrugged. "But he knows everything about everyone. He is Sammael."

The way he said this made Danny not want to hear the name Sammael ever again. Just the sound of the word filled him with small pricks of icy pain.

"He must have made a mistake," he said tightly. "I've never done anything wrong. It was *you* who told my parents about the Book of Storms, at a fete in Hopfield."

Something stopped in Korsakof's face.

"I did . . ." he said eventually. "I did. That is right—they told me that their child had died in a storm."

"Their *daughter*," Danny found himself saying. "I'm their child as well."

"Of course, but they merely said that their child had died, and they had taken to studying storms. But they *knew* storms. No ordinary human knows that much about storms, not in the way they did. People may know all sorts of science about the weather, but they don't talk about storms as *beings*, like your parents did. They must have been close to a storm—closer than any normal person could ever get. So I just assumed they must have called on Sammael too. I thought they would know about him, and about the book, and then I realized that they did not, and I stopped talking, and I forgot. . . ."

Abel Korsakof fixed his eye on Danny. The manic stare crept back. "What does Sammael want from you?" he asked suddenly.

"I keep telling you, I don't know," said Danny. "Who is he, anyway?"

Korsakof ignored the question. "You must have found something recently. He said it was a thing that had to be done."

Danny realized that by "a thing" he meant Danny's own

murder. How had he escaped it? How had he ended up being the one with the knife in his shaking hand, still living and breathing? He ought to be dead, if someone else wanted to kill him. He'd never been strong enough to win a fight before.

Korsakof surely wouldn't try again. It took the old man so long to move after that fall that Danny would be out the door and back in Hopfield by the time he'd even gotten to his feet for another crack. Unless he was only pretending to be frail. Some of those swipes with the knife had seemed pretty swift and powerful.

But Korsakof was the only person Danny knew who might be able to help. So he pushed the creeping fear aside and said, "I did find something strange this morning. I don't know what it is."

He pulled the stick from his pocket with the hand that wasn't holding the knife. He didn't want to let the knife go, not quite yet.

The stick seemed more ordinary every time he looked at it.

"What is that?" asked Abel Korsakof.

"I don't really know," said Danny. "Well, it's a bit of stick, I guess. I picked it up from a tree that got struck by lightning, but it isn't burnt."

He hesitated, remembering again the words of the

sycamore tree. *Be careful.* But you couldn't be so careful, or you never found out the things you didn't know.

"Why do you think it is strange?" asked Korsakof, although he could tell it was strange just by looking at it. From where he stood, small white flames seemed to be lapping at the edges of the stick, like cats' tongues at a bowl of milk.

"It makes me hear stuff."

"Hear what?"

"Like . . . everything. The tree. And plants. And that cat." He pointed at Mitz, who was sitting smugly on a bookshelf, and got ready to be told he was crazy.

Korsakof's fingers twitched.

"Is that all?" he asked. "Just hearing things?"

Danny frowned. Abel Korsakof was an adult. Adults were normally sensible. Even Danny, although he wasn't exactly an adult, had thought he was past the age of being able to believe that trees could talk, before he'd actually heard it for himself. But Abel Korsakof hadn't heard it, and he didn't seem in the least bit surprised or skeptical.

"Yeah . . . I can talk to them, too," he mumbled, a bit annoyed that the old man wasn't more impressed.

"And that is it? You can hold conversations with other creatures, using this stick?"

"Not just creatures," said Danny. "I told you, plants

and things. They can all talk." He had a feeling that Abel Korsakof wasn't going to even raise an eyebrow at this, and he was right. The old man just stared at the stick. His eyes weren't quite still.

"Can you talk to . . . to *storms*?" he asked finally.

Danny felt his feet clench, as though they were trying to grip the ground and keep him upright.

"I don't know," he said. Could he?

"But you found this after a storm? From lightning? It is . . . a thunderbolt?"

"No, don't be stupid," said Danny. "I mean, yes, I found it, but it's just a bit of tree."

"It is something . . . it is something . . . not of this world. Not of our world. Something of his world, perhaps. From a storm . . . A piece of storm . . . that is what he wants." His pupils had gone large, as if he'd been hypnotized. "That is what Sammael wants you dead for. But why should it matter to him . . . ?"

"This? He can have it! It isn't any use to me—once I've got the Book of Storms, I'll find my parents and go home. I mean, this is kind of cool, but I don't need it. If I give it to you, maybe you could give it to him and he'll leave me alone. Here, take it!"

Danny thrust the stick forward to Abel Korsakof. The old man flinched away.

"No!" he cried, flinging up his arms to shield his face.

"It isn't anything bad. It's just a stick," said Danny. "Just give it to him and tell him I'm going to find my parents and I won't get in his way." He tried to push the stick forward again, but Abel Korsakof's face had gone whiter than his beard in terror. His lips were moving as though he was calling on someone for help.

Danny stopped waving the stick around. "You won't help me, then?" he asked, rubbing his nose. He only remembered that he was holding a knife when the blade grazed his cheek. Perhaps if he threatened the old man again, he might get him to say where the Book of Storms was hidden. But Abel Korsakof seemed more afraid of the stick, and how could you threaten somebody with that?

The heat left his legs and he was trembling again. Whatever I am, I'm no hero, he thought. This should be happening to someone like Paul. He'd just charge through it, like he does when you're standing in his way in soccer, and be out the other side in seconds. I've no idea what to do.

Abel Korsakof said, very slowly, "I think I am understanding something. I think there may be only one way out for us, Danny. Even that will not be easy."

Us? He was going to help, then. Danny sank back against a bookcase, needing to prop himself up. Relief made all his tight muscles start to breathe again, and that only made him aware of how exhausted they were.

"What?" he asked, rubbing his eyes and putting the stick back in his pocket. Life seemed safer without it now.

"Is it really true that you do not know anything about Sammael?" asked Korsakof. "Tell me truly, now. Something will happen in a few minutes, and you will not like to know you have lied to me then."

His face had taken on color again, but it was a quiet shade of gray-green, and his piercing eyes seemed to have darkened.

"It's true," said Danny. "I've heard his name, but I don't know anything else about him. And I don't care, as long as I get my parents back."

"So you are not trying to destroy him?"

"No," said Danny, finding that his fingers wanted to cross behind his back.

"Because you must understand that I made a bargain with Sammael," said Korsakof. "He always keeps his word, and so I must keep mine. I can no more help you harm him than I can help him harm you anymore. And faced with the choice, it seems as though I must take a third way out."

Danny didn't understand what the old man was on about. He'd gone back to not making sense again. But he was forever old, and there was probably a huge load of stuff in his head that he just wasn't bothering to explain.

"I cannot kill you"—the fifty years of life, the apprentice that he could teach about storms, the thousands of days of study, vanished from Abel Korsakof's grasp—"and you are in possession of something far more powerful than you know. When Sammael told me about it, I thought you had stolen it. But I see now that you have not, you just came on it by chance, so it belongs rightly to you. And I have lived for ninety years on this earth, but today I have learned something entirely new. It seems that, perhaps, just one single person might be able to find the secrets to Sammael's power, to threaten that power, simply by talking to other creatures. . . ."

He was rambling now. Danny didn't follow half of what he said.

"The book is his," went on Korsakof, beginning to mutter rapidly. "I could never keep it by my side for long—it burned corners out of my soul. But I think that with that stick—perhaps—with that stick, you may have some sort of protection, or perhaps you will be able to read every word from the very beginning. . . . Oh, it is such a sadness. . . . Had I been the one to find that stick, what could have been. . . . But the world never fulfills our desires, my boy. It only burns them to ashes before our eyes, at the very moments they seem finally within our reach. . . ." He pulled himself up short and swallowed. "There is nothing more I can do now, except help you find your parents. Perhaps they will continue my work, with your help. The Book is in my blind in Butford woods. I will draw you a map."

Grabbing a scrap of paper from the shelf next to him, he scribbled a few lines on it and thrust it at Danny. It was totally incomprehensible.

"Find the Book," he said, "and stay out of Sammael's way, if you can. The stick! The stick belongs to you—you will never let it go, not now . . . but while you have it, he will always be after you. . . . If you want to find your parents, you must go quietly, stay low. Leave as little trail as you can. Only speak when you must. Be wary of the plants, the grasses, the trees, and the wind. Be wary of the rain, the birds, the dogs, and the earth. The world is watching you, Danny—the world is always watching. If you want to escape Sammael, do not let it see who you are!" He finished, his finger pointing toward Danny's heart. His blue eyes had turned a dark shade of purple, and a thin trickle of blood dribbled from his nose.

Danny watched it trail down his lips. His spine tingled. Korsakof must be mad. That must be it. Yes, he *must* be. How could anyone be wary of the earth?

He wanted to close his eyes and push it all away. If he could open them again and be in his living room, watching Abel Korsakof on television ranting at some other skinny boy, someone with quiet courage who would nod and bravely bear his fate, instead of someone whose guts were trying to churn butter and whose heart felt very small and weak like a baby bird, then maybe he'd think about the mystery a bit and enjoy the story. But he was here and this was him. And soon he'd have to step outside the walls of this shed and set off again to find the Book of Storms.

It was impossible. He could never make that journey. He just wasn't brave enough.

"Now give me the stick," said Abel Korsakof, in a voice that sounded like fingernails on a blackboard.

"What?" Hadn't he just said nobody could take it from Danny?

"The stick." Abel Korsakof held out his hand, calm and steady.

"But you just said no one could touch it, apart from me. . . ."

"Give it to me. You will get it back, but I must have a look at it first."

"No," said Danny, his heart beginning to quicken. The old man was trying to play a trick on him. He'd been lulling Danny into a false sense of security with all this ranting and rambling, and now he was trying to do something sneaky.

"Trust me," said Abel Korsakof. Which of course meant that you shouldn't.

Danny gripped the bookshelf behind him. He'd have lots of time to react if Abel Korsakof started doing anything, given how long he'd taken to get up the last time.

But it was the final effort of the old man's life, and he found the last pieces of his strength for it. More than ninety years of laboring and scrambling up hillsides and flinging himself sideways to dodge falling trees brought him to Danny's side in an instant, one skeletal hand snapping tight around the boy's wrist, the other around his neck.

Danny struggled for breath, trying to stab forward with the knife, but Abel Korsakof's wiry old muscles held their own for a few vital seconds, forcing Danny's wrist back so that he had to drop the knife or let his arm be broken.

He dropped the knife. Korsakof let go of his arm but kept hold of his throat. The grip of the bony fingers froze into stone around Danny's neck.

"Remember, Danny," the old man said, his face so close that his beard tickled Danny's nose, "not everything that hurts you is an enemy. And not everything that helps you is a friend."

Danny stared at him. Did he mean himself? Which was Abel Korsakof, friend or foe?

"Now give me the stick," said Korsakof.

Danny pulled it from his pocket. Abel Korsakof released his neck, took a step backwards, and put out his hand.

As soon as his fingers curled around the stick, his body stiffened. For a second Danny thought he was covered in hair—white, fluffy hair wriggling and rippling as it pushed against his skin. But it wasn't hair, it was the same white flame that the old man had seen around the stick, and it was eating him alive. In another moment it brightened into yellow, then orange, then red, and for the briefest of seconds it burned midnight black, then Abel Korsakof flung his arms out and fell onto the spread mess of his life's work. The stick dropped from his hand. Korsakof's legs sprawled over the storm map; he took a last rattling breath and was still.

Blood dribbled from between his blue lips, and the skin of his arms and face took on a mottled crimson color. But in the V of his shirt neck, his chest faded to pale yellow. And as his heart gave its final, faint lurch, his eyes returned to a gentle cornflower blue.

✦ ✦ ✦

Danny closed his own eyes and covered them with his hands, wanting to shut out the picture. If he couldn't see that slumped body, those streaks of blood, that blotchy skin, maybe it would all go away. Or maybe those flames would come back and eat up the entire corpse, not just whatever it was that they'd already fed on.

The scream waited for a couple of stunned seconds and then burst from his lungs. He screamed in an awful, endless roar that sent the cat flying out of the shed in anguish. If he stopped, the flames might leap out of the stick again and run over the floor toward him, but surely nothing could touch him while he was yelling so loudly. He screamed until his eyes were bleeding with tears and his face was stinging with the pain of his stretched cheek muscles, and even then he couldn't make himself stop.

What ended it was a touch on his wrists, trying to pry his hands away from his face. He tried to twist away, but he was held fast, and then arms were around him, hugging him close, pulling his face into a soft, warm shoulder.

For a second he thought it was his mum. But the smell was wrong, the body too solid and fat. His mum was bony, with tighter-hugging arms.

It was Mrs. Korsakof. When at last Danny stopped screaming and began to breathe again, she stroked his back a couple of times and let him go.

"What happened?" she asked. But Danny couldn't speak.

Mrs. Korsakof bent over her husband's body and knelt by his side. She didn't seem to notice the stick. It lay just beside the hand that had grabbed it from Danny.

Danny didn't want to touch it. He wanted somebody to come and take him away. Where was Mitz? Danny looked around for her. Brave, fearless Mitz—she'd probably gone after another weasel in the hedge. But without picking up the stick, he couldn't talk to her.

A crumpled piece of paper had wedged itself between his fingers—Abel Korsakof's illegible map. Great Butford. He had no idea where that even was, just that it had been drawn by the shaky old hand that had deliberately set fire to itself in front of him.

He shivered until his knees knocked against each other. And he knew that it was all impossible.

Mrs. Korsakof took Danny back to the house, grasping his arm tightly. She told him to sit down and breathe deeply, until he could speak and tell her who he was and where he belonged. Her low-beamed kitchen smelled of bread and sweet cakes, and her hands trembled as she clutched the telephone and called for an ambulance.

She made Danny a cup of hot chocolate by melting a couple of squares of real chocolate into a saucepan of milk, and she put a plateful of lemon cake in front of him. It was coated in syrup that had crystallized into a sugary crust, but Danny couldn't eat it.

He held tight to the straps of his schoolbag. Mitz did not return. He wanted to go outside and call for her, to have her running over the lawn toward him, pushing her soft head into his palm. But he didn't trust himself to speak.

"The ambulance won't be long now, dear. And the police. Are you sure you can't tell me your parents' names?"

Mrs. Korsakof made herself a cup of tea and tried to raise it to her lips. Her hands were shaking so much that she spilled it all down her blouse.

"Oh dear!" she said, dabbing at herself with a dish towel. "Oh dear!"

For a moment her hands slumped to her sides, and she seemed to be about to do what Danny had done—bury her face and scream. But instead she took a deep breath.

"I must go and be with him," she said, more to herself than to Danny, and then she went out of the room.

He stared at the table for one more second. She had called the police. There would be questions, and he would have to answer them, and he would have to tell the police officers that, yes, his parents sometimes went away at night and, yes, he was eleven, but it wasn't as simple as it seemed because they hadn't meant to stay away, he was sure they hadn't, because now he knew about Sammael and the storms and he was pretty sure that something had been done to them that no policeman on earth could unravel. And the police wouldn't believe a word of it. They would try to be nice and put him in some home somewhere with "responsible" people who weren't his parents and who never would be.

Then he pushed himself to his feet. He didn't want questions, or people trying to be nice. None of that would make anything better. He wanted to crawl away into the night and find a hole somewhere, and wait for things to put themselves right again. And outside, there was Mitz, his friend. She wouldn't ask stupid questions. She would curl up beside him and keep on breathing.

The shadows were drawing long as he slipped from the house and made his way back toward the hedge, calling softly to the cat and peering for her shape in the fading light.

But Mitz had vanished. She wasn't waiting out in the lane, and although Danny stood for five minutes, calling her as loudly as he dared, she didn't come to him. There was nothing to do but stumble back to the railway station and get on a train to somewhere—anywhere—that he knew.

CHAPTER 6

THE FARM

A s Danny hurried back toward the railway station through the deserted streets of Hopfield his ears caught the distant sound of police sirens. Without Mitz to look out for, he kept his head down and tried to ignore the warmly lit windows of other people's houses. What would those people behind the windows say if he marched up to one of the doors and knocked on it, explaining that he'd lost his parents and then watched an old man die, both on the same day? And what if he explained too that the old man's death had really been his fault?

He tried to push the thought of Abel Korsakof away,

right out of his mind, but that wasn't going to work now; he couldn't imagine his head without that memory inside it playing over and over like a flashing neon sign. He tried to wrap the memory in other thoughts: of Mitz, of the reddening sunset, of his own, quiet bedroom with the shelf of books and computer games, and the pictures he'd drawn stuck up on the walls. That didn't work either. No matter how closely he tried to picture them in his mind's eye, none of those things could be bigger than death.

Because death changed everything. When his Uncle Mick had died, Danny had only been about five or six. He might not even have remembered it if he hadn't been staying at the farm and seen Aunt Kathleen running up the lane, bursting into the house, and grabbing the duvet off the closest bed, which happened to be Danny's. After the ambulance left, he saw his duvet bundled up in the hallway. It looked sort of the same, except that there were smears of blood creeping out of the creases. He still wondered what his uncle had looked like under the turnedover tractor—he'd even tried to draw it once, in the secrecy of his room—but he'd never really been able to picture more than just Uncle Mick with the duvet on top of him, covering all the places that were bleeding.

And then Aunt Kathleen hardly spoke for weeks, even to say things about the cows, and Tom got all obsessed with badgers and spent the rest of the summer dodging around the woods in the middle of the night, with Aunt Kathleen trying not to shout at him when he came home. Danny followed him once and got almost as far as the edge of the woods, but Tom saw him and sent him back to the house, and after that his visit quickly ended.

The farm. It was the closest place to home Danny could think of just then. At the farm, he always stayed in the same room and ate breakfast from the same bowl, and suddenly that was all he wanted—just to see a room he knew and eat from a bowl that was his. He'd never taken a train to get there before, but at Easter they'd caught a bus down to a station called Blackthorn Halt, when he and Tom had gone to see Tom's sister, Sophie, off on holiday. It wasn't far away: it had to be possible.

He managed to put the thought in the front of his mind, over all the other things. Blackthorn Halt. Blackthorn Halt station, and then a bus up to Sopper's Edge. Repeating the names to himself, he quickened his pace.

It wasn't until he was sitting on the bus, grinding up the lanes toward Sopper's Edge, that the other thoughts forced their way back in: not only had he left Mitz behind, but he'd also left the stick lying there on Abel Korsakof's shed floor.

Good. At least without that stick, he might be safe.

But as soon as the memory came back to him, he couldn't shift it. The piece of wood had stamped itself across his mind's eye; the feeling of it curled in his palm began to worry at his blood, like a collie nagging sheep.

The stick had stuck to him. He closed his eyes, and in the blackness it was still there. Every knot, every splinter.

Night had fallen by the time he trudged up the lane to the farm. The lights of the farmhouse shone ahead: those ones were the living room windows, blazing away, and the one upstairs was Sophie's bedroom. She didn't do much around the farm; she wanted to pass her exams and go to university. In the living room, there'd be Aunt Kathleen and Tom, their heads together over feed bills and stock lists and magazine articles advising them how to improve their grassland. They were always trying to get Danny to take an interest in the cows, asking him to help feed them, check them over for cuts and scratches, and clean out the barns, but he preferred cows in computer games to real live ones that stamped their hard feet and swung their heads about, spraying the walls with sticky snot from their huge noses.

When Aunt Kathleen opened the door, she didn't see

Danny for a second. She was a lot taller than most other women, and she had to peer down to make out the slight figure in the navy blue sweater, his brown hair blending into the darkness.

"Danny? What are you doing here?"

"Can I come in?" Danny said. His voice was very small.

"Yes, of course you can. You look fair done in! But where're your mum and dad?"

Danny shrugged hopelessly. Aunt Kathleen looked hard at him for a long second and then stepped back into the hall, letting a cloud of cooking smells waft out into the night air.

"In," she said.

Aunt Kathleen knew how to do food. Although her family had already eaten their dinner, there was plenty left for Danny. She put plates in front of him: cold roast lamb and potatoes, thick slices of pork pie, bread and jam and half an iced cherry cake. He found, after forcing himself to eat a mouthful, that his appetite had come back despite all the horrible things that had happened.

When at last Danny had stopped eating for long enough to draw breath, his aunt stopped putting more food on the table and sat down. Aunt Kathleen looked a bit like his mum—her hair was the same toffee blond—but her face was much wider and flatter and she didn't smile quite as often. And she was even less of a comfortable motherly sort, tall and broad and a lot like a man, with a voice that seemed to rumble up through gravel stuck in her stomach—but at least he knew her.

"Right. Where're your mum and dad?" she asked.

Should he lie? He'd lied loads of times to his own parents, of course, but he couldn't remember ever having tried to lie to his aunt. She had quite a big nose, as if she'd be able to sniff out lies before you'd even said them.

So he took a very deep breath and said, "I don't know. They've . . . disappeared."

"What do you mean 'disappeared'? Disappeared where?"

Danny shrugged. Really he wanted to say, If I knew that . . .

"They're not at home?"

He shook his head.

"Are you sure?"

He nodded.

"When did they go?"

"Last night."

"Last night? In that storm?"

Danny stared down at his food. Aunt Kathleen narrowed her eyes at him.

"Danny, I want you to tell me the truth now," she said. "Have they really gone, or has something else happened? Are you in some kind of trouble?"

How stupid was it to ask someone to tell you the truth? Like you just assumed that the rest of what they said was a load of rubbish. It was always adults who did it—no one his own age had ever said, Now, Danny, tell me the truth. His friends might say, Yeah, right, when they didn't believe him. But they waited until he'd spoken before they said it.

"No, I'm *not* in trouble," said Danny, breaking a bit of bread and stabbing it against the plate. "*They* might be, because they've *disappeared*, like I told you. *I* went to school and then tried to look for them, but they weren't anywhere."

Aunt Kathleen raised an eyebrow. He could tell she was wondering why he'd gone to school when his parents weren't around. But she obviously decided to believe him, because all she said was, "You've no idea where they went? Did they say anything?"

Danny shook his head again.

"I'll try ringing them," said Aunt Kathleen. "I'll try their mobiles. And if they don't answer, I'll call the police."

"Don't call the police," Danny said, before he could stop himself. "Please don't. Please."

Aunt Kathleen narrowed her eyes again. "We've got to find them, Danny. Something might have happened to them. Why wouldn't we call the police?"

He felt his face go red at the embarrassment of knowing something he wasn't supposed to know. Now that he was fairly certain they weren't dead, there was even more reason to find them himself and not get any authorities involved. "Because . . . well . . . they aren't supposed to leave me alone, are they? I don't mind, it isn't a bad thing, I don't care . . . but the police wouldn't think that, would they? If you call the police and then they find Mum and Dad, they might . . . they'd send them to prison, wouldn't they? They might . . ."

"Hmph." Aunt Kathleen snorted through her long nose, considered him for a moment longer, and then picked up his empty plate. "Of course they won't send them to prison. Don't be silly."

"But they will! Or they'll at least get into loads of trouble, and it'll be all my fault, and I'll get taken away, and . . ."

"Danny!" Aunt Kathleen stopped, plate in midair. "Of course it isn't your fault. Your mum and dad shouldn't go off like that—you know they shouldn't. I've told them they shouldn't. Maybe it *is* time someone else told them that they shouldn't, someone they might actually listen to, for a change."

Danny felt his heart begin to beat faster. This was what happened when you got stupid adults involved. They did everything wrong.

"If you call the police, I'll run away!" he said, half shouting, half getting up from the table. "I will! Don't call them! I'll run away right now. You can't stop me!"

Aunt Kathleen grabbed his shoulder and then put the plate back on the table with a tight hand that stayed clenched around the white rim. Her fingers dug into Danny's shoulder, making him wince.

After a moment, she relaxed and took her hand off the plate but still held on to his shoulder. "All right," she said. "Calm down. I'll make a bargain with you. You stay here tonight, safe where I can see you, and I'll try calling them on their phones, now and in the morning, and if they haven't come back by then and I still can't get hold of them, we'll call the police. Agreed?"

He was going to say, I've tried calling them and they don't answer, but it was better for her to think she was doing something useful. At least it would keep her mind off calling the police. So he said, "It's probably nothing, really. I mean, they're always going off to look at storms. It probably isn't anything bad at all."

She snorted again, quietly this time, and as her hand released his shoulder, a tingling rush of warmth shot down his arm.

+ + +

Tom came wandering in to keep Danny company while Aunt Kathleen used the phone in the study. He was supposed to be studying for exams but instead had his face buried in a copy of *Farmers Weekly*.

"Hiya, Danny," he said, sitting down and reaching for a cold potato without looking up from the page. "Whatcha doing here?"

Tom was always eating, although he never seemed to get any fatter. He was tall and broad like Aunt Kathleen, but with much paler blond hair, and his arms were longer than Danny's legs. He was the kind of powerful big that Danny wanted to grow into, but whatever his parents promised him, Danny had a suspicion that he was never going to be as tall or as strong as Tom. What was nice about Tom, though, was that he wasn't always trying to prove how great he was. He'd chucked Danny over his shoulder and thrown him into the duck pond a couple of years ago, but he'd never tried it again.

Danny said, "My mum and dad have gone. No one knows where they are."

"Mum'll find them," said Tom, taking another potato.

In about three seconds, thought Danny, he'll ask me if I want to see the cows. One, two . . .

"D'you want to come and see the cows?" asked Tom. "We've got some nice calves at the moment."

"It's dark," said Danny.

"S'okay, there's lights in the barn. I'm going to do the last round in a bit. Come round with me."

Danny really didn't care about the cows. He quite liked feeding bottles to the orphaned calves, but there was something about the way cows looked at you that made you think they were plotting something.

"I'm all right," he said. "I'm kind of tired, actually."

"Okay," said Tom. He never really talked for the sake of it.

There was silence for a few moments.

"Tom?" Danny asked eventually.

Tom turned a page. "Yep?"

"What would you do if you woke up and your mum was missing?"

Tom raised his eyes and looked at Danny. His bangs had grown too long; he had to peer out from underneath them.

"Dunno," he said. "Well, I'd get the milking done, obviously."

Really? But then, Danny had gone to school, hadn't he?

"You wouldn't, like, have a party or something?"

Tom grinned. "Yeah, maybe later."

"Would you call the police?"

Tom shrugged. "Dunno. I guess I don't know what I'd do. What did you do?"

"I . . . went to school. . . ." said Danny.

"Dork," said Tom.

"And then I found this notebook and it said about this old guy, so I went to see him. . . ." Danny trailed off, no longer sure which bits of his conversation with Abel Korsakof had been unacceptably weird and which ones hadn't.

"And he didn't know anything?"

"Well, he sort of did. . . ."

He could show Tom the map, see if Tom knew where it was and how to get there, and then Tom might come along with him too, just to keep him company.

It was sort of a plan. He was just trying to work out the best way to introduce the idea when Aunt Kathleen came back into the room.

"No answer," she said. "Sounds like their phones are off. And as for you, mister, if you're not going to help Tom on the evening rounds, I think it's high time for bed."

For once, Danny didn't wait to be told a second time, or to argue over the hands of the clock. The day had been long enough. He stumbled upstairs to the little yellow guest room where he always stayed at the farm, and Tom found a pair of old striped pajamas that were huge on Danny even though they hadn't fit Tom for years. Then, too tired even to be haunted by thoughts of Abel Korsakof's scarlet face or the blood that had dribbled from his leathery nose, Danny sank into bed, closed his eyes, and let sleep overpower him in one huge, snapping gulp.

CHAPTER 7

THE ACORN

"Wrong!" Sammael snapped, striding into the shed. "He's mine. Put him down!"

The short woman paused. She had already gathered up the corpse of Abel Korsakof into her arms and was cradling him like a baby, her tangled silver hair falling onto his face.

"Er . . . no?" she said, flicking her hair back and double-checking the corpse's eyes. They had the full amount of soft humanity left in them. He was definitely hers.

"I bought him fifty years ago," said Sammael, thrusting an open notebook under her nose and indicating a line with one of his slender fingers. "Abel Korsakof. He's mine, not yours. You might be Death, but you don't get them all, not even in the end."

Death read the entry, her scarlet eyes hardening to crimson. Sammael didn't usually get things wrong. In fact, she made more errors than he did, which she blamed on relentless overwork. The entry was all correct, signed by Abel Korsakof himself. He'd received something called the Book of Storms and fifty years to read it in.

"But the date's wrong," she said. "The fifty years aren't up until next month. He shouldn't be dead. He shouldn't *be able* to be dead. What did you do to him?"

"Nothing!" spat Sammael, although he had his suspicions as to how Abel Korsakof might have died. "But whatever's gone wrong, his sand is still mine. He got his bargain."

"He *almost* got it," said Death. "Except for that final month." But she was getting ready to put the corpse down and concede defeat. She had too much to do, and she wasn't altogether sympathetic toward humans who chose to sell their souls to Sammael. If they wanted to, that was their own affair. It was hard enough these days finding time to gather up all the ones who'd lived natural lives, and then returning them back to the earth, without having to fight Sammael for the odd one who'd died in an ambiguous way.

But Abel Korsakof's eyelids lifelessly lolled open again,

and she caught sight of his gentle blue eyes and couldn't give him over.

"Give!" Sammael reached out an arm.

"Don't touch him!" Death swung the corpse away and closed her eyes. When they opened again, they'd changed from red to the exact blue of Korsakof's.

Around them, ghostly shadows began to creep from the shed walls and slide into the air. They didn't form shapes that could be seen and traced, but they began to eat the air with whispers. It was a language even Sammael didn't understand: the most ancient tongue of all, formed at the first moment a single cell had slipped from existence into death. To Death herself, who indeed knew everything, the sound of the whispers was as clear as a tune played on a single violin.

She listened. Sammael watched her. They rarely met, but he was always struck by her ugliness: her shapeless, plain face and drooping mouth. Her red eyes were usually as dull as ancient garnets, dragged from the earth covered in dust. Sammael hated creatures that tried to stand in his way, but he hated dull things even more. Death was both. All work and no play, he'd taunted her once, and she hadn't argued.

"I see what went on," said Death quietly as the shadows began to disperse.

"I couldn't care less what went on," said Sammael. "He's mine and I want him."

He had plans for Korsakof's sand.

"He isn't, though," said Death. "He laid down his life for that boy, the one you're after. Who, I'd like to remind you before you get any ideas, you *cannot kill*."

"He shouldn't have laid down his life for anyone!" roared Sammael. "His life was *mine*! Either bring him back to life and let him live for another month, or give him to me now! It's the law of the universe and *you* can't change it!"

His ears appeared to be steaming, but Death knew that it was smoke. Whatever made up Sammael sometimes combusted when he got very angry. But he couldn't harm Death.

She supported Abel Korsakof's corpse on her knee and reached up to push her silver hair back from her face.

"It is the law of the universe," she said. "There's no way I could bring him back—he touched some kind of storm fire. It burned his life away, protecting its owner. But he knew it would, and he still wanted to let it. I guess he knew that you'd try again to make him kill that boy and he didn't want to. So he sacrificed himself rather than become a tool for killing innocent children."

Death fixed her stare on Sammael. Not that it would make any difference at all whether she approved of him or not, but sometimes she had to let him know.

"*We* both know he was wrong, don't we?" she went on, grimly. "We both know that you can't *make* anybody kill, you can only suggest it and wait to see if they do. We both know that if you killed anyone, *I* wouldn't take them anywhere."

Sammael glared back at her and then smiled. It was a smile that curled the corners of his thin lips up into a tight arc and stopped just below his eyes.

"You forget," he said, "that I'm a lot cleverer than you."

"And *you* forget," said Death, letting her eyes relax back to their usual red, "that I'm stubborn and consistent and I know what you're up to."

"But you don't," said Sammael. "For every way that I've ever tried to do anything, I've got at least a thousand more up my sleeve. I could list a million ways in which I've managed to cheat you over the ages."

"You leave that boy alone," said Death. "And you leave storms alone, whatever you're trying to do with them. You're playing with fire."

"That's exactly what I'm doing," said Sammael. "And with storm fire, actually. Except I'm not playing. I mean it. And soon those wretched, ungrateful humans will know how *much* I mean it."

He reached into his pocket and pulled out an acorn.

"Do you want to see what *I* can do with taros?" he asked.

Without waiting for an answer, he threw the acorn onto the floor, then cast a few grains of sand on top of it and clicked his fingers.

"Kalia," he said. "Get out. A long way."

The lurcher shot from the shed. Sammael gave her a few seconds, then raised his eyebrows to Death and looked up at the shed roof.

" 'Come, friendly bombs, and fall on Slough. . . .' " he said.

It wasn't a single bolt of lightning, or even a few. A torrent of electricity spewed from the sky, pouring down in a blinding river. What had once been Abel Korsakof's shed erupted into a castle of flames.

"Lightning?" said Death as they faced each other through the fire, which neither could feel. "Very impressive."

"Ha!" said Sammael.

And the castle of Korsakof's shed roared up into the tumbling lightning, seeming to feed on it like a bird swallowing a dangled worm. Blazing into a golden fireball, it gulped and spat and chewed, reaching out to the trees, to the little cottage, to the hedges, and to the sign that hung in the old oak, devouring them in a single bright flare. Within seconds, Puddleton Lane End had become a great black scar, and Storm Cottage a smoking skeleton.

Sammael shrugged and the fire stopped. Death was watching him closely, trying to work out what he'd done.

"Only an acorn," said Sammael. "Plenty more where that came from."

"It's just fire," said Death. "I've seen worse."

Sammael smiled again. This time it reached his eyes, and even Death wanted to shiver.

"And another corpse for you in the cottage," he said. "Old lady. And even if you say I killed her, you'll find it a lot easier to take her away than to try and piece her back together. She was killed by storm fire, don't you know."

He turned on his heel and went to fetch Kalia. It was infuriating that the boy had gotten hold of that taro; storm fire couldn't kill a creature protected by such a thing. But there were still plenty of other ways. He had a good idea for the next attempt, which would hopefully be the last one. And then he could get on with collecting more taros. Shame to have wasted one flattening a shed and a single old woman, but it had been worth it to see the surprise on Death's smug face.

Sammael reached the farm in seconds, unlocked the door, and found his way upstairs. He crouched down by the woman's bedside. Another ugly one. She had a wide, flat face and toffee-colored hair, and she looked like she'd spent her life in a cowshed too close to the back ends of the cattle.

He got a few grains of sand out of his pocket. He always kept a handful in there, but his supplies were getting low—it would soon be time to go back to his room and get some more. Dropping the sand onto the woman's face, he watched it dissolve into her skin.

"There are logs in the bed," he said. "Logs in the yellow bedroom bed. Logs that need chopping in two. And when you've spent a lifetime chopping logs, you know exactly how to do it, don't you? You could pretty much do it *in your sleep.*"

He stood back and watched her rise. Her eyes were open but sightless. She walked as calmly as if she'd been awake, knowing exactly how many steps to take to reach the doorway. Then she headed off down the stairs.

Down the stairs and toward the barn, where the axes were kept.

CHAPTER 8

MIDNIGHT

Death was dancing with Abel Korsakof, her tears falling freely to the ground in great streams. They formed puddles so deep that the dancers were soon splashing, except, whereas Death seemed to dance with greater relish as she kicked up spray, Abel Korsakof was dragging his feet, weak against the depth of water.

Soon Death was holding Abel's body entirely in her arms, holding him upright to stop him from sinking. But the old man was a deadweight. His legs splayed out, catching on the waves and causing Death to trip. She gathered him up under the knees and cradled him. His head lolled back, and his arms swung out into the high-flung water as if reaching for something so tiny that the only hope he had of catching it was to sweep through every inch of air. But whatever it was, he wasn't finding it—all the swinging and swiping was only pushing Death further off balance, causing her to stagger hopelessly about in her lake of tears.

And then Death dropped Abel Korsakof. With a great splash he fell into the pool, and Danny woke up, sure that the sound in his ears must be more than part of a dream, waiting for his brain to clear and reassure him that it wasn't.

Clarity came but brought with it a terrible silence that crawled across every inch of his skin until it had prickled into a carpet of goose bumps.

There was something in his room, he was sure of it.

His own breath, normally so silent, began to catch at the hairs in his nostrils and whistle softly like the wind down a chimney. The more he listened to it, the louder it became, so that he was sure he wouldn't hear any tiny sounds of danger unless he held his breath.

After he'd stopped breathing, the pounding of his heart filled his ears, blood rushing round his eardrums in a pulsing rhythm. It set off a high-pitched, electronic whine that made him clench his fists under the duvet and screw his eyes shut, trying to will the sound away.

When he opened them again, the room seemed even blacker.

He saw a silver glint in a shaft of moonlight, and some vital instinct possessed his body for just long enough to make him throw himself to one side as it flickered. There was a whisper, a rush, a silent swing, and the shrieking, screaming, spine-piercing howl of every nerve under Danny's skin as for an endless moment everything in the room flashed myriads of color and the air turned to molten gold.

The axe thudded into the mattress beside him, pinning down the yellow covers under which he lay.

Danny couldn't move. For a second he feared that he, too, had been pinioned to the mattress, but through the darkness he saw that the lumpy shape of the axe head was next to his shoulder. Cold air was emanating from the metal. He wasn't bleeding, nothing hurt. But his heart was beating as though it were the size of a bucket.

The bedroom door swung shut. And something hung in the air: a trace of flowery scent. A scent so impossible that Danny knew he must be imagining it: there was no way his aunt would ever have played such a trick on him. His eyes must be inventing that whisk of white nightgown disappearing into the shadows.

Slowly he pulled himself away from the axe, inch by inch, until he had crept so far over the edge of the bed that there wasn't enough of him left on it to balance and he fell onto the floor.

From whichever place he looked at it, the axe was still there.

With an enormous effort he overcame the paralysis in his limbs and posted them, one by one, underneath his body. For a moment it seemed the safest way to be, curled up as tight as a hedgehog, but without an armor of spines on his own back he knew it wouldn't be safe for long. He scrambled to his feet.

The axe had not moved.

Danny switched on the light. The axe was Aunt Kathleen's wood-cutting axe, the two-handed monstrosity that Danny couldn't even lift. He had watched Jake, the hired hand with muscles like bricks, felling a tree with it the summer before. It was an old warrior, and it had fallen blade-down right where Danny's chest should have been.

He must have bitten his tongue in the fall: the sharp lemon taste of blood filled his mouth. His legs still wouldn't hold him—either he must move now or he would fall like

Abel Korsakof onto the hard, cold floor and Death would gather him up in her arms.

Danny's hands scrabbled frantically over the door until he found the handle and yanked it open. He ran into the passage outside and stood for another few seconds in the moonlight. The air seemed five degrees warmer than it had been in his room; it was a living air, a breathing air, soft and gentle. And he thought, The air in my room was cold. It was full of . . . of . . . full of . . .

But the only word he could think of to describe the difference was a single name that stayed mute on his lips and threatened him with terror if he dared speak it out loud.

"Danny?" Tom took his binoculars away from his eyes, seeing Danny come out of his room. Danny leapt, as startled as a rabbit at the sound of a gunshot. "Were you having a nightmare?"

"What?" Danny's eyes didn't seem quite focused.

"I just saw Mum coming out of your room. Were you having a nightmare?"

Danny didn't answer. Standing in a shaft of moonlight wearing Tom's old pajamas, he looked very small and thin.

"There's badgers in the yard," said Tom. "A whole family. Come and have a look."

He held out his binoculars. Danny was staring at the blank wall, his palms pressed against the plaster behind him. Even through the half light, Tom could see that he was shivering.

"Hey, Dan." Tom took a few steps toward him, and Danny flinched, then swallowed. "Danny, you okay?"

Danny shook his head rapidly. "Look," he whispered. "In there." He pointed back toward the doorway of the yellow bedroom.

Tom put his head around the door. There was enough moonlight that he didn't have to switch the light on to see the axe; it sat embedded in the duvet, bathed in patches of silver and shadow.

He withdrew his head and took a closer look at Danny. He hadn't thought his small cousin could even lift that axe, never mind carry it upstairs.

"What did you bring that inside for?" he asked.

Danny's knees, exhausted from all the shivering, gave way again. He slid down the plastered wall and seemed to sigh with relief when he no longer had to worry about controlling his limbs. They were apparently not quite trustworthy.

"I have to go," Danny mumbled. "It's not safe here. They're watching. . . . I don't know where to go, though. . . . They're everywhere. . . ."

"Who's everywhere? What are you talking about?"

"Everything's everywhere. I don't know what wants to kill me and what doesn't. Maybe my parents are already dead. . . ."

"Dead? I thought you said they went away. . . . They can't be dead. What on earth are you talking about, Danny? Danny?" Tom crouched down, binoculars still hanging from his hand.

Danny looked as though he were slipping into a trance. "And now he's trying to kill me. . . . I dreamed about Death and Abel Korsakof, and they were drowning in this massive lake. . . ." His eyes rolled up into his head.

Tom, who had seen plenty of death on the farm but never much shock, had no idea what was happening. Danny's body began to knock against the floor as it shuddered.

"Danny! Danny!" Tom reached out to shake him by the shoulders. "Come on, wake up! It's just a bad dream, that's all! Tell me about it! Come on, Danny. Danny! I won't be cross if you're having me on. 'Cos you don't look like you are . . . but you're scaring me, Danny. Come on, stop it. Wake up!"

Danny's eyes rolled back down, and he stared at Tom as though he were staring into the mouth of hell.

"He's trying to kill me, Tom. He knows where I am. I can't go back in there."

"Okay," said Tom, relieved back to his old sturdy self

by the refocusing of Danny's eyes. There would be time for explanations in the morning. "You can sleep in my room, if you like."

"No, no! You don't understand! I've got to leave! To go somewhere else! Oh, but there'll be nowhere, not by now. Why wasn't I careful? It told me to be careful. The most important thing, it said . . ."

Seeing Danny's eyes rolling skyward again, Tom straightened up and yanked him onto his feet. There was only one way he knew to calm anybody down, and that was to go outside, to feel the living world around your body, the sharp sky above and the solid earth below. Half pulling, half carrying his cousin down the stairs, Tom unlatched the back door and dragged him out into the night.

At once Danny seemed to revive. He looked around at the house, the hulked shapes of the farmyard buildings, the stars that simmered in the heavens.

"Feeling better?" asked Tom, sitting him down on an upturned bucket.

Danny nodded.

"Good. Now explain."

"There's something I didn't tell you about," said Danny.

"Well, yeah," said Tom. "I get that. What's going on?"

"The old man I went to see . . . he . . . he . . ." Danny swallowed hard. "He died. Don't ask me how. But he gave me a map. It might help me find my parents, but I can't understand it. I'm not good at maps and stuff."

"Okay, let me have a look," said Tom.

"It's . . . back in the bedroom."

Tom looked at him. "I'll get it," he said. "As long as you tell me everything. And I mean *everything*. Wait here."

Tom disappeared through the door. Now that Danny was fully conscious and calming down again, he knew that he needed the stick back. He needed more eyes, and the stick could give them to him. It was the only weapon he had against an enemy he couldn't even picture.

And he wanted Mitz. She'd have kept him warm while he was sitting in the yard in his pajamas, waiting for Tom. She'd have kept away the shadows that lurked around the barns and outbuildings. Not that he was frightened of shadows. But still.

Tom came back with Danny's school trousers and sweater.

"You'll feel better when you're warm," he said. "Put 'em on."

Tom was right. Warmth did amazing things to you. The moment Danny pulled them on over his pajamas, he felt braver somehow. Maybe this was what knights felt like when they put armor on: like they had a shield against the world. Except that they actually did. And he didn't.

He showed Tom the map. Tom had picked up a small flashlight, which didn't give off much more light than the moon, but they could see the scrawled lines clearly enough.

The "map" consisted of a wobbly blob with the words "Great Butford woods" scribbled inside it. Over the writing Abel Korsakof had also drawn a number of lines across the blob and a small square with an *X* in it. Danny had no idea what the lines were supposed to represent, except clearly the *X* must mark the spot where the Book of Storms was.

"So, this is Great Butford woods," said Tom. "Yeah, it's about that shape—I've been there before. And these are the paths that run through it. I remember this one that starts at the southeast corner; it's the way you go into the woods from the path behind the village green. It comes out at the top of Sentry Hill. There." He ran his finger over one of the lines and stopped at the top of the paper. "But what's the square with the *X*? Is that where you think your folks are?"

Of course Tom understood the map. Danny had never been out for a walk with Tom where Tom didn't know every inch of the paths and hillsides. He would have been a proper wild man of the woods if he'd had a long tangly beard and not been so keen on hanging out with the Young Farmers.

"He said it was a 'blind,'" said Danny. "I guess he meant a bird blind."

"Or a badger blind." Tom grinned. "Well, that's fine, we can get there easy. I'll ask Mum to take us when you're back from school tomorrow. I'm supposed to be studying, but my next exam isn't till Friday, so she won't mind."

At the mention of Aunt Kathleen, Danny's shoulders froze into his spine. He couldn't see her again. She had tried to *kill him*.

"No . . ." he whispered. "She mustn't know. . . ."

"Of course she'll have to know," said Tom. "If your parents aren't here, she's supposed to look after you."

Danny could only shake his head, hoping it might somehow convey his desperation. He needed to find out exactly what was going on. He needed the stick. Aunt Katheen wasn't on his side—that much was clear.

"Have you ever heard," he asked Tom, "of someone called Sammael?"

"No," said Tom, looking at him curiously. "How about you start from the beginning?"

So Danny did. And Tom didn't believe a word of it. Oh, he believed that something had happened to make Danny's parents temporarily uncontactable, and he believed that

Danny had managed to find his way to Abel Korsakof's house. But the rest—the storm, the stick, the cat, the Book of Storms—Tom listened to it all with a small smile that indicated he knew full well that Danny was making the whole thing up. Even the bit about Mitz didn't get him any closer to wanting to believe it. Danny would have thought that talking animals were just the kind of thing that Tom would be interested in. He was mad about animals, always looking out for badgers or talking to his cows, scratching their backs and calling them "Old Lady."

"Okay," said Tom, when Danny got to the bit about getting back on the train at Hopfield and making his way to the farm. "Great story. I mean, very inventive and all that. But don't you think you're a bit old for all this, Danny? Whatever mess you're in, you can't just make up kids' stories about it. I mean, whatever you've done, try telling the truth. People will still help you. They'll probably help you more, in fact."

"But you saw that axe!" cried Danny. "I didn't put it there!"

"Who did, then?"

Danny reddened, but everyone kept telling him to be truthful, so he was. "Your mum! Aunt Kathleen! I woke up and she was there, trying to chop me in half! I mean, she must have been sleepwalking or something, but who

tries to kill people in their sleep? It's Sammael, I keep telling you!"

He saw Tom's shaking head and cast desperately around
for a way to get his cousin to believe him.

"I'll show you my parents' notebook," he added. "I'll
take you to Abel Korsakof's house—you can talk to his wife.
She probably knows all about whatever he did. There's all
his storm stuff spread everywhere—we could sort of . . . work
out . . . where their storm went, maybe, sort of . . . and we
can get the stick back! I'll show you what it does. Please,
Tom! Please! You've got to believe me!"

"Easy!" Tom held up both hands. "Calm down, Dan.
You'll have another fit. Come on, stop making up stories
now. This is a right load of old hogwash."

Danny slumped. There was no way Tom was ever going
to agree to go with him. He should have realized that Tom
was too much of an adult, and adults could always think
of a hundred reasons not to do a thing before they came
up with one reason why they should. Milking cows and
reading *Farmers Weekly* was obviously much more important than Danny's entire life.

Why did everyone assume he was lying? They'd be
sorry when Sammael did manage to kill him and they all
had to admit he'd been telling the truth.

Although if Sammael had killed him in either of the

ways he'd tried so far, people would have thought that Abel Korsakof had been a terrible old monster or that Aunt Kathleen had gone temporarily insane in her sleep and had a tragic accident. No one would have linked it to Sammael at all.

Because nobody *knew* about Sammael. Or they pretended they didn't.

If I showed them, thought Danny, then they'd know. Sammael might be hidden now, but if I took away his power, everyone would see things change. And didn't Abel Korsakof say that, with the stick, I could find a way to do that?

He had to find his parents first. That was the most important thing. And then, once they were safe again, he'd try and use the stick to ruin Sammael, whoever and whatever he was. And then they'd all see.

Danny stood up and took a deep breath. He needed to find his schoolbag and his shoes. He was going, by himself if need be. Tom was right: he was too old to be making up stories. So he would prove that the stories were true.

"I'm going," he said simply.

"No way," said Tom. He tried to spring up and grab Danny, but Danny dodged away. They faced each other, tense.

"I'm going," said Danny. "No one believes me, but it's

all true. If I don't go, my parents will never come back. I *know* it. And Sammael will get me and he'll kill me. *You'll* be fine, although you'll be sorry you didn't listen. So I'm going, and you can't stop me."

"Danny, don't be stupid," said Tom. "It's the middle of the night. You'll get lost."

"I don't care," said Danny. Then he added, "I wouldn't get lost if you came with me. You know everywhere."

"Not quite everywhere," said Tom, but he was giving in.

"It won't take long," said Danny. "Just tomorrow, maybe, if we go now."

"There's no point in going now—there aren't any buses or trains at night. I don't see why you won't wait till the morning."

He still didn't get it. But, then, *he* wasn't the one who'd just woken up to find a mad axe murderer trying to turn him into kindling.

"I'm not waiting," said Danny. "I'm not staying here any longer."

"Do you even know how far Great Butford is?" said Tom. "Hopfield's not far, but you won't get to both of those places by tomorrow if you're walking."

Danny said nothing. He'd said all he needed to. What was it about the dark farmyard that had pulled his fears away? Perhaps it was those streams of silver and black moonlight, or the comfortable noises of cattle chewing and shuffling inside the barn. Perhaps it was only being outside, knowing he'd managed to survive at least ten minutes exposed to the night already. But that feeling he'd had in Korsakof's shed, that the journey ahead was impossible, seemed to have gone forever.

Tom said, "For God's sake. Get your shoes. I'll get my phone and leave a note for Mum. I should wake her up . . . but she was up all last night with that bloaty heifer. Ach, you're a pain, Danny. I guess we can just call her first thing in the morning. She's going to kill me. And if you don't do *everything* I say, I'm bringing you straight back. Got it? Right. We'll take the horses."

What he meant was that he would take his big brown mare, Apple, and stick Danny on the ancient black-and-white pony that both Tom and Sophie had learned to ride on. It was so old that no one remembered its real name and just called it the piebald, after its color.

"Quick way or long way?" asked Tom. "Forest or road?"

The forest was dark and gloomy, but Danny didn't care. "Let's go through the forest."

"Hangman's Wood?" said Tom, reaching up his hand to pull an imaginary noose up from his neck.

Danny nodded. "Yeah. There."

He tried not to think about what Tom had just done, or how the forest had come by its name.

"Okay." Tom grinned. His face was suddenly shining with the thrill of unexpected wildness.

They turned the horses toward the forest and trotted out of the yard.

Hangman's Wood was full of oak and beech trees. By night the shadows piled on top of each other, leaf upon leaf, branch upon branch, until what existed in the spaces between the trees wasn't clear night air but towers of shifting shadow-bricks. Night birds whistled, and insects retreated from shafts of moonlight as the horses padded along the soft earth.

After ten minutes, when the trail began to widen and the trees thinned, Tom thought, There's light enough from the moon, so why not? Waving his arm to catch Danny's attention, he put his heels to Apple's flanks so that she sprang into a gallop.

Together they ran, the horses dreaming of fire in the wind. Old friends that they were, they put their shoulders side by side and dispatched the distance as though they were not earthly horses but ghosts running toward freedom, their tails streaming out behind them.

CHAPTER 9

PUDDLETON LANE ENDED

D anny had never seen dawn break before. The first he
noticed of it was that he began to think he'd developed an extraordinary ability to see in the dark. Then he
caught the movement of Tom's arm as it swept up to point
at something, and saw that the horizon over a distant field
was shining royal blue.

They ambled down a long, straight road in the rising
twilight, keeping tucked into the verge in case a speeding
car came along and spotted them only at the last second.
Danny caught a faint scent on the air. He sniffed.

"Can you smell that?" he asked Tom.

"The burning? Someone's had a bonfire in one of these fields, I'd guess. It's an old smoke smell."

Something pinched at Danny's skin.

"Are we near Hopfield?" he asked.

"Yeah," said Tom, not really in the mood for a chat. "It's at the end of this road. Another half a mile."

"And are we near Puddleton?"

"Yeah, that was the last village, where we came off the bridleway. Didn't you see the sign?"

So they must be approaching from the opposite direction. They'd get to the Korsakofs' house before they reached the village. The old piebald pony stumbled over a pothole in the road. She wasn't shod; her hooves made a soft scrapy thud as they hit the tarmac. If anyone was awake nearby, they probably thought that only one horse was clip-clopping by: sleek brown Apple with her sturdy iron feet.

A skeleton reached up from one of the hedgerows ahead, dark and spidery.

"What's that?" Danny pointed at it.

"Dead tree."

Danny couldn't recall having seen any dead trees around Abel Korsakof's cottage when he'd been there before, but then, he hadn't come this far out of Hopfield.

Puddleton Lane End had been on the left coming out of the village, so this time it would be to their right, which was where the dead tree was.

Was the smell of burning getting stronger, just a little?

There was no need to look for the road sign in the thicket this time. Neither road sign nor thicket existed. Puddleton Lane End was a scorched streak across a blackened waste, roped off by yards of blue-and-white police tape.

It seemed much smaller than before. Danny was sure he'd wandered quite a way down the lane before he'd seen the sign for Storm Cottage, but as they reined in the horses and stood at the end of the lane, a charred timber frame was almost the first thing they saw. It was surrounded by twisted totem poles that had once been trees. The riot of colorful flowers had shriveled and dropped away into ashes; the emerald lawn between Storm Cottage and Korsakof's shed had withered into a patch of soot. The shed itself might never have existed, save for the mound of charcoal and ash that rose slightly higher than the black detritus around it.

The stick! How would the stick ever have survived that? It must have been an inferno, the fire that had devastated this place. And Danny had left the stick on Abel

Korsakof's shed floor, which looked like it had been right in the middle of the blaze.

"Crikey," said Tom. "Was that his house?"

Danny wanted to say, Do you believe me now? But he was too worried about the stick. Should he be cautious about approaching the pile where the shed had been? Was this some kind of a warning?

"Yeah, it was," he said instead. His voice didn't seem to be working properly.

Tom jumped off Apple's back and untied the police tape, but the horses weren't keen on going near the ashes. They snorted, threw up their heads, and planted their hooves in the earth, refusing to budge. Tom looped the reins over Apple's head and tied them around one of the less-singed trees. The grass verge was only brownish, rather than sooty black; it seemed this fire had been intense but had burned out before it spread too far.

Danny slid off the piebald and his legs turned to jelly. He wasn't used to horse riding like Tom was. It made your muscles feel like they'd been wrung out.

Using the pony's shoulder to steady himself for a moment, he watched Tom stamping off to explore the burnt cottage. When finally he managed to stand properly and rejoin Tom, his cousin was kicking at a lump of twisted metal just inside one of the rooms.

"That's iron," Tom said. "How can a house fire have gotten this hot? I wonder what happened."

Sammael, thought Danny. This was probably his punishment for Abel Korsakof not killing me. Even though the old man was already dead when he got here, Sammael probably just destroyed everything else in revenge.

But what was the use of saying that to Tom?

Danny went out the gap where the back door had been, across the scorched garden, and toward the shed-mound. He could see clearly in his mind's eye what had been around him when he'd taken the same path yesterday. White-washed cottage, pink flowers, green grass, rust-brown shed. How could they no longer exist? How, in the space of a single night, could they all have become black and made of powder? Even if the stick had survived, which was possible—after all, it had survived the lightning—Danny would have to dig through a mountain of ash to find it. And if Abel Korsakof's charred old bones were still in there, too . . .

But they wouldn't be. The ambulance would have come along and taken him away. There would definitely be nothing left of Abel Korsakof here.

And when Danny stood by the mound, he knew exactly

where the stick was. He could feel it, as if he had buried his own hand in there, still attached to his arm. All he had to do was pull it out.

He pushed his hand into the still-warm ashes and found it quickly. It wanted to stay with him. It wanted to nestle into the curve of his palm, to have his fingers around it. It was his, much more than a loyal dog or a favorite sweater: somehow, it was just his.

As he stood brushing the ash off its bark, he heard a small mewling cry and a whining close by. It was a voice he knew well.

"Mitz!" he said. "Mitz, are you here?"

The mewling stopped. "Danny?" came a tiny voice.

"Mitz!" he said again. "Where are you?"

"I'm stuck," she said. "It's dark. I don't know where."

She'd been trapped by a tree that had fallen over the mouth of a burrow, where she must have fled for shelter. He found her after five minutes' search, following the sound of her cries. Digging her out with a bit of branch was easy, but when he pulled her body from the burrow, he was sure he'd found a different cat.

Mitz no longer had a long, fluffy coat or a plush tail. Her fur was burnt and matted into clumps. She was coated with a thick paste of soot, ash flakes clung to her back like white spots on a black leopard, and her fine whiskers had all gone. One of her eyes was half closed and oozing something sticky. The other glared angrily at Danny, then began to swivel around.

Danny cradled her in his arms, not knowing what to do to help her. She struggled to leap free, but her strength seemed to have gone.

"Hey . . ." he said, "what happened to you? How did you get down there?"

Mitz wriggled and then lay limp. "Put me on the ground," she whispered. "I don't like being held like a baby."

He turned her the right way up and placed her gently on the earth. Her grimy legs crumpled and she lay on her side, resting her head against the soil.

"Mitz?" said Danny. "Are you okay? You're not going to die, are you?"

"Not if I can help it," said Mitz, swallowing.

"What happened here? Did you see it?"

Mitz closed her eyes. For a terrible moment Danny thought she'd stopped breathing, but her belly gave a little jerk.

"Was it Sammael?"

A shudder ran down the cat's body.

"It was, wasn't it? I knew it! He was probably trying to

burn—" Danny stopped himself, remembering that he hadn't told Mitz about the stick. "He was probably trying to burn everything the old man had, after you stopped him from killing me."

The little creature, who had flung herself so boldly through the air to push the striking knife away from Danny, now tried to gasp but choked on her own breath.

"He didn't burn everything," she said. "There's something in that hole. Not a tree root, not a rabbit. It stopped me going farther down, where I wanted to be."

The fur around her neck was still long, sticking out like a ruff. Danny smoothed it down with his finger. Her skull was tiny without all the hair. She didn't respond to his touch. Reluctantly, he took his hand away.

He reached down into the hole and felt around, hoping that nothing had died in there recently. He found something wrapped in a piece of cloth, rectangular and thin.

Danny sat beside Mitz and unwrapped the cloth. Inside, there was a collection of scraps of paper, stapled together between two pieces of cardboard. It felt as fragile as a kite.

Another notebook. Did everyone leave their lives in notebooks?

CHAPTER 10

THE LIFE & WORKS OF ABEL SEBASTIEN KORSAKOF

Danny opened the notebook. It was much smaller than the spiral-bound book from his parents' bedroom, and some of the pages weren't even made of writing paper. Brown and thin and badly trimmed, they'd been salvaged from parcel wrapping or bags of greengrocers' fruit. He tried not to bend the cardboard covers, for fear the whole thing might fall apart in his hands.

The Life and Works of Abel Sebastien Korsakof, the book declared in a shaky, age-cramped hand.

Abel Sebastien Korsakof, the subject and author of this work (who shall henceforth be referred to as ASK), was born in Poland, of parents who had fled Russia in the winter of 1917 (the year of revolution). His early childhood was a hard one, poor and frugal, the ordinary hardships of life exacerbated by the cruel and inclement weather prevalent in the area in which he grew up. Being the ninth child of parents who earned a pittance laboring on their impoverished farm, ASK learned early in his life of the devastating effects that shock weather events such as floods, freezes, and storms can have on the ability of a family to survive. In his twelfth year, two of his elder sisters were drowned by the rising of the Orsat, the local river, and in his fourteenth year he watched his younger brother Torwek being struck by lightning. Although Torwek survived, he suffered afterward from terrible headaches that he said felt like an axe trying to cleave his skull apart.

After a third sister was crushed by a falling tree in gale-force winds, ASK determined that he would dedicate his life to the study of weather. But as he had neither the opportunity nor the money to attend college, he was left to do his own research, which led him to begin contemplating the actions of the weather in a radically different way to the so-called scientific

thinking of the day. This was prompted by a conver-
sation with his brother Torwek, whom he came upon
one day standing under a tree watching rain fall from
the sky.

"What are you watching the rain for, Torwek?"
ASK asked his brother.

Torwek said, "The rain soothes my headaches. It
promises me that the lightning will make me better,
next time."

"What do you mean? You are not ill, are you?" ASK
asked.

"No," said Torwek. "But the headaches, they hurt so
much. And the rain says that's because the storms were
making new lightning to see what it did. She says it'll
be all right, next time."

"She?" asked ASK, wondering if his brother had
been struck a little simple by the lightning.

"The rain," said Torwek. "Oh . . . I can't explain it
to you. But she promised that it would be better soon,
that soon I'd fall into sand and never hurt again."

With this he began crying softly, and ASK could not
provoke from him a single further word on the matter.

But it was a small step to deduce that if the rain
could communicate with Torwek, then the reverse might
also be possible. And if Torwek could speak to the rain,

might he also be able to beg that it send no more floods but only pour gently onto the earth at the times it was needed?

Torwek was adamant that he neither could nor would attempt to ask any such thing. He said only that the rain was always different but he could not explain how. The following summer he was struck by another bolt of lightning and killed instantly, thus bringing to four the total number of siblings ASK had lost, in one way or another, by means of the weather.

When ASK reached the age of seventeen, his parents died within a month of each other, and he was left with his remaining brothers on the useless family land. He realized quickly that if he truly wanted to discover the mystery behind Torwek's rain, then he should go elsewhere and seek other people with similar interests. Besides which, he did not particularly want to talk to the miserable farmland rain that had so blighted his life. So he bade farewell to his brothers and headed for the capital city, Warsaw.

However, his hope of discovering an enlightened and broad-minded section of people in Warsaw was an entirely vain one. ASK became an outcast in what little society he found around his job sticking labels onto jam jars. The outbreak of the Second World War brought some hope of change, but the production of jam continued largely uninterrupted, and after seven years ASK was promoted, partly due to his not-insignificant contribution to the Polish resistance, to the peerless heights of label-sticker supervisor. By then, ASK had saved enough money to afford his passage to England, a land then regarded by a great many people as the center of the freethinking world. So he bade good-bye to his own country and set off for distant shores.

What can a man say when he feels he has finally reached the home for which he has been searching all his life? It was England's green, golden, and brown fields that welcomed him, England's quiet lanes and blue mottled skies. He soon discovered, however, that these skies never remained blue for long: they could roll through every shade between white and black in a single afternoon and turn from sweet fluff into lashing hail as quickly as a squirrel could scamper up a tree. Clearly, England was a crossing point for all possible kinds of weather.

In his first month in England, ASK found a job working at a telephone exchange in which the hours were irregular, giving him the opportunity to be outside at *different times of the day. At the telephone exchange he also met a young woman, Sarah Ellerton, with whom he began to enjoy a kind of lively banter.*

It was to Sarah that he first admitted his reasons for having come to England, and her response was not to ridicule him but to show a genuine interest in his theories. After some while, she admitted to him her own wishes for the future: that she would be able to live in a small village and become a teacher. ASK began to see a future in which he, too, might live in an English village of the kind he found so beautiful and welcoming after Poland's cold fields. And so it was that when he was twenty-nine, ASK married and came to live in Puddleton Lane End, Hopfield.

However, although ASK missed no opportunity to closely observe the patterns and behavior of the weather, he found that in general, the English were as ignorant about weather as the Polish. They discussed what was going on but came to no more spectacular conclusions than that a lot of rain would indeed fall when the skies turned gray, or that it would indeed be a cold night when the skies were black and clear.

But one morning, in his fortieth year, ASK woke up with a strange notion in his head. He became fixated with the idea that he could invent a machine that would produce both clouds and lightning, with which he could replicate an entire storm, thus enabling him to understand better how to control aspects of storm formation. A few months later, he was gathering dewdrops in a nearby field, so he could analyze the difference between them and some wisps of cloud he had collected, when he met a man picking mushrooms. The man asked him what he was doing.

"Gathering dew," said ASK. He was always wary of revealing his true purposes.

"For a cloud machine?" asked the man.

ASK's breath caught in his throat. "How did you know?" he said.

"I invented it," said the man.

"No," said ASK. "I invented it. I have the prototype in my shed."

"Got the idea in a dream, did you?" asked the man.

ASK took a better look at him. He was a very thin man with a face the color of rain and hair as black as the darkest thundercloud.

"No," said ASK. "I've been inventing my machine for years."

"It came to you in a dream," said the man. "Three months, two weeks, and four days ago."

This was entirely true, and ASK himself had taken

to counting the days, so he knew that the man was correct.

"How did you know?" he asked, beginning to tremble. Had he found, at last, a man to share his dreams with?

"I put it there," said the man.

ASK didn't understand at first. And then he looked at the man and realized that he was not quite a man, in the proper sense. His arms were too thin, for a start, and he looked both like ASK's mother, a small, fat woman with a bulbous nose, and like a streak of lightning. ASK's mother had looked nothing like a streak of lightning: the exact opposite, in fact. To have both of these things combined inside the same body—it was beyond any possible contortion of humankind.

"Am I dreaming now?" asked ASK. That would have been acceptable, although it would mean that he had to gather another supply of dewdrops when he did wake up in the actual morning.

"No," said the man. "Or you wouldn't see me. I can put ideas into people's dreams, but I don't put myself in them. Nobody would want to follow an idea that they'd dreamed about if they remembered me standing next to it."

The man was correct. No one advised by such a disturbing creature would feel comfortable about following his suggestions.

"Then why are you here?" asked ASK.

"I've got something you might like," said the man. "I follow the ideas that I plant closely: you seem to be making a good effort with yours. Perhaps you'd like something else to help you with your study of storms?" He took out a book from inside his coat and held it out.

ASK took the book. It was entitled the Book of Storms.

"Who are you?" he asked the man. "What is this book?"

"You know who I am," said the man. "And this book will tell you almost everything you want to know. And it will protect you from storms, so you can study them right up close if you want to."

And ASK looked at the book only once before he made the unforgivable decision. For each of us, there are one or two terrible things we have done in our lives of which we may not write. They are made all the more terrible because they are the things we cannot find it in our hearts to regret. We know they pull us beyond redemption, but we cannot repent them.

And so for possession of the Book of Storms and the assurance of fifty years of life in which to read it, I made the unforgivable decision.

———

The man had not lied about the book. ASK took it up onto a nearby vantage point to watch a storm and was struck by lightning. And although Torwek, all those years before, had cried out in pain as the lightning coursed through his body, ASK found to his surprise that the feeling he got was more as if a giant snake were coiling itself about his skin. He felt crushed, like a nut in a nutcracker, but at the same time with the conviction that his body would easily resist the external pressure, imbued as it was with the force of the lightning.

From that second, ASK began to hear the voices of storms. He discovered that at the height of their fury they would often crack jokes and pass around the kinds of stories housewives might swap, before wreaking their devastation on the lands below. This careless attitude upset ASK greatly. He remembered his long-dead sisters and brother, in particular Torwek, who had suffered so much, and he determined to at least try and ask the storms whether or not they realized the seriousness of their actions.

A month later, when ASK was sure from the feel of the air and the bunching of the clouds that there would be another storm, he fought his way to the top of a nearby hill and the storm broke over his head. Once at the top, he hailed it.

"Storm!" he said, loudly. "Can you hear me?"

The storm broke off its chattering and listened in shock.

"I can talk to you, then!" said ASK in triumph.

The storm turned, one part to all the rest, and said, "By the breath of a rancid stoat! Get the lubber!"

Then a cloud of hailstones as big as golf balls lashed onto ASK's head, and the only way he could protect himself was by curling up on the ground. After the hail had passed, ASK had no wish to endure another deluge. So he listened to the storm's voices as it continued on its dreadful way and then he went home.

Never would any voice respond to ASK's questions. He tried all methods that he could think of, from politeness to the curses that he had heard the storms themselves use, such as "elf-bladdered windbag" and "oozing nettlespit." Use of this type of insult generally just provoked laughter and sometimes an increase in hostility.

Many times ASK came close to death; trees were pushed over toward him, gales tried to sweep him off his feet, rain tried to blind him so that he could be pelted with roof tiles. But carrying the Book of Storms, he survived them all.

And now, as the last few moments of that long and

fruitful life draw close, ASK has compiled a chart of all that he has come to know about storms. He has learned many things, although he cannot claim to have understood the whole, and he never did manage to create a storm entirely from scratch using the cloud machine. But he came to know very well the truth of the old phrase "You rest the way you have made your bed." Because when the time comes for him to rest, he will put down the Book of Storms and go gently, with no fear, and know that he has lost himself utterly in lightning.

Except, thought Danny, it hadn't been like that. There had been nothing gentle about the way Abel Korsakof had died. Danny had been there, he'd seen it—he'd *caused* it—and it had been horrible. And Korsakof's bed, the bed he'd made—Danny looked around at the dead garden, the ruined cottage—that bed had been black, and burning.

Mitz began to cough and choke beside him, her body heaving with spasms. Spittle ran from between her tiny jaws, and a milky white sheen settled over her eye.

Tom would know what to do. Danny shoved the old man's story into his schoolbag, slung the bag over his shoulder, and picked up Mitz with both hands, carrying her like a tray over to his cousin.

"I found Mitz," he said. "She was stuck in a hole, but she keeps choking. D'you reckon she's okay?"

Tom stopped trying to identify burnt things in the ruins and tickled the top of the cat's writhing head with the tip of his finger.

"Poor thing," he said. "Needs a bit of a scrub, doesn't she? Put her down. She can't breathe properly with you carrying her about."

Danny put Mitz back onto the ground, where she gave three retching gasps, coughed up a hairball, and immediately began to lick herself again.

"You'll make yourself sick if you do that, lady," Tom said.

Danny felt the stick under his palm. "He says you'll make yourself sick if you lick that," he said to Mitz.

"Translating my words into Cattish, are you?" said Tom. "Sounds a bit like, well, English, really. . . . I'm not sure you're quite fluent yet."

Danny tried to ignore Tom's mockery. The cat stopped licking and glared at Danny. "So how am I supposed to get clean?" she said.

"I could wash you? In a stream, or something?"

Mitz's single eye remained still. "Not even if I lose my tongue in a freak mousetrap accident," she said, "will I ever let *that* happen."

Danny turned to Tom. "Can't you hear her?" he asked. "She's talking—you must be able to hear her."

Tom sighed. "Don't be stupid, Danny. Cats can't talk. Come on, there's nothing left here. Let's go to your bird-blind place, then we can go home. It's a long way to Great Butford, and that old pony doesn't do fast."

"But what about Mitz?"

"Bring her," snapped Tom, deliberately misunderstanding the point of Danny's question. "Stick her in your bag, or put her on the pony's back if she's steady enough to stay on. Don't put her anywhere she'll be able to dig her claws in, though, or I won't be responsible for you. This is ridiculous. I should be doing the milking, and now I've got to call Mum, and she's going to rip my head off. Sticking that axe through your bed. What on earth were you doing?" And he stamped back to Apple again.

It wasn't me! Danny wanted to say again. He couldn't quite believe that Tom thought he'd put the axe in his own bed. Tom had seen Aunt Kathleen come out of Danny's room, hadn't he? And Danny had been about to show him Abel Korsakof's story. Maybe all that stuff about Sammael picking mushrooms and Korsakof talking to storms would make him see sense. But there was something hard about Tom when he stamped like that.

"D'you want to come with us," he asked Mitz, instead. "Tom says we've got to go."

Mitz looked up at him and considered. "I will sit on the back of that animal," she said eventually. "Providing it doesn't try to frolic."

"She's not really the frolicky sort," said Danny.

Tom made them stop again outside the village shop in Hopfield, to get breakfast. He came out with a couple of sandwiches and a pocketful of chocolate bars.

"The woman in there said the police reckon it was arson," he said, climbing back onto Apple and handing Danny a sandwich. "Kids, they reckon. Said the place must have been drenched in gasoline—it went up like a light and burned itself out really fast. An old woman died in the house—that must have been your Mrs. Korsakof, I guess."

Danny remembered the lemon cake that he hadn't managed to eat, and tried to shake the thought away. At least his parents would be sure to believe him, once he found them. They'd be glad to see the scrappy little book written by the old man. They'd know that Danny must have been telling the truth when he said that Mitz could speak, because how else would he have known about the book down the burrow? They'd know that even when all your rational sense told you something was impossible, it might still happen. Like talking cats. And talking storms.

Danny put an arm around Mitz to keep her steady and hurried the pony on through the morning sunshine, to catch up with Tom.

CHAPTER II

THE DOGS OF WAR

"Would you believe me if I showed you I can talk to the horses?" Danny tried. "Like if I asked them to do something and they did it?"

"Go on, then," said Tom. "Ask Apple why she's such a prat about phone boxes. I'd love to know that. Ask her to stop imitating a crab."

Apple was bending her body into a banana shape, trying to keep as far away from the red booth as possible as they walked up the high street of a waking village.

"Okay," said Danny, taking his reins into one hand, tucking Mitz safely against his stomach, and putting the other hand into his pocket. "Apple, why are you doing that? Tom wants you to go in a straight line."

"Absurd! Ridiculous!" said Apple. "Evil, evil, *evil* thing!"

Danny thought she was probably referring to the phone box, not Tom. "It's just a phone box," he said.

"Of course it isn't!" said Apple. "That's what it wants you to think, naturally. You humans are so foolish."

"I see no sign of mutual understanding yet," said Tom, keeping his legs tight against Apple's sides so she wouldn't go skittering across the road. "Don't think horse whispering's the career for you, Danny."

"She thinks the phone box is evil," said Danny.

"Yeah," said Tom. "I could've told you that."

"She's an idiot," said the piebald pony.

It was such a quiet remark that, at first, Danny wasn't sure he'd heard it. "Was that you?" he asked the pony.

"Don't see anyone else around here," said Tom. "Unless you're still talking to the trees, of course."

"Not the trees," said Danny. "It was the piebald. She said Apple was an idiot."

"Again," said Tom, "I'm not sure that's something you'd need a magic stick to find out."

"Oh, shut up!" said Danny. "Don't believe me, then."

But he wanted to carry on talking to the piebald. She was such a silent, plodding animal, her head always down, none of the sidling and shying and prancing that Apple seemed to find necessary. How to do it without Tom making fun of him?

Danny tried to drop back a bit, but Tom stayed with him, pulling Apple into a slower walk. After a few minutes, when they'd dawdled nearly to a standstill, Tom said, "Come on, leg her on, Danny, we haven't got all day. I'm supposed to be studying, remember?" and Danny had to stop holding the piebald's reins quite so tightly. As they went faster, Mitz clung grimly on to him with her sharp claws, but he was getting used to that.

He got a brief chance when a post van shot out of a side road and Apple sprang forward to escape it. For a few moments Tom couldn't focus on anything but bringing his leaping horse under control.

"That was you, wasn't it?" Danny said, tucking the cat under his arm again and taking hold of the stick. "You said Apple was an idiot."

"I did," agreed the piebald.

"What's your name? Tom said you didn't have one, but you must, mustn't you?"

"Of course," said the piebald. "I have the name my mother gave me. Shimny."

"Shimny?" Danny frowned. "That's not what Tom and Sophie called you, was it?"

"As neither of them could lay claim to being my mother, then no, it wasn't," said the pony. "But why the fuss about names?"

"It's so strange," said Danny. "The whole thing. All these creatures . . . all these things that have lives and names and can talk to each other. Don't you think that's strange?"

"Will it be a long journey?" asked the pony, apparently not thinking much of the oddness. "I'm rather elderly. I don't know if you're aware of that."

And then Tom came trotting back on Apple, hooves everywhere, and Danny wasn't going to talk to his horse anymore, because he didn't want to feel stupid in front of Tom. Except he did wonder, for a long while, why it was that some creatures seemed shocked to discover that he could talk to them, while some apparently didn't think it was remarkable at all.

By the afternoon, they had run out of chocolate and were hungry again. Unfortunately, they were out on a long bridle path, well out of any village. His stomach grimacing, Tom put Apple into a smart trot and then a canter, letting her scrape along the edge of the young wheat they were next to. Danny, hand tucked into his pocket, heard it hiss like a field of adders as it was trampled. The sound made him wince, and he wanted to tell Tom to stop, but it would only have led to an argument, and he had enough to deal with trying to keep hold of two reins, a squirming cat, and a stick.

For a long time they were both quiet, the miles disappearing beneath them with the rhythmic pounding of hooves.

They came to a small copse at the top of a slope, surrounded by scrubby fields. The copse was dark, but above the hum of traffic drifting up from the road below there bubbled the song of a nearby stream. The ponies ground to an exhausted halt, their ribs flapping in and out, sinking their heads to a few inches above the ground. They gasped. Danny was shocked.

"They're knackered. We went far too fast," he said to Tom as both boys dismounted and Mitz collapsed into a grateful heap on the grass.

Tom, listening to the stream, cast a quick eye back to his horses.

"No, they'll be fine," he said. "Give them a few minutes. Ach, I'm starving. There's got to be something we can eat round here."

Danny sat down near the ponies and watched them transform from heaving bellows into quietly dozing beasts. Their eyes trembled shut as they felt the sun on their noses and stretched out their tired limbs, each resting a hind leg. Time ticked away while Tom scrambled around the trees and undergrowth, lost in the quest for food, but tired as he was, Danny couldn't settle himself to waiting. He was thinking too much about what he had to do and what he had to fear, although on a day like this one, with summer strong in the air and the sun promising to shine for hours to come, it was hard to properly fear anything. He held the stick in his hands and turned it over, looking at it for what seemed like the thousandth time and seeing nothing new.

"Come on, Danny," something whispered to him. "What are you waiting for? Don't you know the dogs are out? Don't you know they're on your trail?"

He jerked his head round to try and see what had spoken. There was nothing to be seen. All he could think was that it had sounded like the wind.

"Dogs?" he said, trying very hard to concentrate on the voice he had just heard. "What dogs? Who are you?"

"Do you have to ask?"

"Yes—I can't make out who you are. What dogs?"

"The Dogs of War!" hissed the voice. "The Dogs of War!"

"What are they?" said Danny, not sure if he'd heard properly.

Somewhere in the distance, he heard a bark.

"What are you doing, Danny? Don't you know they're coming? Look behind you, look behind you!"

Dogs . . . dogs . . . why would dogs be coming . . . ? Danny whirled around to look behind him.

There was the copse. And way away down the hill, a black mass of racing, baying dogs. Even at this distance Danny could see that they were as big as rottweilers and bounding in great, leaping strides across the fields, over the ditches, through the streams, and up the hill toward him. He didn't stop to count them.

"Tom! Tom! *Tom!*" he cried out, jumping to his feet and running over to the edge of the trees. "Tom! Get out! There's a pack of dogs!"

"It'll just be a hunt—oh, hang on, wrong time of year. . . . Don't worry, I'm sure someone's with them," Tom called back from the darkness.

"No, it's just dogs! Loads of them! Come on!"

Danny swung his schoolbag onto his back, grabbed Mitz and stuck her on his shoulder, and then took hold of the piebald's reins and put his foot in the stirrup to mount, but Tom had loosened the girths and the saddle slipped sideways, round Shimny's belly. The pony shifted nervously, her head high, ears stretched in the direction of the yelling dogs. Danny fumbled at the girth buckles, trying to take the saddle off, but his hands were like potatoes on the ends of his shaking arms. For a moment it seemed that he'd never undo them, but as he gave a last despairing yank, they gave way and the saddle thumped onto the ground.

There was no time to replace it. He dragged Shimny over to a grassy ledge, scrambled up onto her back, and let her go, grabbing her mane tightly with his hands. As she began to gallop, he was thrown from side to side and his head whipped backwards, tears streaming at the stinging of the air. The cat flattened against his shoulder, pushing her head into his neck and sinking her claws so deeply into his sweater that they pierced his skin.

Tom! Danny wanted to scream. But he'd shouted and Tom hadn't listened, and now he was galloping away to somewhere only Shimny knew, somewhere Danny couldn't even see anymore, and Tom was still back there in the copse with those dogs racing up the hill toward him. . . .

He twisted his head around and saw Tom stepping out of the copse at the same moment that the dogs reached it. The pack split into two—half flowed on toward Danny, and half rose in a wave, knocking Tom off his feet.

An arm flung into the air, Tom's blond hair caught the sunlight, and then he disappeared underneath the black mass and Danny saw no more.

Shimny stretched every muscle and tendon in her hairy old body and tried to remember how sure-footed she had once been, how she had galloped down hills five times as steep and leapt over ditches twice as wide. She tried to pretend she was still young, tried to ignore the aching shoulders that strained as she reached forward, the joints that grated as bone scraped along bone.

When she couldn't ignore any longer, she clenched her teeth together and said to herself, I am not me, I am not me, I am not me, so that her chanting was in time with the beats of her four hooves and she couldn't hear Danny sobbing on her back that he had left Tom, that Tom would be killed by those black dogs and be torn to pieces and never be seen again.

Their own half pack of dogs was gaining on them, the barks and howls louder with every hundred yards. Where on earth had those dogs come from? But it wasn't time to think, only to gallop.

Shimny careered over a small stream, but Danny's hands were tangled in her mane and his legs gripped her sides so tightly that he didn't fall. Feeling firmer ground beneath her feet, she tried for one last effort. I must lose them now, or I never will.

And with her last ragged scraps of energy, she held off the advance of the dogs for vital seconds until the edge of a wood was approaching so quickly that she barely had time to see the trees before dodging between them. Sunlight streamed through the forest canopy, lighting a path that pulled them toward a fast-flowing river.

The horse did not hesitate to throw herself in.

Danny fell sideways, slipping off Shimny's back. For a second his legs tangled with her kicking hooves; only his hands stayed attached to her, still knotted in her mane. The horse fought to pull her neck away from his weight, and his head went under the water, bubbles pouring into his nostrils.

He choked and coughed and lashed out with his feet, trying to find the bottom, but it was deeper than he could reach.

"Stop!" he tried to shout, but when he opened his mouth, it filled with water.

He tried to breathe one more time, before the flood drained down to his lungs. He spat and yanked hard at his hands, using his whole strength to try and get them away. All that happened was that he pulled Shimny's head down, and then somehow they were writhing together and his leg was over her back again and she was floating level in the water, her neck held high.

Danny's hands were white from the tourniquet of mane hairs. Clumsy and stiff, his hands refused to move. He gnawed at the hair with his teeth until at last it broke, and the panic of being tied to another living creature began to subside, leaving a slow fizz in his bloodstream.

Looking around, he couldn't see the dogs, whose baying still floated on the wind toward them. What would they do when they reached the bank? Dogs could definitely swim, although perhaps once they were in water it would be more difficult for them to bite. Even then . . .

Just as Danny reached into his right pocket to check that the stick was still there, he heard the pony speak his name.

"Yeah?" he answered. The dogs' barks were getting louder as they neared the riverbank.

"Ask the river to slow a bit. We're near a corner, and I'll be beached or drowned at the rate we're going."

Danny didn't want to slow down. They ought to put as much distance as possible between themselves and those howling, yowling dogs. But back on land, without the pony, he'd have no chance at all. He turned his attention to the river. "Sorry, river," he asked, "can you slow down a bit? The old mare can't swim."

"Yes, yes, of course!" the river said, dragging its heels along the stones of its bed so that the flow of water calmed. "Hello! Hello! The stream said you were coming! Pack of dogs just behind you, I see!"

Danny lurched round to look at the bank they had jumped off, nearly pushing Shimny over sideways. Were the dogs following them along the river?

It appeared not.

"I did a bit of, ah, hydraulic engineering back there. Shallowed out so's it'd look like you'd gone across. And they just ran straight over, away to the other side! They're, um, not the brainiest creatures in existence and they won't stop to ask anybeast where you've gone until they're well and truly confused."

Danny's hands trembled in a strange spasm. He closed his eyes and opened them again, to clear his vision.

"Thanks," he said to the river. "We had no chance. . . . They just came out of nowhere. . . . Tom . . ." But he couldn't think about Tom, not just yet.

"Well, shall I put you on the bank, then? I think your horse is about to have a heart attack. Don't worry, I'll put you back on the side you came from. Those dogs are still haring after you way out west somewhere! The other side of the bank! Hah!"

Before Danny had a chance to answer, the river drew back and flung itself in a huge arc over the bank. Boy, horse, and cat were swept into the air in a rushing swell that slapped them down onto the earth and pounded them with an afterthought of water, pressing their limbs into the mud. It was like lying under a waterfall.

As the river drained away, Danny lay on the riverbank, coughing. Every time he coughed, water rattled in his lungs, but he couldn't seem to get it up to his mouth, no matter how hard he hawked. He needed to climb into a tree and hang upside down by his feet from a branch to drain it out, but he was too exhausted to do anything except let his arms sprawl out and press his cheek against the smooth earth. His legs didn't feel like they'd ever hold him upright again.

He ought to talk more to the river. If he was ever going to get anywhere, if he was ever going to find his parents, he had to keep asking for help. But he couldn't even move his hand to check whether the stick was still in his pocket.

The image of his older sister came to him. What would life have been like if Emma had been there, leading the way? She'd have been like Tom, confident and strong, sure of herself. She'd have shown Danny what to do.

Except that hardly mattered now. Emma didn't exist, and Tom was probably dead, lying ripped apart somewhere, his legs bleeding, his blond hair chewed off, like those pictures of mangled foxes on the animal-rights stall outside the library.

Danny shivered and forced himself to sit up. The horse was lying on her side, her legs straight and stiff. Her rib cage was mountainous, an upturned bathtub, but it rose and fell to the rhythm of her feeble breathing. He could talk to her, now Tom wasn't around. But she didn't look like she'd relish a conversation.

The stick was still in his pocket. He'd known that, really. He'd have felt its loss, like when he'd left Abel Korsakof's without it. It wasn't even damp: the outside world didn't seem to touch it much.

Mitz was a bedraggled ball of rage. She was shaking and licking, shaking and licking, in a furious attempt to dry herself. At least the river had washed off all the soot.

"Hey, Mitz," Danny tried softly. "Are you okay?"

The cat gave him a filthy look. "Ask me that again," she said, "and I'll scratch your eyes out. Do I look okay?"

"Better than you did. I'm sure you'll dry and look fine," Danny said, coughing again. His lungs hurt, as though someone had first overinflated them and then punctured them with a knitting needle. Mitz arched her back and hissed at him. Without all the fluff, her body was skinny and sharp and her eyes looked too big for her face.

Another sound came up from the water. It was the river again, its thousand voices straining together.

"Are you recovered?" it asked.

"Yeah," said Danny, although he wasn't really. His legs were made of string, and now he'd never find the Book of Storms, without Tom. He didn't know one end of a woodland path from another, and the map was still in his schoolbag, which he didn't dare take off his back. Once he knew that the map had become a fistful of soggy gloop, then he'd know for certain that all was lost.

"What were you doing, being chased by the Dogs of War?" the river asked.

"I don't know! I just looked around, and they were running up the hill. Who keeps that many dogs? They're killers! They should lock them up."

"The Dogs of War? No one keeps them, not all together in a pack. They belong to the moon—just normal dogs, owned by people, living in houses all around the place, except when she calls them together. But she only sends them out on very special occasions. You must have done something pretty bad."

Danny wanted to stick up for himself one last time, although he was sure he'd stop bothering soon.

"I haven't done anything," he said. "I'm only looking for my parents. And Tom came with me, and then the dogs got him, and he's . . . he's . . . I dunno, and Sammael's after me. He wants something I've got—but he's never even asked me for it, just keeps trying to kill me. I guess next time he'll probably succeed. I must be running out of luck by now."

"Sammael?" The river bubbled deep underneath, causing the surface to shiver. "Ah, then it must have been him who asked the moon to send the dogs. He's old friends with the moon, you know—she always owes him a favor or two. How did you come to be mixed up with him?"

"Not my fault," said Danny. "I just found something. He wants it a lot, I guess."

The river was silent for a moment. Danny couldn't hear its normal slippery streaming sound quite so well when he was listening out for its real words.

Eventually it said, "I did hear that he was plotting something. I mean, he's always plotting something, but this one's big. Something to do with humans—he wants to hurt them badly, to destroy them all, I think."

Danny clutched at the stick. His other hand balled into a fist. What on earth *was* Sammael? How could this river speak so casually of him destroying people?

"All people?" he said. "But . . . *why*?"

"Oh, I assume it's because he's tired of endlessly doing his job with no recognition or reward. He's been doing it a long time, you know, and people have changed a lot. Perhaps he thinks they're not as interesting as they once were—perhaps he thinks they're not as imaginative. Whatever it is, he's certainly angry these days. Angry at the whole lot of you, I'm sorry to say."

Danny wrestled with the idea of all the humans on the planet in one single blob, all looking in the same direction at Sammael, and Sammael facing them back, hating every single one.

"But . . . there're, like, seven *billion* of us. There's no way anyone can destroy us all!"

"Oh, he's got a lot of time," said the river. "And a lot of patience, I'd say. I'd heard he was working on something to do with storms."

This was way too big. All humans? Everybody? But by the way the river was talking, it was something that would take ages. Maybe years. Maybe centuries, and then Danny wouldn't really have to worry about it at all.

"How much time?" he asked. "I mean, will it take him, like, years?"

"Oh, I should think so," said the river cheerfully. "Maybe years. Maybe days. You can never be sure how fast Sammael is working. He just has to collect what he needs—he's found out that storm taros can give him the ability to gather and control storms. It's because of that coat, you know."

"His coat?" Danny tried to picture what kind of coat Sammael would wear. For a moment he wished he could see him, there in front of his eyes. At least then he'd know what he was running from.

"Mmm. Long black thing," said the river. "There're all sorts of stories about it—legends about how it came to be, what it was made from, all that sort of thing. No one knows whether any of them are true, but each set of creatures has its own. Some say the coat was made from the hide of the Great Ox Xur, who pulled the sun up into the sky on the first-ever morning. Some say the coat's made of deerskin, from one of the black stags that pull the moon across the sky. I know that its origins are shady and that it was bought at great cost. But whatever the truth, he discovered that when he put that coat on, it gave him the power to control the storms he gathered up. So that's what he's planning to do, I think. Collect enough taros to be able to call up a storm so vast, it can destroy a huge area, and then another, and so on."

"But . . . he can't kill people, can he?" said Danny. "He has to get other creatures to do it for him, doesn't he? That's why he's never tried to, I dunno, strangle me or something. I didn't believe it at first, but those dogs . . . Why would you go to all the trouble of trying to get *dogs* to kill someone if you could just go and do it yourself?"

"Clever!" said the river. "Not lacking in brain, are you? You're right: Death's job is to go around collecting people's sand—or souls, if you like—and then to return that sand to the earth so it can become part of new lives. If Sammael tries to kill people, then Death won't take their sand away—she says his job is to create, not to destroy, so she brings them back to life. But if a storm killed them, too much of their sand would go straight into the earth with the lightning. It'd be impossible for Death to get it all back and make them alive, and whole, again. She wouldn't refuse to take the rest of them, then—she wouldn't leave people in limbo just to make a point to Sammael. So his plan will work fine, unless something stops him. Frankly, I'm not sure that anything can."

Danny pulled the stick from his pocket and looked at it. It still just looked like a stick. But he was talking to a river, and the river had said Sammael's power to control storms lies in his *coat*. . . .

He slowly twisted the schoolbag off his back, plonked it on the ground between his knees, and opened it. Water had wriggled through the seams. Both notebooks were damp, their pages sticking together, but still readable.

When he fished around for the map, though, all he found was a lump of wet mush that had bled blue ink all over itself. It was too wet to fold out.

So the map had gone. No Tom, no map, no Book of Storms. Would he ever find his parents again? Should he just give them up for lost?

"I've got to go back there. . . . I've got to find Tom. Is there even any point . . ." he said, not quite knowing what he was trying to say.

"Any point in what?" The river was still cheerful.

"Any point . . . keeping on trying," he said, finding the thought. "I don't actually know if my parents are even still alive. I sort of think I'd know if they weren't, but maybe I wouldn't. Maybe they have just gone, forever, and I'll never see them again. And now Tom . . ." He didn't have to fight back tears; he was past crying.

The sun eased round in the sky, and a thin ray hit the side of his face. The river was silent for a moment and then said, "But you still need to find the answer, don't you? And there're always places you can find answers if you keep looking long enough. It's just that looking is sometimes harder than you want it to be, that's all."

"There aren't any answers," said Danny. "Every time I get near one, Sammael kills it."

"That's because *he*'s only interested in posing questions,"

said the river. "He's interested in ideas that take you somewhere else, instead of just returning you back to the place
you started from. You'll understand when you meet
him. But here in the world, there *are* answers."

"Where?" challenged Danny.

"Everywhere," said the river. "In the sand, for a start, if
you're looking for human-type answers. Try talking to
earthworms—they sing about the sand. They know a lot,
the earthworms—all day, every day, they eat earth. It's
what everything on the planet has been and one day will
be again, and they *eat* it!"

Everything on earth. That meant his sister, too. If
nothing else, maybe he could at least find out more about
Emma. Then he'd have *something*. Because, of course,
worms wouldn't know about anything aboveground, so
there was no use in hoping that they'd help him find his
parents, unless his parents were already dead. And the
same went for Tom.

"Questions work like water," continued the river. "There's
little bits of them everywhere, spread around. The answer
is just a matter of gathering all the bits together. Even the
secret of Sammael is probably lying around the world in
little fragments. One day, some creature will find all the
fragments and unite them—maybe they'll even find out
how to destroy him. But perhaps whoever finds out his

secret won't want to destroy him in the end. You never know."

"I'd destroy him," said Danny. "I'd do it now if I could. But I don't know how to find him. Perhaps the worms could tell me that."

"They couldn't," said the river immediately. "Sammael isn't a creature of the earth. He's made of ether. Do you know what that is?"

"No," said Danny.

"It's the upper air," said the river. "It's where the gods traveled in ancient times. It holds more than we earthly creatures could ever dream of. It's where Sammael lives, and *you* couldn't go there unless you sold your soul to him. And something tells me you're unlikely to do that."

"It tells you right," said Danny.

Whatever his soul was worth, he was certainly keeping it.

Danny left the riverbank, trying to peer through the trees and see back up the hill. Had the dogs gone? He should go back up there now and find Tom. But then there were the worms—could he maybe find something out from them that might help him call off the dogs? If he'd been brave, he'd just have gone up there anyway. But he wasn't brave. Or at least, not brave enough.

He dragged his eyes away from the woods and walked a few paces along the river, scanning the ground. The earth looked moist and crumbly: surely there would be worms down here.

Behind him, Mitz the cat stopped washing and looked up. She'd been listening to every word he'd just said. What could he have been talking to? All she'd heard besides Danny had been the sighing of the wind through the tree-tops, the chattering life of the woodland, and the hideous burble of that hateful river. But he'd claimed to be able to talk to everything, hadn't he?

He'd claimed. But then, he'd claimed he was just look-ing for his parents and instead had dumped her in a river and tried to drown her. Why should she trust him?

She got to her feet and slunk away between the dark tree trunks. Her paws didn't disturb even the tiniest leaf as she went.

CHAPTER 12

WORM

D anny found the rusted lid of a biscuit tin and began
to dig. Somewhere in the distance a dog barked and
then another answered. He shuddered.

I want a normal life, he thought as he dug, stabbing
the lid into the ground so fiercely that pieces of it began
to break off. I want a normal life where you don't have to
find out about things that shouldn't exist by talking to
things that shouldn't talk. I want to talk about normal
things, with normal *people*. And to have them believe me.
Maybe Tom was right not to believe me about all this. If
I heard me saying it, I wouldn't want to believe it.

The worm paused with a sinking feeling as the earth around her shook with the pounding of some object from above. It didn't automatically mean death—she had survived being dug up once before—but you could never tell. There was the hot sun to kill you if you got flicked out onto a hard surface. There were human tools that sliced you in half, and hands that burned your blood. Birds were always waiting to eat you up, and a worm was powerless against them. It had nowhere to hide now.

Danny tried to pick the worm up, and it screamed at the touch of his fiery fingers. He dropped it back into the soil, and it tried to slink back underneath.

"Hey!" he said. "Please stay. I need to talk to you."

The worm stopped its slither and wriggled so it was just below the crumbly soil, away from the sunshine.

"How can you talk to me?" it asked in surprise.

"Don't you know? I thought earthworms knew everything. At least that's what I was told." Danny settled himself down on the leaf mold. He had a good feeling about this worm.

"Oh no," it said. "That's not true at all. Whoever told

you that is probably confusing what we *know* with what we *sing*."

"So you sing about things you don't know about? How's that?"

"It's the sand that sings, really," said the worm. "The sand that we swallow tells us of the lives it's been, the world it's seen, and we sing its songs as we work. It isn't like the legends that other creatures have, explaining how the world came to be created and suchlike. We just sing what the sand is telling us."

Danny looked at the soil around the worm. Dark, damp earth and grit, small rocks and sand. The closer he watched, the more movement he could see: a beetle marching over a familiar trail; some tiny creature shifting fragments twice the size of its body. Which lives had he known that had ended? His sister's, and of course Abel Korsakof's. Were they both underneath him in the soil, singing through worms?

"Could you ask the sand something for me?" he asked the worm.

"I don't know," it said, dubious. "We don't pick what the sand knows, to sing of. We just sing of what it says. I've never tried asking it anything . . . and I don't think I could."

"But will you just sing anyway? I'd like to hear it."

"I will," agreed the worm. Its voice echoed a little, slinking away to the edges of Danny's ears.

It took a mouthful of earth and began.

> *"In Dublin's fair city, where the girls are so pretty,*
> *I first set my eyes on sweet Molly Malone,*
> *She wheels her wheelbarrow, through streets*
>   *broad and narrow,*
> *Singing, 'Cockles and mussels, alive alive O!'*
> *'Alive alive O! Alive alive O!'*
> *'Cockles and mussels, alive alive O!'"*

This was not what Danny had expected. The secrets of the worms couldn't be that pointless, surely? But then, he'd only asked the worm to sing whatever it normally sang. He needed information about specific things, not just ramblings from random grains of earth. But if he couldn't ask anything . . .

Then he had it. He could find out about the things within his own grasp. Himself. The stick. Where had the stick come from? And was owning it changing him into somebody—some*thing*—else?

He pulled a hardened piece of his own skin from his fingernail, flaked off a tiny fragment of bark from the stick, and dropped both of these just in front of the worm.

It chanced upon the grain of skin first and vacuumed it up. At first no song came out. Perhaps it wouldn't work—skin wasn't sand, after all. But Danny waited, and a small, whining voice began to croak from the worm.

> *"Somehow the future's more than us, and somehow*
> *the past is less.*
> *And somehow, somewhere, there's a peaceful place*
> *and where I am is a mess.*
> *But if I close my eyes and ask enough times,*
> *maybe someone will tell me the way,*
> *And I won't have to think about storms anymore. . . ."*

The skin evidently wasn't up to much, because this trailed off. If it was a reflection of his life, it was pretty rubbish. Just a bit of doggerel . . . Was that really all he was made of? Then the worm inhaled the piece of stick, and her voice changed again.

> *"The world is deadly, the world is bright,*
> *The creatures that use it are blinded by sight,*
> *But there's no sense in crying or closing my page,*
> *Sense only battles in fighting and rage.*
> *So come all you soldiers and answer my call,*
> *Together we gather, together we fall!"*

Danny had never heard the voice before, but he knew at once whose voice it was. The words settled over his shoulders in a freezing cloud, and a thin crackle of static rushed through his head. It was nothing like what he would have expected—surely lightning should have spoken with great, sharp speed? But this was certainly the voice of lightning—it prickled through his blood until his skin was crawling with spines.

So the storms were inside the stick. The storms, whose anger everyone feared so much—he was carrying a part of them around with him, in his trouser pocket. What would they do to him if they knew? Reclaim it, surely, with gales and hail and fire. It wouldn't be just his parents who got killed then, it would be him, fried right down to the last fingernail. The only person who'd survived the lash of a storm had been Abel Korsakof, but then, he'd already sold his soul to Sammael for it. If Danny knew one thing, beyond how large the lump was that choked his guts, it was that he wouldn't be seeking out Sammael's protection against anything.

Danny stared at the disturbed earth, watching the worm burrow her way slowly back into it. She was strangely perfect and unblemished, next to his own grubby and scratched hands. For a long moment he wished he was the worm, tunneling his way underground into darkness. Worms didn't have these problems. Worms didn't have parents to do stupid things. Worms looked after themselves.

But then, worms had no one to take care of them either. And Tom had looked after him. He hadn't needed to—he could have gone home and told the police to find Danny. But he'd come along and known the way. All those twists and turns, the paths and villages—Danny would never have found the route alone.

He tried to push away that last, horrible memory of the dogs sweeping over Tom, the arm thrown into the air like it was waving. What had happened to him? Was his body lying back where he'd fallen, next to those trees, bleeding itself out onto the ground?

Without knowing, Danny couldn't go on. Whatever the stick was, Tom was real and normal, and the idea of him being dead was terrible. Danny had to face it—he had to go back up there and find out.

What if the dogs were still there? What if they were standing guard, waiting for the other half of the pack to return?

Danny's heart began to patter, but he refused to listen to it. He forced himself up onto his feet, feeling like a very small person inside a huge, reluctant body.

Mitz was nowhere to be seen, and Shimny was still

lying on her side, her coat sticking up in wet bristles. He would leave her be—he'd have a much better chance of going unnoticed without her.

"I'm going back," he whispered to her, unsure if she was asleep.

The pony gave no indication that she'd heard. Her eyes were closed.

I suppose I must be a coward, thought Danny. Doing frightening things is so hard. And as he looked back along the rows of pines, he could see that the edge of the wood was bright and stark. He'd be exposed out there. He'd be seen for miles.

But Tom was out there too. He would just have to take his chances.

He could see quite clearly from the edge of the wood that the dogs were still up by the copse, patrolling like beetles around the spot where Tom had fallen. Of Tom he could see no sign, but the grasses and plants were tall and the shrubby undergrowth crowded around the bottom of the copse.

Between Danny and the dogs was a huge field. He hadn't taken proper notice of it before, but it stretched, rough and tufty, crossed by the ditch that Shimny had jumped, and then sloped upward. How on earth had they escaped those dogs? There was no cover anywhere, nothing that would have hampered their pursuers. Shimny must simply have managed to outrun that black, baying mass, stride for stride. That was all.

Danny lay on his front, watching the dogs. A couple of them were nuzzling at something hidden behind a bush. He craned his neck to try and catch a better glimpse of it, then wriggled forward, pushing against the earth with his knees. For the moment the dogs didn't seem to have noticed him. Maybe if he kept low, they wouldn't pick up his scent on the wind.

He wriggled on, inch by inch. But the grass around him wasn't tall. Soon, the dogs would be bound to see him.

His knee came down on a sharp stone, and he bit his lip to hold back the yelp. The dogs must have sensed something, though, because their ears pricked up. Muzzles went into the air, nostrils twitching.

Danny buried his face into the earth, spread himself as flat as he could, and stopped breathing.

He knew that when he put his head up again, he would see them bounding toward him. Or even just walking calmly on their thin black legs, knowing he hadn't a snail's chance of outrunning them this time. Just his own two legs against their many sets of four—they'd be on him in an instant. He eased his hand into his pocket to find the stick, although he knew there was no way he'd be able to find words once the dogs were slavering down his neck. He would rather just keep pressing himself against the ground, feeling it solid beneath him, trying to believe for a tiny bit longer that nothing too awful would happen.

When the first whiskers touched his ear, he screwed his eyes tightly shut, clenched his fists, and braced himself. What did his parents' faces look like, exactly? He tried to summon them up, to hold them one last time in his mind, but all he could picture was the tufty mane on Shimny's neck, tangling in the breeze as she galloped. If only there could have been one more morning back at home, one more normal breakfast, one more call from his mum as he left the house.

The nuzzling stopped, then moved around to Danny's cheek. This must be the smallest of the dogs—its nose was tiny. Its teeth were probably even sharper, to make up for its lack of size.

Soon it would bite him, and he would find out.

A small weight thudded onto his back. That must be a paw, ready to hold him down. And then it moved, lightly, up to his shoulders.

By the time he felt its claws digging into his hair, he was almost sure that it wasn't—couldn't be—the paw of a dog. It was something with four tiny paws, each one little bigger than the size of a dog's claw.

In the quietest whisper he could find he said, "Who are you?"

The words were so faint that he hardly heard them himself, but the little creature on his back froze and flexed its tiny claws against his sweater. He tried again.

"You're not a dog, are you?"

"Not a dog," it said. "Not a dog."

"Oh, Jesus . . ." Danny's arms lost their tightness and turned to jelly. He felt the soil pressing, grain by grain, into his face.

"Not Jesus," said the creature. "Not Jesus."

Danny had to work hard to squash back the hysteria that bubbled into his mouth.

"Shaking," said the creature. "Shaking and talking and humaning. Peculiar."

"What are you?"

"Squirrel, naturally," said the squirrel. "Just off nutting."

"Haven't you seen those dogs?" Danny dared to move his head a fraction toward the dogs.

"Pah! Dogs! Little bit running, jumping. Beat the dogs anytime!"

The squirrel bounced on its tiny feet. It weighed scarcely more than a pile of leaves on Danny's back.

Beat the dogs anytime. Yeah, if you were tiny and fast and could run up trees. How had humans taken over so much of the world, again? Everything else seemed to have its own set of resources. The more Danny thought about it, the more he didn't seem to have any at all. Except cunning.

"Do you reckon," he said slowly, swimming through the fog of fear in his mind to find the thought that was waiting there, hard and bright, "do you reckon, if you ran past those dogs, they'd chase you?"

"Ha! Stupid dogs! Chase me always!"

The squirrel sat down and had a good scratch at its ear, kicking furiously with a hind leg that drummed off Danny's back. He hoped he wouldn't get fleas.

"There's no way they'd catch you?"

"Never!" shrieked the squirrel. "We race dogs! Set them running! Dogs chase, squirrels taunt! Then we sit in trees . . . and laugh! Ha! Ha! Ha! Throwing nuts! Hee hee!"

It flung itself about so wildly in a pantomime of running and leaping and throwing that Danny was afraid the dogs would notice. He didn't fancy the idea of them running for the squirrel while it was still on his back.

"Will you?" he said quickly. "They've got my cousin, up there. I need to get them away somehow. If some of them follow you . . . maybe I could deal with the few that were left. . . ."

This thought made his throat contract, but the squirrel's enthusiasm was a bit shaming. He had to at least try to appear as if he might be brave.

"Of course! Of course!" it said. "Many squirrels running! All dogs running! You seeing!"

Danny barely felt it gathering its legs together and springing from his back. He dared not raise his head to watch it go. All he could do was wait, and listen out for the sound of thundering paws, and try to keep breathing.

He heard the barking first. A couple of isolated shouts, followed by three or four more. Even holding the stick, he couldn't be sure what they were saying—perhaps it was something like "Oi!" or "Hey!"

Danny risked a look. All the dogs had turned to stare up at the treetops of the little copse. On the breeze came the crackling of twigs as a cloud of tiny, leaping creatures streamed through the branches.

And then the squirrels began to dive from the trees, down onto the ground, up the next tree, sprinting across gaps of grass, hurling themselves back up the shrubs in the hedgerows. They weren't faster than the dogs, but they twisted and jumped and zigzagged, never still for a moment, impossible to follow.

The dogs went mad. As they barked, jaws open, they lost sight of the squirrels for a fraction of a second and then saw them again, somewhere entirely new. They lunged, teeth snapping, capturing nothing but the scent of tail hairs on the tips of their tongues. All duty forgotten, they bounded and bit and fell over their own scrabbling feet in their eagerness to get to the squirrels. In moments they were gone.

Danny picked himself up and began to walk over the field, toward the spot where he'd last seen Tom.

There was a foot sticking up out of the grass, from behind a bush. It wasn't moving.

Blood roared up in Danny's ears. He closed his eyes for a second and made himself keep walking, step by step, until he was a few feet from the bush, and then he tried to find his voice again.

"Tom? Tom?"

There was no answer, but then, he'd done little more than whisper. So he tried again, clearing his throat.

"Tom? Tom, it's me. . . ."

"Danny?"

Tom's voice was much stronger than Danny had expected. Much more normal, and alive. He walked around the bush, hope rising.

Tom was sitting propped up against a tree stump. His face was muddy, and there were twigs and bits of green stuff caked over his hair and clothes. A couple of rips in his sweatshirt flapped open, showing patches of bleeding skin. He was holding his left arm with his right hand, but he didn't look anywhere close to death.

Danny nearly threw himself onto Tom's feet. He wanted very much to give in to the weeping and wailing that was trying to blow his chest up like a balloon. But that would only make Tom go back to treating him like a little kid again, just when he'd done something that might earn him a bit of respect. Or had gotten some squirrels to do it, anyway.

So he tried very hard to stop himself shaking and went to kneel at Tom's side.

"Are you okay?"

Tom looked at him curiously. "Yeah," he said. "Yeah, just a bit grazed. They didn't really have a go at me. Just backed me into a corner and growled a lot and then . . . left. Some squirrels came along. Dogs always chase them."

The boys stared at each other for a few seconds.

"There's a river down there," said Danny. "We went into it—me and the piebald. They couldn't follow us."

"Clever," said Tom. "Your own James Bond moment."

But it hadn't been like that at all, not for a second. It had been terrifying. Danny wanted to reach out to Tom. He wanted Tom to stand up and say, It's over, we're going home, and to give Danny no choice about it.

"Where's the piebald?" said Tom.

"Still down at the river. She was lying down. Where's Apple?"

Tom looked around. "Gone," he said. He didn't follow it with "Someone'll find her" or "She'll go straight home." He just fixed his eyes back on Danny with that curious gaze.

"Should we look for her?" Danny asked, hoping the answer would be no, but knowing that it ought to be yes.

"We'd better get hold of the piebald first," said Tom. "Losing one horse is pretty shabby. Losing two . . ." He took his hand away from his arm. It had been covering a slightly deeper bite, but even that wasn't bleeding too much anymore. And although he got to his feet stiffly, he was able to walk without leaning on Danny as they started to walk back across the grassy field.

Shimny was still lying on the riverbank, asleep in the quiet, green morning. Without disturbing her, Tom took his shirt off and went to clean his grazes in the river. He couldn't reach the one on his back, so Danny tore a few strips off the pajama top that still flapped out from underneath his sweater and wiped away the thin streaks of dried blood.

Once the wounds were cleaned off, they looked much better. Mere scratches where the skin had been broken. But the blackening bruises that smoldered under Tom's skin made Danny think of the piebald pony.

"You look like Shimny," he said without thinking.

"Shimny?" said Tom.

Danny knew that he should raise his eyes, look Tom in the face, and swiftly make up some plausible lie, but he couldn't.

"I mean the piebald," he muttered, crushing the cloth in his fist.

"I know. But why'd you call her Shimny? *Shimny?* What kind of a name is *that?*"

"It was just . . . a name I thought of. . . ."

Tom raised an eyebrow. He looked as though he was about to ask something serious, but then he sneered. "Been reading those pony books again, have you? We could go to the next village and find some ribbon, if you want to plait her mane?"

"Shut up!" said Danny, pushing him.

"I could get you some brushes, too, and some paint for her hooves, Danny—or d'you prefer *Danielle* these days—oof!"

Danny thumped him on the side of the face, and Tom swung up his hands to grab his cousin. For a minute they wrestled, rolling over and over on the riverbank, smearing Tom's carefully cleaned cuts with mud, until Danny's foot kicked too close to the punctures on Tom's arm, and Tom decided it was time to finish. He neatly pinned Danny to the ground, a knee in his back, both of Danny's thin wrists held fast in one of his massive hands.

"Surrender?" he asked.

"Git," said Danny, spitting out a piece of reed.

Tom cleaned himself up again. And then, as the boys sat down to take some rest and wait for Shimny to wake up, they heard the most marvelous sound in the world. Somewhere in the quiet wood a horse was trotting, its hoofbeats thick and dull on the soft leaf mold. It was definitely the sound of a horse, rising above the birdsong and the faint whispers of rustling leaves. Not a woodpecker, not a rabbit thumping the earth, but a horse trotting through at a good pace, putting out its head and bellowing a call for its lost companion.

Shimny lifted her head and screamed just next to

Danny's ear. If it hadn't been so painful, he would have been gladder, but Tom had already leapt to his feet.

"Apple!" he shouted. "Apple! Here, girl!"

The hoofbeats stopped. For a moment Danny doubted that he'd really heard them. But there was an answering call: Apple's high, shrill neigh.

"Apple!" Tom yelled again, and Shimny looked sharply at him, which he did not see.

The padding of the hooves started up once more, and this time they crescendoed rapidly. Danny followed the sounds with the space of his mind—There! There! Behind that tree, coming from there! She must be there!

Then Apple came into view and stumbled to an exhausted halt, her head hanging low. Her brown coat was wet with sweat, and her smooth legs had been torn, leaving ribbons of blood glistening like slug trails down the dark hair. She looked horrible, to Danny's eyes—a picture of defeat and pain.

But Tom had spent his life tending to injuries. He just shrugged his shoulders, said, "Thank goodness," and went forward to take hold of Apple's trembling head, and she pushed her nose into his stomach.

Danny got to his feet and gathered up the bloody strips of cloth to chuck them in the river, while Tom ran his hands down Apple's legs.

"Don't chuck those," said Tom. "Rinse them out again and bring them back."

Danny did as he was asked. Tom fished out his mobile and dialed a number, clamping the phone to his ear with his shoulder and taking the bundle. It wasn't difficult: this was how he normally made phone calls. He held Apple's rein out to Danny. "You hold her head. Talk to her."

The phone sparked into life, and Tom began cleaning the cuts on Apple's hard brown legs.

"Hi, Mum, it's me. Yeah. Yeah, everything's fine. Just had a bit of a scare with some dogs. Apple's got a few cuts and scratches. We're in Butford woods, just down by the river. . . . No, no, everything's fine. Really . . . Could you come and meet us with the box, maybe?"

Danny's heart froze as Tom waited to hear the answer on the other end of the line.

"Oh, crap, I'd completely forgotten about that. Sorry— really sorry. I know I said I'd help you with the tagging. . . . I know, I'm really sorry. But . . . yeah, yeah, it's ridiculous. Yeah, call them again. Try the police, too, if you like. But he was just going to run away. I thought it'd be better if I stayed with him. . . . I did leave you a note! Sorry, Mum, I'll bring him back as soon as I can. . . . Yeah, definitely before supper, I promise. . . . Mum? Mum? Crap . . . it's dead!"

Tom swore and took a hand away from Apple's leg to put the phone back in his pocket. He didn't look at Danny. Apple pranced.

Danny didn't want to ask about what Tom had promised and obviously failed to do. He didn't think the answer would be friendly. Instead he asked, "Is this Butford woods?"

"Yeah. I said keep her still. I need to get this leg cleaned up. Talk to her, just any old rubbish. She's a fusspot."

Danny looked at Apple's rolling eye. He put his hand in his pocket.

"Stand still," he said. "Tom's trying to wash your cuts."

"It hurts!" whined the horse, snatching a leg away.

Tom swore. Normally he was infinitely patient with wounded animals.

"For crying out loud, Danny, I don't think she's in the mood for an intellectual conversation. Just use the sound of your voice to soothe her."

Danny said, "There, there," and patted Apple's neck. It didn't seem to work any better to keep the horse still, but at least it didn't annoy Tom.

Tom went to chuck the last of the rags in the river. The afternoon sun was darkening from clear yellow to pale orange. No sign of a storm in the air, no black threat hanging over them in the—what was it the river had called it?—the ether. Danny looked up into the sky. Just blue sky. No tiny creature watching them from the high heavens.

Perhaps it really was all a dream, some kind of fantasy he'd imagined. Now everything in the woods was so peaceful that it seemed impossible anything could be wrong.

He closed his eyes for a second, one hand still clenched around Apple's reins just under her throat, the other in his pocket, and listened to the sounds around him. The breeze in the treetops, the sweet chattering of the river, the twittering birdsong. Only it wasn't birdsong. The birds were bellowing out obscenities to one another.

"Yeah! Yeah! Come on, then! Come on, you petal-spleened excuse for a worm's bum! I'd like to see you twitch one atom of a pinkie toward this tree! You call yourself a robin? A robin? I call you the blacky purple bit of my poo! Gaaargh! Graagh! Come on! I'll 'ave yer! I'll 'ave yer!"

The sparrow near Danny's right ear almost fell off its branch in indignant rage. An apoplectic robin ten feet away began to spit furiously back.

"And what kind of bird are you? A cow-dung bird, that's what! You eat the grain that other animals eject out of their back ends! Nobody's ever put you on a Christmas card, have they? You take your pathetic excuse for a lady and get out of my tree, or I'll pull out every feather on your pale little pigeon chest! You hear me! You hear me! I'm not telling you twice, you sack of ear wax! Out! Out!"

Danny laughed, taking his hand off the stick. The sound flew into the air and sent the birds shrieking away to continue their argument in another tree. It felt like a long time since he'd laughed. But once the laugh started, it woke him up like a glass of lemonade on a stifling day.

"What's so funny?" said Tom, coming back from the river.

Danny shook his head. "You wouldn't get it," he said.

"You're nuts," said Tom. "Well, let's go, then. It isn't far now."

"I don't have the map anymore. It got soaked. And I can't remember all the little lines and stuff on it."

Tom shrugged. "Doesn't matter," he said. "I know where we're going."

"*You* remember it? You only saw it once."

"Course I do!" said Tom. "I'd be a poor excuse for a country boy if I didn't know every inch of the land like the back of my own hand, now, wouldn't I?"

He grinned and tapped the side of his nose.

Danny said, "Show-off," and went to take the piebald's reins. Then he stopped. "Where's Mitz?"

"Did she go in the river? Cats and water aren't exactly best mates, you know."

"Of course I know," said Danny. "But she got out. I spoke— I saw her."

Tom shrugged. "Probably crawled off into a bush somewhere to lick herself dry. She'll find us again if she wants to be found."

Would she? Danny remembered Mitz's sharp little face hissing at him, the fury in her eyes. But of course she would. It wasn't his fault they'd gone in the river. Going in there had saved their lives, and Mitz would surely understand that. She was probably just lying low for a bit, recovering and watching them from the bushes.

Tom gave Danny a leg up onto Shimny's back, and Danny peered into the undergrowth as they set off, but all the sparkles that could have been yellow eyes were just sunlight catching on shiny leaves.

CHAPTER 13

THE BOOK OF STORMS

T he bird blind was tucked away in a close thicket of trees. Tom seemed to know exactly where it would be: he led them up to a path, they padded along it for twenty minutes or so, and then he steered Apple between a beech tree and a huge clump of yellow thorny shrubs and jumped off her back as soon as he could safely avoid the thorns. When his feet touched the ground, he winced but said nothing about it.

"There you go."

Danny tried to see where he was pointing. It just

looked like more overgrown bushes. But, yes—there in the middle of them were a few planks of dark, rough wood, and a low roof covered in moss, underneath a thatch of thorny branches. Danny slid off his pony.

"I'll go in first," he said.

Tom must have caught the reluctance on his face, because he looped Apple's reins around a branch and said, "I'll come with you. D'you think something's happened to them in there?"

Danny shook his head, his mouth dry. He let go of Shimny—she wouldn't leave Apple—and brushed past Tom to find an entrance to the little hut.

Inside, it was dark and damp. Things were growing over the walls, or through them—soft leaves and scratchy little twigs reached out to stroke and claw at Danny's skin as he ducked his head through the doorway.

At first he couldn't see anything in the blackness, but as his eyes adjusted he made out a small bench and a tiny shelf. On the shelf was a single hardback book.

"Anyone in there?" Tom stuck his head inside. In the few seconds it took for his eyes to widen and start picking up the thin light, Danny had taken a step toward the shelf and was reaching out for the book.

"What's that?" asked Tom.

Danny stopped his hand. He didn't want to share the Book of Storms with Tom. Tom would laugh at it, tell him it was just a silly old book, and then he'd make Danny go home. But what choice did he have?

"No parents here," said Tom, as if he'd known there wouldn't be. "No parents, just a book. Is this some kind of treasure hunt? Is that what you've dragged me all the way out here for?"

The book wasn't big. No gold lettering, no leather binding. Just a flat black shape in the darkness, full of some kind of promise.

Tom tried to reach over his shoulder and take the book, but Danny grabbed it first. As soon as his hand closed around it, he knew he was right to keep his cousin away.

For it didn't feel like a book. The cover had the dry, papery texture of snakeskin, but it yielded slightly to the touch, as though still wrapped around a snake. Not quite firm, not quite dead. The secret that lay inside this book was breathing.

Danny clutched it to his chest so that Tom wouldn't get it. It was like holding a coiled python. Every nerve in his stomach knotted itself into a tiny ball.

"Let's have a look," said Tom. His voice was harsh in the darkness.

"No," said Danny. "You mustn't touch it. It'd . . . it'd hurt you."

He knew it could kill Tom. Or bind him to something far beyond understanding. But explaining either of those things was too complicated, and Tom wouldn't believe him anyway.

He pushed past Tom and took the book outside into the bright air. The golden light made him blink for a few moments; he held the book more tightly to his chest, afraid, for the most fleeting of seconds, of himself and this strange new power.

Then he took a few steps away from the ponies, sat down against a tree, and rested the book on his knees.

Tom came out of the bird blind. "What is it?" he asked.

"Don't try to take it," said Danny. "Just don't. You don't believe me, but it's Sammael's book."

"But your folks aren't here. Did you know they wouldn't be?"

Danny nodded. "I was looking for this."

"That book?"

"The Book of Storms." Abel Korsakof's voice hissed out from Danny's throat and stained the dusty air. He'd given up his *soul* for this small, dark book. What, inside it, could be worth giving up an entire soul for?

"Can I look?" asked Tom. "If I don't touch it?"

Danny didn't know. But there must be so many things that you just happened to see in your life. If you didn't try to take them, could they really hurt you?

He shrugged. Maybe at least it might mean that Tom believed him a bit more.

Tom came to sit beside him, and Danny put his fingers once again on the snakeskin cover, then opened the book.

The Book Of Storms
By Danny O'Neill

Danny stared. The print was old and uneven, and he'd never written a book in his life. He'd certainly never written *this* book.

On the title page was an engraving of a low range of hills under a stormy black sky. Through the clouds a single bolt of lightning had been thrown; it forked toward the ground.

As Danny looked at the picture, he saw in his mind's eye exactly what that fork of lightning had struck. The hills were those that rose up behind his own town. His house lay just below the hill with the smooth, egg-shaped top, and the fork of lightning was the very same one that had struck the old sycamore tree in his garden. Which was, of course, impossible—this book was much older than that.

He turned the page. There wasn't a list of contents—the book launched straight in at the first page.

The house is falling in.

He read this and stopped his eyes. His heart began to quicken. Was this the proof that everything he'd been telling Tom was true?

"Look!" he said, putting his finger by the words. "It's the storm! It's the storm they went away in, just like I told you!"

Something crackled on his fingertip.

"What are you on about?" said Tom. "It's in some foreign language, isn't it? All jumbled up—looks a bit like Polish. What's the point of staring at it? You won't understand a word it says."

The Book of Storms, thought Danny. Written by . . . himself? Was this a book that only he could read?

Danny took his finger from the page as it grew uncomfortably warm, and read on.

The house is falling and Danny is falling, knees and elbows crumpling onto the floor, and an earsplitting crash is tearing through the air—that's surely the roof, breaking in two, about to come pelting down on top of him.

He knew this bit. And it was all there: the meeting with Abel Korsakof, Aunt Kathleen's axe, the big black dogs, the frenzied dash into the woods. He skimmed the book, faster and faster, galloping toward the river, pulling himself out, finding the worm, finding Tom, watching Mitz creep away behind his back, finding the bird blind. . . . He tried to skip forward a few more pages, but he couldn't understand the words until he'd gone back to throw his eyes over the previous ones.

"What are you on about?" said Tom. "It's in some foreign language, isn't it? All jumbled up—looks a bit like Polish. What's the point of staring at it? You won't understand a word it says."

The Book of Storms, thought Danny. Written by . . . himself? Was this a book that only he could read?

Danny took his finger from the page as it grew uncomfortably warm, and read on.

The page ended. So that was the whole story: Sammael had done something to a couple of people he'd called "idiots," who had lived in the same house as Danny. He'd shown them "a little bit of what they were up against." And what, exactly, that must have been, Danny didn't want to imagine. Tell me how to get them back, he urged the book. Please tell me.

He turned over the page, holding his breath. A cloud puffed up, covering his face in freezing mist and making his eyes sting. Tom didn't seem to notice it at all.

As the cloud cleared, he read,

Don't start asking questions. The Book of Storms exists to give answers to those who are prepared to pay for them. If you will not make your own bargain and pay, you must take what it chooses to give.

This book was made from the first taro ever left by a storm: the first bolt of lightning that ever fell onto the steaming earth was captured in a single crumb of bark, from which the cover of this book was hammered out by Sammael, the Master of the Air.

The process of leaving taros was devised by this first-ever storm, in order that after every storm, a token would be left on the earth, inside of which would remain the song used by storms as a gathering call. This, it was hoped, would prove a safeguard against any force or creature who managed to devise a method of supress-ing storms as they manifested themselves. Storms well know how devastating and unnecessary they are per-ceived to be, and they are aware of the measures they must take to protect themselves and their futures. Indeed, one might think of the taro as an imperishable seed from which a particular flower might always grow again, even should all the currently flowering examples be put to the sword and the bonfire.

So whoever finds the taro, if he or she can unlock its song and hear its voice, can call up a storm. The taro binds itself to its finder and imbues that finder with the forces unique to storms. No storm can kill the finder, nor take from him or her that taro, which must, according to the laws of Nature, belong entirely to the finder, for the duration of his or her life.

He was—what was the word?—*imbued* with the forces of storms? They were inside him, for*ever*? For his entire life?

Danny saw his own hands steadily holding the book. He saw his legs dressed in the black school trousers, and his feet inside their leather shoes. Were those hands, those legs, those feet—were they wrapped around storms? It was impossible. But it was written in the book, wasn't it? He, Danny O'Neill, *was* a storm.

An angry, raging, violent storm. Inside him, until he died . . .

But beware! To contain *something does not give a creature the means by which to control it. No earthly creature can control a storm. A storm will do what it likes, once gathered.*

He had learned the song from the worm. So he could call up a storm, and it couldn't kill him, but he couldn't *do* anything with it. And he had no idea how to call up the particular one that his parents had gone after, anyway.

Have more faith, wrote the book. *There are always paths to travel. And it's certainly true that bravery can be its own reward. There is a creature to whom the secrets of storms are partly known—the farthest-traveling bird of all, which spends its days and nights flying and sleeping on the high currents of the air: the swallow. A swallow will know where the weather has gone. A swallow will know what remains of it.*

The page stretched away, blank. Danny tried to turn more pages, but his fingers kept slipping before he could separate them.

Ask a swallow. It was a sort of clue, he supposed. But not much of one.

"All that," said Tom, "for a book written in Polish."

Danny closed the Book of Storms and tried to think. It must have said very different things to Abel Korsakof, all about types of storms and how they gathered up, and how they worked. It must have said just enough to make him feel like he had something to work on, or that he was learning things that nobody had ever known before. There must have been something in there that had convinced him he'd gotten a good deal in return for his soul. But had he known that the book would change for Danny?

Probably not. And if Abel had known the stuff about taros and swallows, the old man could just have told him, instead of making him come all this way.

But perhaps he'd thought there was something special about the Book of Storms itself. It certainly wouldn't hurt for Danny to take it with him. Better than leaving it to grow mold in that damp old bird blind, anyway. At least, having read the whole story, he knew now that Aunt Kathleen had only been following a dream and wasn't really intent on killing him. And he knew what had happened to Mitz. The faint worry that had been nagging away since her disappearance began to drain out of his chest, leaving a tiny nut of needling betrayal in its place. Mitz had simply stopped trusting him. He'd saved her from the rabbit hole, and she'd turned against him and left.

I didn't do enough, he thought bitterly. I failed her. I couldn't even look after a cat.

This small truth provoked a surge of darkness inside

him that spread through his blood like tar. It was Sammael's fault, all this. Sammael had to be found and defeated, and crushed into a dust so fine, it would make the sand grains of life look like boulders.

Danny put the book in his bag. "I know what happened to my parents," he said to Tom. "Sammael made the storm take them, just because he was angry that they were trying to find out about storms. He didn't want to kill them, just to show them that humans shouldn't think they can control storms, because he thinks that only he should be able to do that. And I think I know how to get them back."

"What?" Tom got to his feet. He had to lean against the tree trunk; he didn't seem able to put much weight on his right leg.

"Yeah," said Danny. "That's it—we'll call up a storm and see what happens."

He hadn't meant to say it. But now, as it was said, his schoolbag felt warm. The Book of Storms was glowing with heat.

"Where d'you reckon we'll find some swallows round here?" he asked Tom.

Tom looked at him for a long time. He seemed to be weighing up a great number of things in his head. Eventually he said, "Danny, we need to go home. I told Mum I'd get you back before supper, she's already raging like a mad elephant and banging on about calling the police, and I've got an exam on Friday and you've missed school, and anyway, you look really tired. Don't you want to go home and get something to eat? And some sleep?"

He didn't mention that he was starting to feel rushes of hot pain every time anything brushed against the wound on his thigh, or that his temples were squeezing tightly into his exhausted brain. But his patience was wearing out.

Danny shook his head. "You go," he said. "I'll be fine."

Because he would be fine now. The Book of Storms was more than a book: it was *his* book, like the stick had become his. It would protect him.

Tom took a deep breath. "For God's sake, Danny!" he said. "I can't just leave you! You're eleven! And you're a wet-behind-the-ears idiot townie—you know jack-all about finding your way around. I *can't* leave you, and I've had enough of running around chasing after stupid fairy stories. It's a load of rubbish! Don't you get it?"

Danny couldn't look at him anymore. Tom was the one who didn't get it. Tom wouldn't get it until it was too late. All Danny wanted was for Tom to see for just one second that he wasn't making any of this up, but Tom was far too practical.

"I won't go home. Not now. I've nearly got them—I'm

nearly there. I know what to do, and I'll do it on my own if I have to. I don't need you anymore." He got to his feet, swung the schoolbag onto his back, and picked up Shimny's reins, then looked at her back. It was as high as his head and he didn't have a saddle anymore. He'd find a tree stump to get on from.

Tom watched his cousin lead the pony away. His leg was hot and sticky; a dark, wet patch still glistened over the dried stains on his torn jeans. His ribs ached, and the skin on his cheek was tight where a huge paw had reached up to rake its claws through his flesh.

His eyes followed Danny's slight body, still dressed in navy school sweater and black trousers, as it walked past a crooked hazel tree, the spindly branches hooking toward him. Danny stumbled over a loose clump of grass and put his hand out, grabbing at a plant to stop himself falling. It was a stinging nettle. He winced but didn't stop to search for dock leaves, like Tom would have done.

What had Danny seen in that book? Spooky old thing. Written in a foreign language, so who knew what it might say? Of course Danny had pored over it for ages, probably thinking that if he read enough of the words he'd find some that were a bit like English and be able to understand what the book was about. But Tom knew that Danny didn't speak Polish, not a single word.

Crazy cousin. Maybe he'd had some kind of accident, hit his head and lost his mind. Maybe something terrible *had* happened to his parents and he'd been involved. Whatever it was, it would become clear in time, no doubt. But meanwhile, it was probably best to look after Danny rather than lock him in his room and have him beating at the door trying to get out. Tom understood the need to roam free when things were wrong.

If Tom didn't go with him, Danny would be all alone. He'd trudge through the shadows, trailing the piebald pony behind him until she, too, refused to move her ancient bones one more step, and then he'd go on by himself. Danny didn't know anything about the world, or how to survive outside at night with only the rustling trees and the bats for company. He'd end up eating deadly nightshade and sitting on giant hogweed, which would turn his skin into a sheet of itchy red blisters. He was a town boy, an indoors boy, and he was totally clueless about nature.

Tom narrowed his eyes against the harsh late-afternoon sun.

"One more hour," he called. "You've got one more hour of this, and that's all. There're always swallows and swifts in old farm buildings. I know an old barn just outside this village. It's the other way. And after that, we're going home, whatever happens. That's it. Okay?" He unlooped Apple's reins, pulling her reluctantly round to face the opposite direction.

Silently, Danny turned and followed him.

CHAPTER 14

INTO THE WOODS

Nearly there, said Sammael to himself. Nearly ready.
He hadn't collected as many taros as he'd wanted
to, but soon he'd know exactly how much power he could
command with the number he had. The boy must surely
be dead by now—the dogs would have torn him apart.
And soon the rest of those dull-witted, ungrateful humans would follow him, down into their fiery graves.

Sammael had told Kalia to go off hunting. Then he
found his way to a mountainous desert, a place as far from
watchful eyes as the earth could provide.

He would allow himself six taros. Back in the room,

he'd stored hundreds, but using six would give him a good idea of how huge a storm he could call up and command when he used all he had.

It was time to practice.

The knot of ash wood hit the stony ground and rolled until it found a little hollow, where it came to rest. Up in the sky, the clouds hunched and began to crawl toward each other. One of them belched loudly, and a swift breath of wind swept down to the mountains below.

It caught Sammael's hair. Having hair that blew in the wind was one of the best things about having taken on a human shape. It made him feel surrounded by energy.

For a second Sammael missed Kalia—he liked the way the wind gnawed at her curly gray coat. But she'd be too much in danger with what he was about to do. She was best back in England, racing through the fields flushing out rabbits, not dodging the wind around these bleak rocks.

Sammael pulled another twisted lump of wood from his pocket. Most of the taros were pieces of wood; even storms, it seemed, had particular places where they preferred to store their messages. Which proved that even storms were creatures of habit.

Habit. What a pathetic thing. Habit was just an excuse for not having any imagination. But they'd regret having made their taros so easy to find, when they saw how he could control them. And maybe once the humans saw his power, they'd start thinking twice about who was behind everything, pulling the strings.

"They won't have time to think, though," said Sammael to himself. "They'll see, in one blinding flash, before they all die, who they really owe thanks to. I'll show them the most beautiful, the most impressive and inspiring, thing on earth, and then I'll kill them all. They'll see what *I* can be responsible for."

He dug into his pocket again. Another lump of wood joined the other two.

"They think I'm a demon," he said up to the bunching sky. "Then I'll show them what *demons* do."

He chucked another taro down onto the pile. And then it was simple. He knew the call. He'd known it since he'd found that first taro and made the Book of Storms from it. He didn't even have to say it out loud, but sometimes he liked to hear his own voice, staining the storm's words like poison onto the air.

> *"The world is deadly, the world is bright,*
> *The creatures that use it are blinded by sight,*

But there's no sense in crying or closing the page,
Sense only battles in fighting and rage.
So come all you soldiers and answer my call,
Together we gather, together we fall!"

The clouds began to scream. Gathering, swarming, they tumbled faster and faster toward a central point in the sky, directly above the pieces of wood that Sammael had thrown. Not for them the slow, threatening rumble over hours and days, the gradual buildup of pressure. This time they were being dragged forward by a call three times as strong as the normal one, pulling them viciously toward each other.

The clouds crashed together, boiling and seething; they were squashed and stretched and yanked through the air. Inside them, electricity crackled, fighting for space. Raindrops began to swell and pour down in streams, bursting like waterfalls from the mouths of the darkening sky.

The wind around Sammael roared up into a hurricane, tearing trees from the earth. He stood, letting it rip through his hair. It wouldn't shift him. He wasn't some lowly tree or flimsy house, to be blown off his moorings and sent hurtling into the sky. He was made of air: he could stand exactly where he liked and command it not to move him.

The storm, too confused to remember its usual voices,

began to shriek. A million cries shriveled out above the crashing groans, twisting like agonized snakes devouring their own tails. Lightning set fire to the rain; sheets of flame spewed onto the mountainsides. Within seconds, the land and sky were ablaze.

Sammael stood exactly where he had first planted his feet, and watched the fire. Flames reflected in his black eyes. He caught a piece of burning twig and ate it, but the sensation of burning wasn't a thing he could feel, no matter how much of it he pressed against himself. He could only watch the fire and listen to the dying screams of the trees, the plants, and the grasses. He listened for a long while as they grew louder and more anguished, and then he smiled.

When he had heard enough, he began to climb up one of the sheets of flame into the sky. If only Kalia hadn't been a mortal dog, she could have followed at his heels. She'd have liked that, haring up a branch of fire, her spindly legs reaching out toward home.

Ah, Kalia, he thought. If only all creatures were more like her, there'd be no need to destroy everything with fire. He'd be master of it all already.

But then again, fire was fun.

The lurcher still wasn't back by the time he reached the room. Everything was just as he'd left it: the boxes of sand stacked up by the far wall, the box of taros starting to look respectably full. A few more storms and then he'd have enough.

But where was Kalia? He missed her, with a strange feeling in his insides that he'd ordinarily only noticed when something was going wrong somewhere. What if she was away talking to old friends, to other earthly creatures who might try to sway her loyalties away from him?

He'd never questioned her loyalty, although he normally held it as a rule never to believe what earthly creatures said. They were notoriously fickle. Not Kalia, though. The great gray dog was a steadfast coward who watched him with her huge eyes and didn't approve of half the things he did but who pressed her head against his leg and tried never to leave his side unless he sent her away with kicks and curses. Kalia was too stupid to leave, he told himself. Although he knew she wasn't stupid at all, not in the common way. She'd been born knowing where he was, and she'd found him the minute she was old enough to leave her mother. And she'd said to him . . .

Sammael didn't want to listen to his thoughts. Where

was Kalia? Damn dog, always running off when he had things to do, and refusing to find her way back home by herself. Now he'd have to go find her.

He knew where she liked to hunt. A short step through the land between the room and the earth and he was standing in an English hayfield, the late-afternoon sun drawing down on his back.

"Kalia!" he snapped. No need to be loud about it: she had ears like radar. And she should know where he was, if she was thinking about him at all.

She came racing up within minutes, a bundle held between her jaws. Tail wagging furiously, she fawned against Sammael's legs for a moment, scrabbling over his feet with her purple paws.

"What've you got?" He reached out for the lump in her mouth.

Kalia released it. "Found it," she said. "Think it's got some news for you. It saw me and started muttering all sorts of strange things about dogs, big black dogs, and I thought it was talking about the Dogs of War. I thought, It must know about that boy, that boy with the taro. . . . Oh, I've missed you! You've been ages!"

Sammael took hold of the lump and held it up by the scruff of its neck. It was a mangled, terrified cat with no whiskers and only one good eye. It looked like it had spent the night in a washing machine, although that was mainly because it was drenched in Kalia's slobber.

The cat twisted in the air, trying to claw at Sammael's hand. He wasn't surprised. His fingers sometimes felt like ice to warm-blooded creatures.

"Stop creating," he said to the cat, gripping it a little tighter.

It stopped struggling and hung limply.

"I know where you belong," Sammael said, looking at its matted head. "You belong in the house next door to that boy, don't you? You've come a long way from home. What are you doing here, I wonder?"

The cat jerked and closed its eye, as if it didn't want to look at him.

"You came with him, didn't you?" he asked.

The cat gulped.

"And you were chased by the dogs. But the dogs got him, didn't they?"

He didn't miss the quiver of the cat's tiny white throat, although it was trying very hard to be still.

"You're saying the dogs *didn't* get him?"

Sammael's voice was so quiet that a fly buzzing past half a yard away wouldn't have heard it, but the quieter it got, the more agony it seemed to cause the cat.

She opened her mouth in a silent meow.

"Cat, cat, cat," said Sammael. "Whatever you've told my dog, you'd better tell it to me. The only reason she didn't eat you was that she thought you might be interesting to me. You're not being very interesting at all, at the moment."

He walked to the side of the field and put the cat down on the branch of a tree, just above the height of his head. The skin he'd been holding settled back down onto her shoulder blades, and she began to lick herself nervously.

"Come on, cat," said Sammael. "Out with it."

The cat stopped licking and blinked her eye a few times. A shudder ran down her skin. "We got away from the dogs," she said. "He threw me—threw all of us—into a *river*. It was so *wet*. I nearly drowned."

"I'll do worse than that to you if you continue to annoy me," said Sammael. "Now spit it out."

"*You* already have," said the cat, growing bolder from its perch. "You set fire to a shed and I got burned and trapped in a rabbit burrow. I used to be an exceptionally fine figure of a cat. . . ."

Sammael reached out his hand. The cat tried to back away, but her feet were stuck to the branch. His fingers closed around her back like the tentacles of a frozen octopus.

"What happened to the boy?" he said.

"He's gone to find the Book of Storms," said the cat, closing her eye again, trying to fight the cold that was hardening her veins. "He knows where it is. The other boy, I mean."

"The other boy? The one with blond hair?"

"Yes. When the dogs came, he got left behind. But then the dogs ran off after some squirrels and he escaped. He's tough, the other boy."

"Have they found the book?"

The cat tried to wriggle out from under his hand. "I don't know. I don't know anything more. Please let me go."

"Do you know where the book is?"

"No."

Slowly, Sammael released his grip on the cat. Kalia was sitting a few feet away, staring again.

"Do you want to eat it?" he asked her.

"No, thanks," said Kalia. "I've got a sort of burnt taste in my mouth just from carrying it here. Let it go."

Sammael flicked his fingers at the cat and it scrambled down the tree, shooting off into a bush. "You'll never make a proper demon dog," he said. "You're supposed to want to savage everything you meet."

"All I want is to serve you," said Kalia, trampling the ground with her forepaws.

"Find me the Book of Storms, then," said Sammael. "Before that irritating boy does. Go on, fetch!"

"Don't you know where the old man hid it?" Kalia stopped treading. Sammael was supposed to know *everything*.

Sammael's face had set, hard. "Touched as I am by your faith, Kalia," he said, "if you question me one more time, I'll throw you into the land between worlds and let the colors eat you up. Now shut up and let me think."

Why had he taken his eyes off the boy? He cursed himself for an idiot. After that stupid woman had missed with the axe, he'd been sure the sniveling wretch of a human couldn't possibly have the mettle to escape the Dogs of War. But somehow he'd gotten away, and he'd thrown himself into the river. And rivers always knew more than they should. That was the trouble with water—it got everywhere.

So he found the river.

"Did you tell the boy about my coat?" he asked.

"I told him what I knew," said the river. It wasn't afraid of Sammael.

"Where did he go?"

"Off to find a way to kill you, I don't doubt. Is that what you're scared of?"

Sammael said nothing.

"He's looking for his parents," said the river. "He thinks they've been taken by storms. They've disappeared, you know."

Sammael did know, and he cursed himself again. Then he caught sight of something. A rag, snagged on a clump of reeds at the water's edge. A pale piece of cotton with a thin blue stripe running down it, and a pink stain splashing over the blue. They'd been wounded, and that was blood.

"I'm a sight hound," said Kalia. "I only follow things that I can see."

"Not now, you don't," said Sammael.

He stepped into the bird blind and felt it, still swimming in the air. It had been here recently and now it was gone.

"They came here," he said. "And they took the Book of Storms." Think, he said to himself. How to kill the unkillable? The boy was protected by storms. He seemed able to thwart every attempt on his life that Sammael could throw at him.

And now the boy had discovered about Sammael's coat.

Then he had it. The boy had the stick—a simple taro, made only of tree and storm. But the Book of Storms was more than that. It was made of tree and storm and one other thing—it was made of Sammael himself. He had hammered out that taro, he had bound together those pages, and he had sewn them inside their black cover.

All he needed was the book.

"Find them," he said to Kalia. "And fast, or I'll get a dog who's better at finding things."

He gave her scrawny backside a kick with his boot, and she fled from the bird blind, sniffing frantically to catch the scent of horse on the forest floor.

The cat licked her wounds for a while and then lay in a ray of sunlight, letting the yellow heat warm her body. She closed her eye and rested her cheek on the ground, but there was no way of shifting the memory of those icy fingers holding her like a cage. What had become of Danny? Would she ever see him return from school again, have him pause to tickle her on his way from garden gate to front door?

Perhaps. Perhaps not. But this wasn't an adventure for cats. She needed to sit down, spend three days grooming herself, and then begin to think about idly swatting a mouse with one of her white paws.

I may be wild by nature, she thought, but being wild is much better inside my own territory.

She got to her feet and began to run. If she'd been any other creature, she might have needed to stop and look at the landmarks around her every now and again, in order to be sure she was still going the right way. But in Mitz's head a single sound kept her straight and true and running, through all the miles and miles that lay between her and her eventual destination.

It was the sound of an armchair, and it called her home.

CHAPTER 15

THE SWALLOWS

The old barn was all but derelict. A farmer had used it for storing hay the year before, but too much rain had soaked through the holes in the roof over the winter, and the hay had been ruined. It was still there, moldering away, waiting to be cleared if the farmer ever decided that it was worth his while mending the roof and then running the risk of storing another year's crop under the ancient structure.

The swallows didn't care about the holes. The rafters were still sound; there were plenty of places to build their nests high up in the eaves. Any creature who could fly for thousands of miles, sleeping on the wing, wasn't going to be put off by the threat of a few drops of rain every now and again.

They saw the boys and horses coming from far away. All four creatures looked like lame old dogs, hobbling on for miles with sore feet and aching limbs. A couple of the swallows took a flight out to have a better look, plunging and whirling like leaves on the wind. They feared very little; few other creatures could ever catch up with them.

"There!"

Danny looked up to see Tom's finger pointing toward the sky. He tried to follow its direction, but Tom's arm was moving too fast, sweeping in circles.

"See it?"

"See what?"

"The swallow! There's another! Whee . . . they're coming to have a proper look at us."

Then Danny saw them. Tiny darts of feather wheeling around his head, flying in great circles. They looked as if they weighed nothing at all, or just enough to keep them steady in the lightest of breezes.

He put his hand in his pocket and called out. "Hey! Hey! Stop!"

Ahead of him, Tom laughed. "Oh, quit, Danny," he said. "D'you really think you can make swallows stop flying?"

The swallows swooped and chattered, racing as close to the boys' faces as they dared. One grazed Danny's eyebrow with its wing tip.

He didn't want to speak again. It was terrible when Tom mocked him. Please, he begged the birds silently. Please stop. Just show him.

"Show who?" said a swallow.

He couldn't tell which swallow; they were both still spinning through the air too quickly for his eyes to follow. But the voice was definitely a swallow's, and it had heard him. He hadn't spoken out loud, though. Unless he was going mad.

"Can you hear me when I *think*?" he said inside his head, to the swallows.

One came full tilt toward him, flapped its wings rapidly, and came to perch on his shoulder. "Ha!" Danny said to Tom, and pointed at the swallow.

Tom stared, rubbed his eyes, and looked again. "Oh, this is ridiculous," he muttered. "My head's spinning. It's the shock . . . those dogs. . . ."

"Not when you *think*, silly," said the swallow. "But I can certainly hear you *talk*. Most birds wouldn't believe that sort of thing if it slapped them round the beak, but we swallows—well, there are so many things in the skies, who are we to discount one more, however unlikely it seems?"

Danny could only just see the tiny bird out of the farthest corner of his eye. It weighed nothing at all, and its claws clung to his sweater like burrs.

"Have you ever sat on a person's shoulder before?" he asked it, again without using his voice.

"Not once," said the swallow. "But you're not an ordinary person, are you? You can't be."

"Yeah, I am," said Danny. "I'm about as ordinary as people get. Or I was, anyway. I don't think I ever will be again, no matter what happens."

So it did work! He could talk without talking out loud, just like they did. If only he'd known that before, he could have said far more to Mitz and Shimny, without having to worry about anyone else overhearing.

"Where are you going?" the swallow asked.

"To find you, actually," said Danny.

"To find me? Why me?"

"Well, all of you, really," said Danny. "But just you, if you can help me. I need to call up a storm."

"Lawks!" said the swallow, losing its balance and falling halfway down Danny's chest, wings spluttering against him. It regained its composure and shot off into the air.

Danny watched it go. Had he offended it? No—it had gone to find the other swallow. They came back to him together and landed, one on his head, one on his shoulder. He couldn't tell which was which.

Tom took a pace toward him and then stopped dead. Suddenly, Danny didn't dare look at him.

"I'm Paras," said the swallow on his shoulder. "And this is my sister, Siravina. Now tell her what you just said to me."

It felt very strange, talking to a creature that was sitting on top of your head.

"Hi, Siravina," said Danny. "I need to call up a storm. I've . . . sort of . . . been told that you might know where it went?"

"Where it went?" echoed Siravina. She had a slightly smoother voice than Paras, liquid honey to his dark molasses. "You want to call up a particular storm, then?"

"Yeah. Is it possible?"

"Is it?" Paras echoed. Siravina was silent.

Tom called out, "Oi, *bird boy*, you going to stand there all day?" with a tightness that made Danny try to pretend he hadn't heard. See? he wanted to say. I'm standing on a grassy path with a swallow on my head, and it's asking me about storms. *It* believes me! But there was a thin anger in Tom's voice that Danny didn't quite understand.

"What's your problem?" he shouted back. "Can't you see they're *talking* to me?"

"They're *sitting* on you," Tom corrected him. "It's probably 'cos you're covered in squashed flies from all this stupid messing about."

"She's talking," said Danny. "I can tell you what she's saying if you like. I can just repeat it. Then you'll know."

Tom looked suddenly exhausted. "Oh, sure," he said. "They're talking. I can see that. Anyone could see that. Look . . . can we just go and sit in the barn for a while? I think we should have a rest."

"You go," said Danny. "I need . . . *I* need to talk to the swallows."

Tom hesitated. It was clear that he wanted to say something scornful, but instead he gave a tired snort that didn't really say anything at all, then turned on his heel and trudged down to the barn, climbing in through a hole in the planking and leaving Apple to graze on the thick grass outside.

Danny tried not to look triumphant. For some reason, proving himself right didn't feel quite as good as he'd thought it would.

"Why would a human," asked Siravina, "want to call up a storm? Storms are dangerous things. And more to the point, *how* could you?"

"I . . . I don't exactly know," said Danny. "But my parents were lost in a storm—and only that storm knows what happened to them. And I've found all sorts of things—a taro, a book called the Book of Storms. I've even found out the song of the storms, I think. So I must be able to call one up somehow, mustn't I?"

"You have the Book of Storms?"

Both swallows spoke at the same time. Siravina's claws dug into Danny's scalp. Suddenly they had stopped breathing; they began to have a heaviness about them that weighed down on Danny's head.

"Well, yeah," he said. "It doesn't say much, though, really. I mean, not for me. It's just got the story of yesterday and today in it, all the stuff that's happened since then, and a bit about Sammael. And then at the end it tells me to ask swallows—it says you know all about how to find a certain storm. I mean, I can tell you loads about the one I want. I can even show you a picture from it. You'll have to look out while I get my bag off my back, though."

Paras dug his feet into Danny's sweater as he lifted the strap of his schoolbag carefully over the bird and swung the bag around in front of him, trying to keep his head steady. There probably wasn't any need—Siravina was holding on so tightly that she wouldn't have fallen even if

Danny had started turning cartwheels, but Danny was anxious not to unsettle either bird.

He crouched down to unzip his bag and carefully pull out the Book of Storms. As soon as he had it in his hands he wanted to sit down and reread the whole story again. Perhaps there was a clue in it somewhere that would tell him whether he had any hope of finding his parents. Perhaps the book would have updated itself, to include what the swallows had just said. And then the book would have a bit in it about him reading the book, as if he were both over and underneath the pages. If it was still writing itself, when would it ever stop? When he found his parents? When he, somehow, one day, no longer had the stick anymore? Or would it just go on writing his whole life, as long as he had it?

Not that the rest of his life was going to be quite so much of an adventure, of course—he planned to spend a lot of it at home. If he could.

He opened the book to the title page. The swallows craned their tiny black heads to see the picture of the storm.

"Can't make it out," muttered Siravina. "Impossible to see, this close up."

It wasn't until she had taken off and flown a good distance away, then swooped down again from quite a height, that she saw the picture clearly enough.

"Do you know it?" asked Danny.

"Well, yes, of course," said Siravina. "I know every inch of the sky. That storm was the night before last, and it came through this way, certainly. But it's died out now, of course. It's long gone."

Danny's fingers tightened on the Book of Storms. "It can't be gone," he said. "I have to call it back."

"That's impossible," said Siravina, "Once a particular storm is spent, it can't gather again. The energy has gone into other things. All that's left is the taro. Storms exist for the moment. Didn't the Book of Storms tell you that?"

"No," said Danny slowly. He closed the book and ran his hand over the snakeskin cover. Did it shiver beneath his fingertips?

"Are you sad?" asked Paras. "Siravina can be a bit blunt sometimes. But she knows a lot."

"No," said Danny. "I was just following the clues. If there isn't anything I can do, I suppose I'll just never find them again."

He had to bite savagely on his lip to stop it trembling, but it wasn't tears of sadness that threatened to fall. It was some kind of boiling rage. His hands began to shake.

"Tell me how they went," said Siravina abruptly. "You mentioned Sammael."

"They just went," said Danny. "In the middle of the

night. I woke up and they'd gone, and I didn't think that was too strange, because they always go to look at storms, but in the morning they weren't back. They always come back. And then I found this notebook, and this old guy, and he told me that Sammael had done something to the storm to make it, I dunno, take them somehow—that sounds stupid, I know. But it's the only thing that makes any sense. They wouldn't have stayed away unless something . . . I don't know . . . I dunno what I thought, really."

Siravina fluttered down to perch on the Book of Storms. She looked at Danny, her tiny black eyes as shiny as beetles' backs.

"It sounds reasonable to me. There are all sorts of ways of hiding people in weather. Perhaps Paras and I *can* help you—we'll fly out and ask the winds what they've seen. We'll see what we can bring back to you."

It was a faint hope, but it breathed inside Danny as if he'd inhaled mint, clearing a path through his despair.

"Will it take long?" he asked. "Shall we wait here?"

"Best thing," said Siravina, "is to go to the top of Sentry Hill. That way, if we do find there's something left of that storm for you to call back, you'll be able to see it coming. Sentry Hill's the tallest point for miles around."

"It'll be dark by the time we get up there," said Danny. "I won't see it coming once it's night."

"Of course you will," said Siravina. "Nights are never dark, once you open your eyes properly. And anyway, there'll be plenty of moonlight. Come, let's go!"

The tiny bird launched herself into the breeze, disappearing from sight within seconds. Danny didn't feel Paras go, but he heard a flutter of beating wings and saw the swallow's movement, sprinting off after his sister. Strange, intense little birds. How could they be so accepting? It had taken Danny nearly two days to accept that Sammael existed and storms were more than just the sum of their parts, and that even the birds could talk in their own language—but the swallows had just agreed that even things which seemed impossible were quite likely to be possible in the end and had made no fuss about it.

He'd miss that when he was back home again. But other things would make up for it.

After the swallows had flown off, Danny put the Book of Storms back into his schoolbag and went down to the barn to find Tom.

Apple was grazing rapidly, tearing up the grass outside the barn in thick tufts. She ate with the fury of a half-starved lion, turning her rump on Danny and Shimny as they approached. The piebald stayed well clear, aiming for a patch of grass ten feet away. Danny tied her reins up into a fat knot so she wouldn't tread on them. She needed to eat, although he was anxious to get going.

"Tom!" he called into the barn, peering through the broken door at the dark mountains of moldy hay.

There was no answer. Cautiously, he picked his way through the strewn hay and let his eyes adjust to the gloom inside the barn, casting around for the shape of his cousin. Tom was lying in a huddle on a huge, stinking bale of hay. He seemed to be shivering, although the air was hot and damp.

"Tom?" Danny said again, but the shivering bundle didn't answer. He must have fallen asleep. Danny edged his way forward, unsure of whether to wake him. Perhaps he was really ill, with some kind of blood poisoning from the dog bites, or water disease from the river.

Every nerve in Danny strained to go find Sentry Hill. He could just leave Tom sleeping, then come back to him later, after he had found the storm. Tom wouldn't mind, would he? He'd never wanted to come with Danny anyway. He'd be happy if he was left to sleep.

Danny shook his head rapidly, trying to dislodge the thought. He'd been lost and scared, and Tom had come with him and kept him safe. What kind of a person would he be if he left Tom now, shivering in a barn? If all this came to nothing, if he never found his parents again, then Tom and Aunt Kathleen and Sophie would be the only family he had.

He sat a short distance away and tried to squash the nerves that were crawling up into his stomach. His cheeks burned and his head ached. If only Mitz were still around, he could have left her on guard, nestling warmly in Tom's arms to quiet his shivers. But Mitz was gone, and that was Danny's fault too. If only she hadn't gone. If only they weren't here. If only he could make his brain silent, just for a few minutes.

He leaned his head back against the rotting hay and closed his eyes.

"If you want to understand me," Sammael asked Danny, "how would you prefer to do it? To picture me as a man? Or would it help if I were, say, a great crested newt? It's all one to me."

Danny looked up into Sammael's black eyes and wished he weren't so short. He knew that if he were taller, he'd be more decisive. It would make sense for the devil to be a man—that's what he usually was. But a man with cloven hooves, horns, a tail. And red. So somewhat similar to a goat, but red. Was a great crested newt really much different from that?

He hummed a little to buy some time, watching Sammael tap his long fingers irritably along a polished tabletop. It was very important to get the answer right. Danny sensed that Sammael didn't deal in second thoughts, or indecisiveness. The words that escaped from your mouth would bind themselves around you like ropes.

What should Sammael be? Man . . . goat . . . dog . . . axe . . . ant . . . moon . . .

"For God's sake, hurry up," snapped Sammael after about a minute of silence. But perhaps it had been longer than that.

"I . . . I . . . I . . ." Danny saw the look in Sammael's hard, narrow eyes and clung desperately to what he might have been thinking. What was the devil on earth? What was the wickedest, hardest, most evil thing he could possibly think of? What did he fear most, apart from this indescribable being before him with its long fingers, twitching foot, and blazing eyes?

Nothing. He could think of nothing. In his eleven years of life, so many things had terrified him: large dogs, dark corners, the door to the headmaster's office, shooting stars that might have been meteors, his father's anger, things hiding in alleyways, under beds, behind the open doors of unlit rooms. But this was a different kind of fear, a hopeless fear that if he was wrong, if he gave Sammael a stupid answer, all would be forever awful and that would be the last word on the matter.

Danny found he was beginning to sweat.

"Come on," drawled Sammael, looking bored. "If you're going to make me into a devil, you must have some idea of what I look like. If not, how can you fear me enough to want me dead?"

Danny's heart began to rush a little faster as if it knew the end might be near and it was trying to squeeze in as many beats as possible before it fell silent. His palms were soggy. What was it he was supposed to be answering?

"Okay, I'll give you until the count of three. One," said Sammael, his voice dangerously quiet. "Two."

"No . . . wait . . ." said Danny helplessly, sure he could no longer breathe.

"Wait? For what? What's the problem here? Are you not *sure*? Are you telling me you want to look at what I *really* am?"

"You're evil!" Danny managed to gasp. "I know that!"

"Oh, Danny," said Sammael. "You're so disappointing. Well, we'd better get on with it, then. We've had one and two. What comes after that?"

"No, wait. Wait!"

"Three," said Sammael. "Time's up."

Danny's eyes snapped open, and he threw his arms over his chest, clutching his shoulders to shield himself. The light outside was fading. There was nobody else in the barn except Tom. Something was happening inside his head that he didn't like at all.

He crawled over to Tom.

"Wake up! Wake up! We've got to go!"

Tom started, grabbed at something, and thrust it toward Danny. Cold metal grazed Danny's cheek; he jerked his head backwards and stared. The fading light from the doorway flashed, once, on the quivering tines of a pitchfork.

"Jesus! What . . ."

"Danny! You scared me! Sorry!" Tom sat up and brought the pitchfork away from Danny's face. "What time is it? Where is this?"

Danny edged back a little farther, although he was safe enough now. "We're still in the barn. You fell asleep. We both fell asleep."

"Damn! Is it . . . what time is it?"

"I dunno. Late. But we've got to go—the swallows went ages ago. We need to get to Sentry Hill."

"We need to get home. I promised Mum we'd be back by suppertime. She's done enough worrying."

Tom began to move stiffly to his feet, clambering past Danny toward the doorway. Outside, he looked up at the darkening sky. Far above, the stars were beginning to glitter.

Danny came to stand beside him. "We can't stop now. It's nearly the end. It's got to be."

"Swallows won't fly through the night," Tom tried again. "They'll have gone to roost somewhere. They won't move again until the morning."

"Well, go home, then. I don't care. You never believe me, but I don't care anymore. Go home to your mum if you're so scared of the dark."

Danny turned his face away. His skin burned. The moldy hay bales back in the barn seemed to be calling him to lay his head down on them, to let himself fall into a deep, yielding sleep. He'd lie there all night breathing in mold spores and dust, and all the insects and mice who had made their homes in the hay would crawl over him, but he'd be too asleep to care.

But then he'd wake up, and he'd have to get up and go on again. And one hour soon, if he was faced with much more, his heart would drop and fail him. He had to go. If Tom wasn't going to help him, he had to go on alone.

He went back to Shimny and pulled her head up.

"We've got to go again, Shimny," he apologized. "I think this is the last time. I think we'll find them now."

She didn't seem to notice that he was talking inside his head. Maybe it still sounded exactly the same to her.

She said, "I'm hungry. Must we?"

But that was all she said, and then she lifted her old, patched head. Her blue eye was close to Danny's face. Her solid old bones, stiff and tired and creaking, stood hard inside her warm skin.

"Sorry, old pony," said Danny as he dragged himself up onto her back from a pile of planks. "We've got to go back to the woods and up that hill. Can you find it? I don't know the way."

"Sure I can," said the pony. "I've been here before. But isn't Tom coming?"

Danny didn't answer. He could only repeat to himself, Soon, I'll find them, and we'll go home, and then all this will stop. It has to stop. Soon, it has to stop, or my legs just won't hold me anymore, and I'll fall off this pony and lie on the cold black ground and let the night swallow me up.

And as he set off into the last traces of the twilight, he heard a call behind him.

"Oi! You stupid idiot! Wait up!"

Tom was trotting after him. Little more than a shape in the gloom, his blond hair shone pale through the darkness. Arm outstretched, standing up in his stirrups, hand gripping the handle of the old pitchfork, he looked like a ghostly horseman ready for war.

For a second, Danny remembered the tines flashing so close to his face. Tom's on my side, he reminded himself. He's on my side, and at least he's got a weapon now. Although we won't get Sammael with a pitchfork. Still, if we're quick, I might get to my parents before he finds me. And they'll know what to do about him. Of course they'll know. They'll protect me.

CHAPTER 16

THE STORM

"They were here. Recently, I swear it. Very recently."

Kalia gazed up at Sammael. He was standing by the barn door, looking at the empty space in front of the barn.

"Of course they were here," he snapped. "But following them is pretty pointless if you can't go fast enough to catch them up, isn't it?"

"It's not my fault," the dog whined. "I told you, I'm a sight hound. I'm doing my best."

She tried to push her head against his palm, but he removed it.

"You're useless," he said. "I don't know why I let you hang around." Kicking her away, he turned his attention to the grass and stamped on it. "Where are they?" he demanded. "The boys. The ponies. Where did they go?"

The grass shivered and stuttered under his feet.

"The p-p-p-ponies . . ." muttered one blade. "Their t-t-teeth . . ."

"Ponies have teeth. I'm well aware of that," spat Sammael. "Tell me which way they went!"

"They ate us. Big, tearing teeth . . . *scrunch* . . . *crunch* . . . They ripped us and tore us. . . ."

"I couldn't care less if they made wigs out of you," said Sammael. "Where did they go?"

The grass, so recently chomped, continued to twitter and gibber. He could get no sense out of it.

Kalia crept forward again, her shoulders hunched. "Where are we?" she whispered. "I think I know this place. Isn't there a hill, with one side of it quarried away?"

Sammael stopped the kick he'd been about to swing again at her. This rage was doing strange things to him; normally, there was no way Kalia would have ever been able to suggest something to him that he hadn't already thought about. He must stop being so fixated on this boy and start being rational again.

"A hill?" he said. "Sentry Hill. Of course."

"Well, wouldn't that be a good place, if he's looking for a storm . . . ?"

It might. In fact, it definitely was—Sentry Hill stood apart in the rolling landscape, tall and alone. How had the damned dog thought of that before him? He had powers beyond all mortal reasoning. His brain worked at the speed of light.

He kicked her, hard. She slunk backwards and crouched in the darkness, watching him.

Sammael looked through the night. Light or dark—it made little difference. He saw by the changing feel of the air, by its patches of coldness and heat. He saw the path that the boys had traveled, up into the higher part of the woods. How long since they'd been here? How far ahead were they? However far, he could walk there in seconds. But the boy mustn't be frightened. He must hand over the Book of Storms of his own accord.

It wouldn't be any use trying to strike a bargain with him, not as things were. Danny must know by now that Sammael wanted him dead. He wouldn't trust an offer, however plain and straightforward, to swap the book for his parents, not if he had an ounce of sense. How to make him believe that surrendering the Book of Storms would save him, rather than kill him?

By rescuing him, of course. That was always the way,

with humans. Sammael could make the boy think he was going to die, then save him. Danny was only a young, inexperienced human; even if he did know how much the taro protected him, he wouldn't want to risk throwing himself under a bolt of lightning to try it out.

And then, once a small part of his trust was won, he would gratefully give over the Book of Storms and Sammael could draw the final curtain.

Sammael dug his hands into his coat pockets and smiled again to himself. Of course there was a way. When had he ever not found a way, in the end?

The first belch of thunder sounded a long way off, to Tom's ears. The air was still thin, too—he should have become aware of a gradual buildup of pressure drifting around their shoulders and cheeks, making them start to sweat.

Still, with thunder that quiet, the storm wouldn't be with them for ages, if it came their way at all. Something that far away was probably just passing by, on its way elsewhere.

Tom shivered a little in the cool night air. If he'd known how far they would come, how long this journey would go on, he'd have made sure of bringing at least a jacket. Damn his half-brained idiot of a cousin. But something odd had happened to Danny—normally he was the first one to turn blue and set his teeth chattering and look like he was about to freeze solid from the cold. Normally he was the first one to stop and suggest going home, or to sit down on every stone and gate that they passed on a walk. Normally he wasn't altogether that keen on going on walks anyway.

Now he didn't even seem to notice that he'd hardly slept for two days, and it was getting dark and damp and cold again. Tom couldn't understand it. Creatures didn't change just like that: the same cows were always at the front of the herd waiting to be milked every morning, and the same ones were always at the back. What *had* happened to Danny? Whatever it was, it had changed him from the person he'd been for eleven years into someone Tom wasn't altogether sure he recognized, or even liked that much.

And that business with the swallows—how had he done that? It was *Tom* who had a way with animals, not Danny—*Tom* who understood how to communicate wordlessly with them, and get them to follow him around. He imagined those tiny bodies clinging onto his own sweater, and his stomach snarled with something that wasn't simply hunger.

Thunder growled again. Tom's hand tightened on the

pitchfork as Apple jerked her head up. Louder this time—a little closer, but still far, far away.

He could hardly see Danny in front of him. They were back in the trees again. There must be some clouds, or surely the moonlight would be filtering through the tree-tops, casting milky streams on the forest floor.

For a second he thought he saw something out of the corner of his eye. A flash of white, or red, or was it both? When he turned his head to look, there was nothing but the branches of the trees, creaking as they pawed at the darkness.

A long-buried hope began to seep into Tom's blood. The woods were changing. They weren't just trees and plants and animals—there was a brilliance in the air between the looming shapes. The woods were *alive*.

He rubbed at his eyes, and there it was again. A dart of color—blue or gold or green. And suddenly he knew why he couldn't keep his eyes on it: it wasn't an earthly thing. He was seeing the thoughts—the voices, the spirits—of the trees, crackling through the air.

It didn't make sense. His mind had been twisted by all this craziness: by the journey, the lack of sleep and food, the dog attack. He had gone mad.

But had he? When he was a child, he'd talked to trees as though they were people just like himself. He'd stopped only when it seemed that growing up meant he should be sensible and rational and accept that trees were unable to think or talk.

Ten years ago, he'd believed that there was some vital spirit in the woodlands, and now he was seeing it. Was it madness? Or was it vision?

Tom closed his eyes and opened them again. Purple . . . silver . . . amber . . .

The third clap of thunder was much closer, and it ricocheted through the sky, zooming toward them from the clouds to their right. Apple snorted, puffing coarse breaths of night out from her lungs. Her walk became spiky as she lifted her hooves higher, muscles tight.

"Danny, there's going to be a storm!" Tom called forward. "It'll be dangerous up on that hill—there's a massive quarry. We should go back and find that blind, wait till it's over!"

"Go on, then," shouted Danny back to him. His tone said clearly that he would not follow.

Stupid idiot. Tom cursed him under his breath. That old piebald pony would plod onward through a burning building at the same, steady pace, but Apple was a well-bred hunter, and she had high-strung nerves. It would take all of Tom's skill to keep her calm in the middle of a thunderstorm.

The ground was rising steeply; they were walking up the wooded side of Sentry Hill now. Tom knew it well—the other side of the hill had been quarried away for years, and a vast cavity now gaped where once thousands of tons of limestone had been. It wasn't too dangerous—the quarry was all fenced off, and there were signs everywhere warning walkers to keep out. But the top of the hill was clear and bald, and up there they would be horribly exposed to the weather.

"We're going to get soaked!" said Tom. "There's no cover up there."

Danny ignored him.

A flicker of color danced in Tom's vision again. He tore his thoughts away from it. This was real. This was dangerous. This was going to end badly, and he was responsible.

"You're an idiot!" he shouted at Danny, to make himself feel better.

It didn't work. Apple stepped on a twig, leapt in the air as it made a loud snapping noise, then stopped dead as a proper crack of thunder split the clouds above their heads. For a moment she waited, unsure of her own fear, and then she reared up onto her hind legs, sending Tom curving into the air.

He leaned forward, trying to pat her neck and calm her. "Easy, girl, easy," he muttered. But as her hooves touched the ground again, he could feel that it would be the devil of a struggle to make her take even one more step.

"Danny!" he called. "Apple's going to go mad!"

Danny came back, hardly visible in the darkness, but said nothing at all. He sat, completely silent, for a couple of minutes.

The breeze picked up and began to hiss through the treetops. Somewhere, a faint flash broke the night sky, and a glimmer of light flickered through the forest.

At last Danny turned away again, and Tom felt Apple relax uncertainly underneath him. She started to move forward.

What had just happened? Danny had clearly calmed the horse down somehow, but what could he possibly have done to her in those two long, silent minutes? *Was he some kind of horse whisperer?*

No, that was absurd. Probably Tom himself had just relaxed while they were standing there, and Apple, feeling her rider no longer tense, had taken heart again. There was no way Danny could suddenly have learned how to calm the hot-tempered mare. Was there?

The rain fell harder and harder. Ahead of them, Tom could barely see the shapes of the trees, but he knew by the amount of rain that was falling straight down onto him that there could only be a few trees left around them.

They were almost out of the wood, almost out onto that wide stretch of heath that crowned the top of Sentry Hill like a monk's tonsure.

Wide-open spaces made Apple want to gallop. Wide-open spaces in the inky night, with the shadowy trees lurking behind them, would probably make her want to flee for her life.

There was the last tree, gone. They stepped out onto the close-growing hilltop, and Tom put his hand up to his face to shield it from the rain. He couldn't see anything anyway, and the rain was starting to drive into his eyes, blown on a slant by the coursing wind.

"What are we *doing* here?" he yelled out to Danny, but the wind took his words away and flung them back at his ears, like a handful of peas. "This is crazy!" he yelled. "We've got to go back!"

Danny turned back and said, "Get off the horse. She reckons you're turning into a monster. That's why she's so scared."

"What? Don't be *stupid*! Let's go!"

"That's what she says!" Danny said. "I told you I could talk to her! That's what she's *saying*! If you get off her, she'll see you and she won't be scared."

"She'll just pull away if I get down," said Tom. "You know jack-all about horses! Don't tell me what to do!"

"Fine," said Danny, turning Shimny away again. As soon as he had plodded a few steps up the path, Apple began to tremble violently. Then she reared. This time Tom knew he had only that one, smooth, rearing moment—the second she touched the earth, she would be running in a blind panic away from all this, and there would be nothing he could do to stop her.

As the world slowed in that endless, final rear, Tom could have sworn he saw a figure standing a short distance away, one arm stretched out to the neck of an enormous dog.

But then Apple touched the ground with all four hooves again, whipped around, and was gone. And Tom, crouching low on her back as she dashed into the forest, was trying not to think of the twisted roots under her feet and of what would happen if she tripped over one and slammed, full speed, headfirst, into the nearest tree. He thought only of the colors he had seen. Save us, he thought to them. Please save us. If you exist at all, guide the horse safely somewhere, and let us both live.

Danny watched them go for a single, incredulous second and then realized Tom wasn't going to be able to make Apple stop. He was alone and completely friendless in the bristling rain.

He was just about to turn Shimny and plod back down the hillside after Tom when two tiny birds flew out of the night and latched themselves onto his sweater.

"We've found it! We've found it!"

"What?" For a moment he couldn't quite understand. "Found what?"

"It's a whirlwind! A twister! They're trapped inside! Call it back and ask it to let go and you'll have them!"

"What?" Danny's head swam. There was no question of going after Tom anymore. He knew where they were! He could call them back!

"Use the song! Use the song!"

The song! He could remember it, couldn't he? Yes, of course. The world is deadly, the world is bright . . .

"How do I call it? That one, I mean. Does it have a name?"

The swallows shrieked with laughter. "A name! What would a storm have a name for? Just open the Book of Storms, and call to it! Think of it, of everything you know about it. Draw a picture of it if you like. Write the words that make you think of it on the page of the book. You don't need a *name* to call a storm! You need an *imagination!*"

The swallows launched themselves into the black air and disappeared. With hands that shook so badly he could barely control them, Danny pulled the Book of Storms once again from his bag. He opened it and stared down at the front page, just able to make out the picture. It should have soaked up the rain and become damp, but the rain seemed somehow to avoid it.

Draw in it. Write in it. With what? He had no pen. Even if he had, his hands would never have agreed to hold it.

But why should he need a pen? If all he had to do was imagine that he was drawing . . .

He reached into his pocket and drew out the stick. It had been tucked away for so long that he was almost surprised to realize it was still a separate object, and not a part of himself. What would happen when he touched it to the pages of the book?

A flame shot from the stick. He snatched it away, thinking for a second that it might burn the book. But how could anything burn a book already made from fire?

Lowering the stick again, he watched the flame diminish until the stick was touching the book's page. The flame became a thin trail of smoke. What could he draw that would identify the storm? It came to him even before the question had died away in his mind. The sycamore tree, of course. He knew the shape of every single bough and twig on that old tree.

When he had finished, he couldn't see his picture very well, but he knew it was good. And even if it didn't look exactly like the tree, it was how he had always seen the tree in his mind when he pictured his own back garden. He'd done what the swallows had said.

Putting the stick back in his pocket out of habit, he held the book in one hand and kept the other on the stick, then took a deep breath and began the song.

> *"The world is deadly, the world is bright,*
> *The creatures that use it are blinded by sight,*
> *But there's no sense in crying or closing the page,*
> *Sense only battles in fighting and rage.*
> *So come all you soldiers and answer my call,*
> *Together we gather, together we fall!"*

Rain began to pound his skull as though the raindrops were being fired from a cannon. They screamed louder, with greater exhilaration, and the wind had to blow harder to drive them sideways. Through his water-lashed eyes, Danny could no longer see. He tucked his head down to his shivering chest and thanked his stars for Shimny, who stood steady as a rock. It was coming! This must be it! And soon—

The first sound he heard was laughter.

"You wouldn't believe how long it got! First time I've ever stretched anything that far in my life!" A voice guffawed. It was a terrible voice, so full of sound and gravel that it made Danny's head rattle like a can of dried peas.

"I said I'd get him! HA HA HA HA HA!" The same voice roared with hearty laughter, and there followed a crack that from a human might have been a hand clap. From the storm it was a bolt of lightning hissing out of its grasp.

"You're a one! The finest I've seen!" called out another voice. "Much better than that last hay dodger we had trundling round the place! Ahahahahahah!"

The sound of its laughter made Danny feel like his head was being shorn in two by a butcher's knife.

"I said to him, I said, You've come up Oak Stovely way, you've seen them old pines torn up by the roots, you've seen that church steeple chucked halfway across the village. I said to him, Who'd you think did that, eh? Crawling mothsniffer! Wretched young weasel-breathed frogspawn! I showed him! HA HAHAHAHAHAHA! E-HEWH! E-HAH! E-WHEEEEEEH!"

What were they talking about? The noise was so painful that it crippled his ears and sent tears running from his eyes, but Danny didn't understand a word of it. Some stupid joke, no doubt. The whole thing looked so angry, but it was worse than that; this was no venomous tirade. This was—Danny fumbled for the word, shaking like his own teeth—this was mockery. And if this storm had his parents . . .

He clenched both fists in rage, one still around the stick and the other pressed, knuckles first, into Shimny's withers. Then he felt such heat boil in the pit of his stomach that he could not identify it until it had spread through every artery, every vein, every capillary, of his body and he knew that it was fury.

"OI! YOU UP THERE! YEAH, YOU!" he screamed, raising his face in the driving rain to the black clouds he could not see. "How . . . How DARE you? How can you sit there and just . . . and just LAUGH? Where are they? What have you DONE with them? Give them back! You evil, evil, EVIL thing!"

Then he closed his eyes, screwed up every muscle he could find, and waited to be struck down.

There was a pause in the laughter.

"I say," said another voice, not one of the first two. "There's a chap on a pony down there shouting at us."

"Not another one," a fourth voice said wearily. "You'd think they'd have left us alone by now. Shall we?"

The storm unleashed a volley of hail straight down at Danny. He had no time to see it coming before he was surrounded by a blinding white tent that made his eyeballs scream. The ground around Shimny's hooves spat like a bonfire. Danny clutched at his face with his spare hand to shield it from the flashing sheet, and fragments of ice drilled into the top of his head. What if they punctured holes in his skull? He tried to cover himself, to pull his head down into his chest, but one hand was no good and he had to use the other, which meant letting go of the stick, so he could no longer hear the voices or talk to them. Shimny was obviously saying something too—she began to shift from hoof to hoof.

Ice found its way under the collar of his sweater and slid down his back, but he was so soaked that he hardly felt it. Was he just supposed to endure this? Where was the whirlwind? Should he use the song again?

He tried to remember it. The last line was easy, but the first? Something about being blinded? He was being blinded by the hail, by the lashing rain, by the tearing wind. He couldn't think, couldn't remember. What if he just shouted the last line, again and again? Would the storm recognize that?

He tried it, screaming into the night. "Together we gather, together we fall! Together we gather . . ." But he wasn't holding the stick anymore: there was no way the storm could hear him.

If he took his hand off his head, the hail would rip into his skin, slicing it apart with its blades of ice. But if he didn't, the storm would never stop. It didn't sound like it was ever going to slacken and move on or give up at all.

And just at the moment he decided to let himself fall forward onto Shimny's neck and see whether he could reach into his pocket by protecting his face in the choking safety of her mane, he felt hands pulling him off the pony's back. They were cold hands, but he was too cold himself to notice.

Then something was shielding him, square between the driving wind and his crouched body. Shimny squealed and tried to run; she kicked him by accident as she trampled the ground behind him but then stopped, silent and still.

And Danny looked up into a face he had never seen before. It was the face of his father and mother. It was Aunt Kathleen's face, Tom's face, Abel Korsakof's face. It had the muzzle of a slavering dog; the patient, long eyes of a horse; the pointed nose of a cat. It was swallows and worms, rivers and axes, all rolled into one. And it was the face of a stranger, with white skin and black hair.

Even through the darkness, Danny could see its every feature. The cheekbones, the pale jaw, the hard black eyes. The thin, cruel mouth, with its nasty grin. And he could see, exactly, how he himself appeared before this creature, how small and twisted and miserable he looked.

"Wrong storm," said Sammael. "Yours is still miles away. But I won't hurt you, don't worry. All I want is what's mine."

CHAPTER 17

SAMMAEL

Danny's hands tightened instinctively around—what? Each other? The stick? Shimny's reins?

The truth was, he didn't know what was underneath his palms anymore; couldn't think about any sensation except the one his eyes were experiencing: looking at Sammael.

Because Sammael wasn't ugly. He wasn't horrendous. The sight of him didn't make Danny's stomach scream and turn liquid, or the hairs on the back of his neck stand on end and pierce his skin like pins. His eyes were those of a kind father. The way he was standing, holding his coat out against the rain and the wind, shielding Danny from all the pain he'd just felt—it was just what his mum had always done when he'd been smaller—closed him in and protected him with her body.

And Sammael was speaking like a normal person.

"The book," he was saying. "The Book of Storms. Hand it over."

Danny couldn't tear his eyes away from Sammael's face. Those eyes—that thin smile—they should be *evil*. They should be making him shake in fear. His heart was throwing itself about his rib cage like a frenzied lion, but the rest of him was perfectly happy. Why wasn't he more afraid?

"The Book of Storms?" said Sammael again.

Shouldn't he be asking for the stick? Abel Korsakof had said he'd want the stick. He'd asked Korsakof to kill Danny long before Danny had found the Book of Storms.

"What?" asked Danny, not sure he'd heard right.

Sammael looked up to the sky; the rain slackened off. The thunder took to growling gently, like a crouched dog.

"The Book of Storms," repeated Sammael. "It's mine and I want it back. Surely you can agree that's fair?"

"But—" Danny stopped himself. Should he even mention the stick? Maybe Sammael had forgotten all about it.

But looking at him, he didn't seem the type to have

ever forgotten anything. Maybe he just didn't want it anymore. Was this really what Danny had been running from all this time? Maybe this was why people said you should face your fears—they were nothing when you looked them in the eye like this.

"Must I repeat it again?" asked Sammael. "The book's mine and I made it. I lent it to Abel Korsakof for the duration of his life. We even signed a contract over it, which I can show you if you really feel the need. Now the old man's dead and I'd like my book back, please."

He let go of the side of his coat and held out his long, thin hand toward Danny.

The bag on Danny's back began to grow warm. He didn't want to take it off; it would leave a horrid cold patch.

"Why do you want it?" he asked. His heart began to gallop, but he was surprised to find that his lungs were still full and clear.

"I told you, it's mine," repeated Sammael. "If I took your schoolbooks, you'd want them back, wouldn't you?"

"And you'll call off the storms if I give it to you? Stop chasing me?"

"Of course," said Sammael. "I've got better things to do than run around after little boys who don't know what they're doing."

"Yeah, I bet you do," said Danny. "Like figuring out how to make massive storms and hurt people."

"No one *makes* storms," said Sammael. "I can play around with a bit of weather, for sure, and I can make it hail on you until it pushes your eyes out of the back of your skull. But, then, you've stolen something from me and I'd like it back, so I think that's fair enough. Most people don't steal from me. They've got more sense."

He didn't smile as he said this. Danny looked at the outstretched hand.

"What'll you do if I don't?" he asked. "You can't kill me, can you?"

"I wouldn't be so sure," said Sammael. "There's usually a way around everything. It just takes time to find it, that's all. But that isn't what I'll do first. First I'll kill your parents. Oh, I know you think I can't kill, but there are ways."

Danny's heart stopped. He looked around for them; were they somewhere here, held in ropes and chains? Had Sammael brought them along to taunt him?

No—all around was just the black night, sweating with light rain. No parents.

"Where are they?" he asked. His voice shrank in desperation.

"Not here yet," said Sammael. "But they're within my

control. You know that I used a storm to take them away. I wasn't interested in killing them then—I just wanted to forcefully dissuade them from their delusions of megalomania. They were planning on going to Korsakof's today, did you know that? They thought that because your sister died, they could go on some kind of crusade against nature and learn how to suppress storms. Frankly, they wouldn't have had much success. But it was the *idea* of it that I found so despicable. What's wrong with *widening* your horizons? Why do you humans always have to work so hard at closing them down? But they're still spinning around inside a twister; it would be easy to arrange something fatal for them. You're welcome to risk it, of course, if you really want to keep hold of that book. Although given that I made it and I know exactly how it works, I can't believe that it would have told you much about anything *you* wanted to know. Has it?"

Danny wanted to lie. He wanted to say, Yeah, it's told me *everything* about who you are and how to take all your powers away, just so he could see what expression those words would bring to Sammael's face. But Sammael wouldn't really believe him. And his parents—they had to survive. More than any amount of petty satisfaction, they had to survive. He couldn't risk making Sammael angrier.

It was time to back down. Give over the book, trust Sammael. Abel Korsakof had said he always keeps his word.

"But what did they ever do to you?" Danny asked. "It isn't wrong to want to make things better."

"Better? What's better? Your parents don't love storms, like Korsakof, or want to be impressed at how powerful and magnificent storms can be. They wanted to *stop* them, to *calm them down*. Can you imagine? A world without storms—a calm, safe world where nothing ever happens to threaten anybody, and all you people just go about your dull, ordinary little lives, doing dull and ordinary and *safe* things?"

Danny couldn't imagine it, because it would be a world in which Emma would be alive, not him, and her parents would never leave her alone in the middle of the night, and she'd never be standing on a hillside in the darkness talking to the most terrifying, most fascinating creature she had ever seen.

"But it's only because of Emma," he said. "They only want to stop other people dying the way she did. They'll never stop wanting that."

Sammael smiled thinly. "But after this recent experience, even they might think twice about leaving their only son orphaned and alone, don't you think? There's not much crusading you can do if you're dead. Now give me the book."

"If I give it to you, will they be safe?" he asked.

"Of course," said Sammael.

Most people might have said, "Trust me." But not Sammael. He held all the cards already. Danny needed his whole life back—his parents, his freedom, his normality. All Sammael wanted was a book.

Danny shrugged his shoulders out of the bag straps and brought his bag to the front. He unzipped it. Miraculously, the contents were still dry: the Book of Storms must have kept the rain away from the two notebooks. Looking at the top edge of his parents' notebook made his stomach wake up for the first time in minutes; it stirred and gave a small sob. That notebook seemed old and familiar now, though he hadn't even read it much. But it was a part of him—it had a record of his birth in it, it mentioned his sister. It had been written by people who'd made him, who'd loved and cherished him. The Book of Storms might know what he'd done in the past two days, but *how* it knew was a mystery. It sat, black and alien, no part of a world he could explain or understand.

Danny reached into the bag, took hold of the book, and pulled it out. There, in the night, it didn't seem quite solid—the edges bled a little into the darkness around them.

He looked up at Sammael and hesitated.

"Who *are* you?" he whispered.

"Don't you know?"

"I think I should, but . . . I don't."

Sammael raised an eyebrow and then let it fall again. "I'm anything you've never thought of," he said simply. "I'm all that no human could ever be. I'm infinite. *You'll* learn to spend your life doing what other people tell you to do, and they'll tell you that to go outside certain limits is bad. Because that's where *I* am. I've spent a long time trying to open people's eyes. But now I know there's no point. Because now I know *everything* that you are, and I know that you, being human, will never even *want* to know the same about me. So just give me the book and we'll be done."

Danny gazed at him one last time. He did want to know. He wanted very much to know how he could fear and not fear, how he could want to run from something and also want to reach out and touch it, how he could see a face that looked like sunshine and hatred both at the same time.

The rain picked up again. It was cold on his back—the brief respite had let him thaw enough to feel pain once more.

Sammael's hand was still stretched out to him, motionless.

Danny rubbed the corner of the Book of Storms, memorizing the papery warmth that seemed to remain dry whatever the weather.

And then he held it out. Sammael's fingers closed over it and took the book away from him.

Sammael put a hand on the cover and looked at his book. For a second, his fingers tightened, then he opened the cover.

What did he read on those pages? Could he read anything at all in this black, raining night? Danny thought he probably could, from the way he was staring down at the book. He turned a few pages.

"You've had quite an adventure," he said. There was nothing fatherly about his voice now.

"Where are my parents?" said Danny. "You said you'd give them back if I gave you the book."

"No I didn't," said Sammael.

"Yes you did!"

Danny's guts began to bubble.

"I said I'd kill them if you didn't give me the book," said Sammael, still reading. "The devil's in the details—ever heard that phrase?"

"Give it back!" said Danny, reaching up. "Give it back, you cheat!"

Sammael stopped reading and looked at him. "I never

cheat," he said. "I never cheat anyone out of anything they've asked for. It's they who cheat themselves, by being stupid. I said your parents would be safe. Did I once say I would give them to you? No. Did I say I would give you *anything* in return for *my* book? No. Did I tell you I'd let *you* live if you gave it to me?"

"Yes, you did!" shouted Danny, springing forward and clutching at Shimny's reins. "You said you wouldn't kill me if I gave it to you! You definitely said that! And you can't, anyway—I've got the stick! It protects me from you. I know that much!"

"It protects you from the storms," said Sammael. "But *nothing* can protect you from this."

He reached into his inside pocket and pulled out a small, thin object. At first Danny thought it might be another stick: it was about the right size and shape. But then something flashed on the end of it—a sharp point of lead. It was a pencil.

Sammael flicked the book on a handful of pages. "It always amazes me," he said, "this human thing about opposites. I say, 'If you don't do this, I'll kill you.' And you just assume that if you *do* do it, then I *won't* kill you. But my rule is, Assume nothing. Take nothing for granted. Or you've only got yourself to blame when the thing you refuse to imagine turns out to be the thing that *happens*."

He began to write in the book, reading aloud as he did so.

"Danny faced Sammael. In his hands, the horse's wet reins felt slippery, like water snakes. Nothing at all like the cover of the Book of Storms."

Danny's hands itched, then burned, then couldn't decide whether to itch or burn. The reins felt like snakes in his hands. Water snakes? No! No, he told himself, they definitely didn't feel like that. A bit snakelike, maybe . . . What was like water snakes but not water snakes? Nothing! They were two thin, slippery water snakes. Nothing at all like the cover of the Book of Storms.

"There was nothing left for him here. Nothing to be gained by fruitless arguments that he was too stupid to understand. He turned back to the fat old pony that was still standing dumbly behind him. The gray lurcher let go of the horse's reins, which she'd been holding between her teeth."

Kalia let go of the reins. Danny hadn't even seen her standing at Shimny's head. From what he could make out, she was huge but skinny, with a pointy face. She didn't look dangerous. Was she Sammael's dog? Surely he'd have a big, black, slavering thing, like those Dogs of War?

"Danny suddenly found that he'd developed the ability to jump onto his pony's back from the ground. Just like his cousin Tom. Well, that was one good thing to come out of all this, wasn't it?"

And then Danny was on Shimny's back, gripping tight to her wet flanks. Her tufty mane scratched at his wrists. Should he get off? *Could* he get off?

"And the pony began to gallop. Fortunately, they were on a nice, smooth hilltop and could get up quite a speed. . . ."

Shimny's legs began to move. They were too far away to hear Sammael now; the pony was galloping with renewed vigor in her tired old legs. Danny wanted to pick up the reins, hold them properly, control her. But the speed was fine, the speed was definitely fine, because of course she knew where she was going, of course she could keep her feet safely. The quarry was fenced off—no need to worry about that. Everything would still be fine if he didn't pick up the reins. The reins were snakes, after all. You couldn't control a pony using snakes.

He put his hand to his pocket, felt for the stick.

"Hi ho, old fruit," he said. "Topping speed, eh?"

Had he really said that?

"I'm enjoying it," puffed Shimny. "I do like a night-time jaunt, myself."

"Good thing we got away from Sammael, wasn't it?" said Danny.

"Rather," said Shimny. "Bit of a blighter, that one."

What on earth were they saying? These weren't his words. Or Shimny's. This wasn't the way either of them spoke. This was a script being written for them, the words slithering out from their minds in unhesitating black streams.

"Tricky devil," said Danny.

"Oh, quite." The pony put her head down and careered against the fence. Danny wasn't scared—of course he wasn't scared. Nice fence. Good fence. Strong fence.

Fence that had been cut by a helpful gang of kids the week before.

The ground vanished from underneath them. Shimny had no chance to claw it back and fell, sliding down the side of the old quarry with Danny clinging onto her mane for his dear life until even his slight weight pulled her too far sideways. She lost her footing and began to roll, faster and faster, in a whirling blur of legs, hooves, tangled mane, flying tail, jackknifing neck, and blood red nostrils gasping for breath.

Danny let go and was thrown clear onto the craggy rock face, where he tumbled for a few wild seconds and then struck his head on a jagged projection.

His neck broke, and the world disappeared.

CHAPTER 18

DEATH

"The story of Danny O'Neill. The End," Sammael wrote, then closed the Book of Storms.

"Right," he said to Kalia. "Home time, I think."

Kalia was lying down, waiting for him. She didn't move.

"Kalia!" Sammael snapped his fingers.

The lurcher whimpered.

"Come on," he said. "We need to get on back."

"I'm caught," said the lurcher in a voice so faint that even Sammael could barely hear it.

"Caught? How caught?"

"I don't know. . . . It's wire or something, and then the horse trod on me. . . . It hurts. . . ."

Sammael chucked the book down and crouched by the dog's long body, feeling it with his hands. She was lying flat—her head, shoulders, and ribs were all fine. Then, as he reached her hind legs, he encountered a sticky mass. She was caught in the wire of a rabbit snare.

"Leave me," she said. "I'm dying—there's nothing you can do. Leave me."

Sammael's jaw clenched. The dog hadn't asked for eternal life. All she'd asked was to be his dog and for him to be her master. That was the only bargain they'd ever made. Her paw print was in his notebook as a witness to it. He owed her nothing, could demand her safety from no one.

Her skull under his palm was narrow and frail.

"You stupid, idiot animal," he said. "Why didn't you make me give you a long life?"

"But then I'd have known how long I had with you," said Kalia. "I'd have known when it was going to end. It would have broken my heart."

"Better your stupid heart than your legs," said Sammael.

"No," whispered Kalia. "My legs are mine to break. But my heart—that's yours. . . ."

She fell into a faint, her eye closing. Sammael put a hand on her ribs: still something beating in there. Still a pulse. She was shivering faintly. He shrugged his bony shoulders out of the sleeves of his coat and laid it on top of her. Only two creatures had inhabited that coat—its original owner and himself. Neither had belonged to the solid earth. Could the coat's mysterious power do anything for a dog?

He felt for the wire of the snare again. Slowly, with infinite patience, he began to untwist it, trying not to hurt her further.

Shimny lay on the slope, not caring to check how many of her legs were broken. She couldn't breathe, at any rate, so soon it wouldn't matter. The end would be quick enough.

She looked up at the moon, unaware that little by little the air was seeping back into her winded lungs. She wondered why she could still see when she ought to be dead. Perhaps death slows time, she thought. For death was surely coming. She felt it in the unsettled throb of the night air, heard it whispering out from the lumps of flesh and bone that had once held both her own and Danny's heartbeats. This short interlude was probably just a last gift to her from the living world, a last chance to taste its sharpness and feel its strong warmth.

Out of the corner of her eye she saw a woman approaching up the slope of the quarry. The woman must have seen her, but as she drew closer she didn't hurry, her short legs dragging a little as if she was used to taking her time.

The woman crouched and put out a hand to touch Shimny's neck just behind the ears. Her hair was white, and she had a steady, sad face.

She smiled and took her hand away.

"You're not mine," she said. "Not yet."

Then she rose to her feet and made her way over to the corpse of the boy, whose neck was twisted back at an angle. The woman stooped, spreading out her arms to gather his body up and cradle him. Her hands were under Danny's knees and shoulders when she cast her eyes down to his face, and then she stopped.

For a full minute she didn't move but stared into his lifeless eyes, then she began to slide her arms out from underneath him.

"I won't do it," Shimny heard the woman say. "I won't be a pawn in Sammael's Machiavellian little spats. How did he *do* this?"

And the whispering shadows began to creep from the rocks, curling up around Death's neck and ears. Lying in a land between death and life, Shimny's walleye saw them too—to her they were black and green and the darkest shade of purple, half spreading into leaves as they flattened themselves out with explanations.

Death listened. When the shadows finally died away, she stood up straight and looked down at the boy's corpse. She was bound to take it—too much of him had been lost already, pulled away into the Book of Storms.

For a moment she clenched her fist, preparing herself. Wishing, not for the first time, that she could kick a stone or punch the ground or scream any one of the millions of screams she'd been saving up since the dawn of life. But Death's job was not to scream. It was to tidy.

Then she caught sight of the horse again, looking at her. That horse—it had seen her. It had seen her shadows. There would never be anything tidy about that horse now—it would spend the rest of its life telling crazy stories about Death and her red eyes to anyhorse who would listen. Sometimes things couldn't be tidy, no matter how hard you tried. And sometimes they shouldn't be.

Death walked away from the dead boy, her hand still clenched into a fist, heading for the top of the slope.

When she returned, she was carrying a small black book. Shimny had seen it before—it was the book that Danny had found in that wooden hut. Death didn't seem to like it much: she sat down on a rock beside Danny and began tearing the pages out, cracking the spine and yanking at the stitching with her teeth. As the pages fell, she crumpled them up, sandwiching them between her knees.

She caught sight of Shimny watching her. "He was seeing to his dog," she said, a touch defensive. "He'd just chucked it on the ground. Didn't notice me taking it. Finders keepers, isn't it?"

Shimny blinked.

"I'm not going to spend my time cleaning up Sammael's corpses," said Death. "I'm part of the natural order of things. It's time he learned that. He might be natural, but he certainly isn't order. Let's see what he says to this, eh?"

With this, she tore the last few pages from the cover and reached out for Danny's limp head. She took his face in her hands, opened his mouth, and began stuffing the crumpled pages, one by one, inside it. Even after she'd pushed a good handful inside, more than ought to have fit into a human's mouth, she kept on going. When the pages threatened to spill out from between Danny's teeth, she began to pack them more tightly, pushing them down into his throat with her bony fingers.

"It's a question, isn't it?" Death said to Shimny as she twisted up the last few pages and crushed them after the others. "Can you eat your words? Does it make any difference if you do? What if someone else eats them for you?"

Shimny had no idea what the mad silver-haired woman was talking about. But she did know that, although paper might find its way through Danny's guts eventually, there was no way he could eat those stiff black covers from the outside of the book. She eyed them.

Death smiled at her. "Don't worry," she said. "I wouldn't even put these on a dung heap. Poisonous things." And she tucked them away inside her waistcoat.

She crouched over Danny for a moment, kissed the boy's forehead, and then, with a grin, stood back up and dusted off her hands.

"That'll really needle him," she remarked to Shimny as she set off the way she had come. "Might make him think for a couple of minutes next time."

She said this as if she didn't really have much hope of it, but her walk as she departed had a slightly cocky jaunt. Shimny would have sworn to herself, had she not been dazed and broken, that as she watched the receding back, a slight breeze picked up toward her and she heard the figure of Death whistle.

Don't go, Shimny found herself thinking. Please don't go. Turn around and come back to me.

There was definitely a tune coming from somewhere—it drifted sweetly into her ears, soothing her. But it must have been Death who was carrying the tune—the notes became fainter with every moment. Pain began to bite at Shimny's body with sharper teeth, and she closed her eyes again. What I'd like more than anything, she thought, is to keep hearing that tune.

As soon as she had enough strength, she resolved, she would scramble to her feet and follow it.

"Danny, Danny, why are you lying here? Danny! Danny!"

Danny swam from oak green gloom up toward where the light seemed strongest. The weeds were holding his feet down, tugging at his ankles to keep him anchored to the bottom. He wanted to break the surface. Although he could breathe, this wasn't his world, where creatures that weren't fish swam and pond weed oozed along the plush silt. It was safe, but too dark for him; the water was thick with tiny particles, and only a few strands of light penetrated down, so he could hardly see.

The world of the dead is a pond, he was surprised to find as he rose higher. But there was nobody here that he recognized: no old man, no horse. Perhaps they were the shapes of the swimming things that weren't fish. Perhaps that's what he was now too.

But no—he still had feet and ankles like a boy. He wrenched them free of the weeds and felt the air in his body lift him up to the light. There was a voice calling him.

"Danny, what are you doing? Get up, get up!"

The voice was pulling him toward the sun. It wasn't the sun speaking, though—from its pure, silver tone Danny knew that it must be Death herself, watching over him. Was she calling him to join her? No—she was *whistling* to him. Notes glided through the water and coiled themselves softly around his ears. His chest began to warm, repelling the cold depths.

For one final second he felt regret at leaving this womb-like place, and then, as the light grew nearer, he saw that it was shining and golden and stabbed straight into his heart. He was powerless to do anything but close his eyes against the screaming, stinging pain as his head broke the surface of the pond and he was thrust back once more into the world of the living.

He was lying on a shelf of rock. Above him, low black rain clouds trundled across the night sky. The rock was cool underneath his head but sharp in places; an uncomfortable lump was digging into his left shoulder blade. His mouth was choked with something soggy: he tried to gather up enough saliva to spit it out but swallowed instead. Whatever it was went down easily, as if it hadn't been made of anything particularly solid. Perhaps it was just a bit of blood from a cut in his mouth—it had that same metallic taste.

He wriggled to relieve the pain in his shoulder and stopped in surprise. Because once he'd dislodged the lump, nothing much hurt. He ought to hurt, surely? Whatever he was doing lying here, he must have fallen somehow—he was halfway down a vast slope that stretched away, both above and below, farther than the darkness allowed him to see.

He'd fallen. Yes, that was it. He'd fallen, together with Shimny, a tangle of legs and snakes and flailing hooves. He'd been galloping away from somewhere—someone— but who was it?

The moon slid out from behind a cloud.

Sammael. Sammael had tricked him. He'd been running from Sammael, and Sammael knew where his parents were.

Danny scrambled to his feet. How did he feel so un-bruised, so strong? No matter—he had to get back up to the top of the hill while there was a chance Sammael might still be there.

Where was Shimny? There—lying a few feet away. The ledge was wider than he'd thought—it must be some kind of path, winding its way up the rock face. But it would take too long to follow it. He'd have to scramble up the slope the direct way.

Could Shimny do that? Was she even alive?

"Shimny! Shimny!" He pushed his hand into his pocket and yelled silently at her. She didn't move.

"Shimny!" he tried again. "I've got to go back up. Now! Meet me up there—there's a kind of path, I think. But I've got to go!"

He should have touched her, but he didn't want to, just in case she was cold under his hand. She couldn't be dead, not Shimny, not after everything. Enough death had hap-pened already. She would come after him as soon as she got her breath back.

He put his hands to the rock face and leaned forward against it. It was too steep to try walking, so he crawled. His knees sank onto sharp ridges, his shins scraped along jagged outcrops of blasted stone. His palms were soon ripped; as the clouds rolled away and moonlight began to let him see where he was going, he saw that he was leaving spots of dark blood glistening on the scree.

But the top was ahead of him. The wind had dropped, the rain and hail had fled. The ridge stood out black against a sky finally shining with moonlight. It wasn't too far for him to scramble now. It couldn't be too far.

He put his hand on a clump of spines and forced himself just in time to bite down hard on his lip and squash the yell of pain. When his knee came down in the same place, even his double layer of pajama and school trousers couldn't protect him. It was like crawling across a lake of broken glass.

But other people did that, didn't they? They sat on beds of nails and walked across burning coconut shells, and they still kept going. They took themselves away in their minds to other places and tried to imagine that the pain they were feeling was a good sensation instead of a terrible one. What if he could do that too? What if he could turn the world on its head and convince himself that it was his parents at the top of this slope, his parents and his own home, instead of the frightening, hard figure of Sammael?

What if Tom was up there, waiting with his strong arms to help Danny, having already vanquished Sammael? Tom would be laughing fit to bust, watching him crawl so slowly up this slope. No, Tom would come down and carry him.

So he imagined arms around him—his parents' arms, Tom's arms—carrying him forward and upward, and he imagined that at the top of the slope, they were all there, lined up and waiting for him.

He put his head down and crawled.

And then there it was, the ridge, so close that he could almost reach out and touch it, and there was the gap in the fence, and he was crawling along soft, springy grass again, so gentle under his knees that it felt like he was sliding along a silk mattress.

There was no need to crawl anymore. He got to his feet and ran along the fence line, keeping low like a monkey. But the fence was no cover at all—he'd be seen a mile off now, with the moonlight so bright. He made for the trees and kept to the shadows, amazed at the silence of his own feet. Something must be helping him—he wasn't breaking twigs as he ran or treading on crunching shrubs. He could hear nothing of himself except his own breathing, which he tried to keep as slow and light as possible.

His foot nudged something hard on the ground. He'd

have thought it was a tree root and run over it, if it hadn't moved just a fraction when he kicked it.

Tom's pitchfork! This must be the place where Apple had thrown in the towel and Tom had dropped the pitchfork as he tried to cling on.

Danny picked it up. Sammael wouldn't be fought off with a pitchfork, he was sure of that, but the feel of the solid handle gave him heart. He wrapped both hands around it, not caring that the old wood was rough and splintery. What were a few tiny splinters after that scree?

He could try and run Sammael through with it, although who knew what might happen? Would it just go right into him and out the other side, as if he were a ghost?

There was only one way to find out: to do it and face whatever happened afterward.

He almost didn't see Sammael. The huddled lump, still crouched over the dog, was lower than Danny had expected. But the moonlight flashed, and there he was, absorbed in his task.

Danny couldn't see what he was doing, but he knew that waiting would mean he would miss whatever small opportunity he had. So he gripped the handle of the pitchfork and charged.

Sammael looked up at the rush. In a second he stepped

over the lump on the ground and threw the entire contents of his pockets at Danny: a hail of acorns, twigs,
beechnuts, and dried-out fragments of wood hit Danny's
face and bounced back onto the earth between them.

Lightning began to fall in a great, white sheet. Danny
saw the first spears and threw the pitchfork before any could
catch him. Eyes closed, hair standing on end, he heaved it
forward with nothing more in his arm than blind hope.

The pitchfork glanced off Sammael's shoulder and
pierced the dark bundle on the earth behind him. Danny
leapt onto the handle, driving it into the ground. Of course!
The coat! Sammael's power lay in his coat—if he could
only keep that coat pinned down—but was the coat made
of air too? Would it just disappear from the prongs of the
pitchfork?

Sammael began screaming up to the storm.

"Strike the boy! Strike him down! I COMMAND YOU!"

But the lightning wouldn't touch Danny. It crackled
into every blade of grass at his feet, it set fire to the trees,
it made the metal fence blaze and spark, but it wouldn't
touch him.

"STRIKE HIM!" yelled Sammael, his face burning
with black fire.

And the lightning, confused, struck the pitchfork.

Danny was thrown back as the pitchfork burst into
flames. He staggered and tried to keep his feet but ended

up flat on the ground a few yards away, looking up at the flashing, howling sky. Rain poured onto his face.

He lifted his head to see what had happened to Sammael, but the night was too black to make out anything, now that the moon had again been covered by storm clouds. As fast as he wiped the rain from his eyes, water ran back into them again, blurring his vision.

The lightning had stopped. Nothing could control the storm, nothing could command it to fight. It had raged for only a few turbulent seconds and then blown gently over. Whatever power had called it together, the various parts of the storm had clearly been reluctant to come.

Those bits of wood Sammael had thrown at Danny— had he emptied his pocket of taros and left himself un- protected against the lightning? Had he *died* on that pile of flame?

No—that wasn't possible. Sammael wasn't made of flesh and bone, to burn away. Danny rolled over onto his stom- ach and crawled in the direction he thought he'd come from. His knees smarted, and his hands bled again.

He tried to play that last vision over in his mind. There had been a lump on the ground—he couldn't be sure, but it might have been that great, thin dog. Had he driven the pitchfork into the dog, too? He hoped not.

Then the lightning had struck and dazzled him, and he

hadn't seen any more. But there was still one thing that should have been lying on the ground somewhere, that he couldn't account for. What had happened to it?

"Lost something?" said a voice.

The schoolbag came crashing down on Danny's head, pitching him forward. He got a mouthful of charred scrub and paddled his hands around, feeling for the bag. It wasn't there. Sammael hadn't dropped it on Danny's head, he'd just swung it, to vent his anger.

He was standing in his shirtsleeves, pearl against the black sky.

"You killed my dog," he said. "Well done."

"You've lost your coat," said Danny, pushing himself up and spitting out burnt mud. Without the coat, Sammael looked strangely thin and ordinary.

"I said, you killed my dog," repeated Sammael.

Danny tried to swallow the spiny lump in his chest. "Yeah? Well, you tried to kill me and you tricked me and you said you'd kill my parents!"

"She was only a dog," said Sammael. "She never did anything to you."

"So? You should have looked after her better, shouldn't you? What are you going to do to me now? Try and make more lightning strike me?"

"You know I couldn't, without my coat," said Sammael,

frowning. He looked around his feet for a moment and then swiveled his eyes back to Danny. The boy was up on his knees, his face smeared with grime.

"Ha! So the river was right! You've lost your coat and you can't do anything! You can't call up storms, you can't make them do what you want, and you can't use them to kill people! You can't even do anything to me anymore!"

Sammael considered the black ground, the burnt spread of ashes where his coat and his great gray dog had been. He looked at Danny once more. The boy's face was the color of old paper—the exact shade of the Book of Storms' stiff pages.

So that was what had happened. Sammael dropped the schoolbag at Danny's feet and took a step backwards. He reached deep into his trouser pocket and pulled out a scant few grains of dirt. Before Danny knew what was happening, Sammael raised his hand to his lips and blew the dirt into the boy's face.

Danny closed his eyes, expecting to be blinded, or at least to feel some stinging grit against his cheeks. But nothing happened, on the outside.

Inside, his brain warmed, as though he had pulled on a woolly hat. He thought about marzipan, thick and sweet, sitting like a blanket on top of Christmas cake. He thought about tiny lights sparkling off the waves of the sea, and the sea foam curling around itself in great tumbling streams. He thought, What if I took up surfing, and pictured those waves as exactly, as clearly, as this—I would sit on top of each wave as though it were made of thick marzipan; I would slide along it as though the wave itself were my surfboard. I could do it—I would *know* how to do it—if I could hold these thoughts in my head. I could learn to sit on the waves, to let them carry me across oceans—

He opened his eyes.

"Coats aren't everything," Sammael said softly. "And neither are storms. There are always other ways. The river didn't tell you *that*, did it? But *I* did. You just didn't want to listen to me."

And he disappeared into the darkness.

Danny blinked once or twice as the thoughts of oceans drained away. Had he really just stopped Sammael building up a great storm to destroy all the world's people? It didn't seem possible. Not Danny, alone there on a hilltop, armed only with a pitchfork.

But was that *sand* Sammael had blown in his face? Was *that* what it did?

He was still trying to puzzle this out, turning the stick over in his hands, feeling its smoothness, when the rain dwindled away to a mist. Two tiny birds flew out of the darkness, toward him.

"It's coming! It's coming!"

What? Not another storm . . . but of course. He had summoned one himself, another lifetime ago. The storm that carried his parents.

Above him, the clouds groaned and grumbled. One gave a bellowing yawn. There was a long, satisfied burp, and the sky began to creak and mutter. Danny waited while winds trailed and zoomed around his ears, while specks of rain danced over his skin and cold plucked at his ankles. For long minutes he waited, ignoring his shivers. If only night were shorter. If only dawn would come. At least then he'd be able to see what was approaching, instead of having to stand here on the hilltop listening to the air swirling around him and trying to work out what was going to arrive first, from which direction, and at what speed.

He felt it before he heard it. If only Tom could see him now. Tom, who always prided himself on being able to predict the weather, who'd stick his head outside in the morning and say things like, "Bit of drizzle, but it'll soon clear up," or "This one's set in for the day." What would he have said if he'd seen Danny sniffing the wind and

Danny had turned to him and said, "This one's a whirl-wind, just wait and see"?

Tom wouldn't have believed it. But then he'd have heard, as Danny now heard, a peculiar stillness and a faint whistling sound. And he'd have been forced to admit, as the wind started raking him horizontally from left to right, that Danny was correct.

Because the whirlwind was upon him almost before he could steady himself. It swept him sideways, pushed him flat to a tree trunk, and pummeled at his clothes. He clutched tight to a branch with one hand and the stick with the other and began the song again. This time he shouted it, for all he was worth, until his lungs were dry and burning and his breath had been completely sucked away.

> *"The world is deadly, the world is bright,*
> *The creatures that use it are blinded by sight,*
> *But there's no sense in crying or closing the page,*
> *Sense only battles in fighting and rage.*
> *So come all you soldiers and answer my call,*
> *Together we gather, together we fall!"*

And when he'd finished, instead of repeating it and waiting for an answer, he opened his mouth as wide as it would go and screamed, "STOP! PLEASE!"

The winds dropped like withered petals to the ground. There was a soft thud nearby, then another. Still blind in the darkness, Danny stumbled toward them, his hands outstretched.

"Mum?" he said, not daring to hope. "Mum? Dad?"

There was a silence longer than any piece of real time. And then a voice.

"Danny?"

It was his dad.

And then, "Danny?"

Which was his mum.

"Where are you?" he called, but they were closer than he'd thought, and a figure, clambering up off the ground, reached out to him.

He fell at it, hugging his mum tighter than he'd ever hugged before, and then his dad wrapped his arms around them both.

"Oh, Anna," Danny's dad said. "Oh, Danny, how did you *find* us?"

Danny couldn't speak. His stomach was so full of heat and fear and coats, of swallows and lightning and the belching of clouds, that he thought he might be sick. He looked up at his parents. Even through the dark, he could see that their clothes were torn and their faces gray and exhausted. His mum's hair stuck out like the fur on an angry cat.

"Why do you go?" he said. "Why do you leave me?"

They looked at each other. "There are things . . ." said his dad.

"Oh, just tell him," said his mum, suddenly sounding like it hurt her to speak. She put a hand up to rub her eyes.

"Not here," said his dad. "Let's get home first."

Danny knew they were trying not to mention his sister. But that wasn't right—she ought to have a name. She ought to be spoken about.

"I know how Emma died," he said. "I found your notebook. I read about Emma and the storms and all that stuff."

He saw them flinch when he said her name, as though they'd both trodden on something sharp. Neither of them spoke for a moment, and then his mum said, "It's very difficult, Danny. You're . . . too young. You'll understand when you're older."

He was about to say that he understood now, but his dad broke in.

"It was the storms, okay?" he said. "Sunday night, we both woke up and we'd had this weird dream, both of us— the same dream. She—Emma—was there, and she was talking about . . . about . . ."

His dad didn't seem able to speak for a long moment, and then he coughed and forced out some words again.

"She was talking about storms. And she said, these days, there're more and more of them, everyone knows that. And she said she knew why, and if we followed her, she'd tell us. So we followed her. Not *her*, you know, just . . . the *thought* of her. And then we were dragged up in that twister, just spinning and spinning . . . and we couldn't get back down. I thought we were done for. . . . We just spun and spun and spun and tried to hold hands so we wouldn't lose each other. . . ."

They trembled and reached out to each other again, reminding themselves that they were safe again, standing on the cold earth together. For a second Danny felt them swaying just out of his reach.

His dad said again, "How did you find us? Did you come out here alone?"

"I came with Tom," he said. "Tom knew the way. We rode horses."

"Tom? Your cousin Tom?"

Danny tried to see his dad's face in the night. The moon broke free from the clouds again, and there he was, the same, familiar Dad.

"Yeah," he said.

"Where is he now? He didn't leave you alone up here, did he?"

He did leave me, Danny wanted to say. He left me his pitchfork. If it hadn't been for Tom, I'd be dead by now.

"His horse ran away," he said. "I think it just went mad. He couldn't help it. But he must be around here somewhere."

His mum opened her mouth, about to say something, then changed her mind and gazed at Danny. She seemed shorter, somehow. They both did. And instead of looking away from him, at his dad, Mum just swallowed and said, "Okay. Where do you think he's gone?"

Good question. Because the storm had died away, and Tom should have gotten control of Apple and ridden her back by now. That's definitely what he would have done, if he'd been able to.

But as the moonlight spread over the hilltop, he saw very clearly that it was just the three of them up there, and nobody else was anywhere near.

CHAPTER 19

AN ENCOUNTER

Tom had tried his hardest to pull Apple up, but her terror was stronger than all the combined efforts of the bit in her mouth, the reins on her bit, and Tom's arms on the reins. She'd pulled him through gaps too narrow for comfort, ducked under low-hanging branches that nearly sent him flying backwards over her tail, and hurdled with huge leaps over shadows as if they were deep black pits. He'd tugged uselessly for a while and then given up, making himself as still and low to her back as possible so as not to further unbalance her desperate, leggy scramble.

What finally stopped her was the river. She arrived at its bank and came to a dead stop, snorting at the inky water. Tom, already crouched forward, was smacked in the face by her neck as she threw her head up. His nose was bleeding freely as he pushed himself upright again.

At least she'd stopped. Tom's heart began to settle, and he swung his leg over the horse's back, letting himself slide to the ground.

His legs were not quite steady. Apple was not a good rock; she shifted away from his hand on her shoulder as he tried to lean on her.

"Easy, Apple, easy," he said.

And the rain slackened off after a while. But soon after that, another raging wind picked up and Apple began to cringe in fear at every waving branch. Tom knew it would be useless trying to coax her back up through the moaning trees—he'd have to wait for the winds to die down before he went up to the hilltop to find Danny again. The best thing to do in the meanwhile would be to find a tree to shelter under and hope that it didn't get struck by lightning.

He was standing under a huge old oak when the man came down the path. Apple pricked her ears at the sight of the white shirt, but the moonlight that was starting to break out from occasional gaps in the clouds showed the figure well enough. Just a poor man, without even a coat. He'd been drenched by the rain, and his shirt was clinging to his bony shoulders. His head was down, black hair plastered to his skull. He was so thin that he must have been freezing.

"Hey!" Tom called out. "You okay?"

The man put his head up as if he'd only just noticed Tom. He'd looked pretty lost in his thoughts. Something bad must have happened for him to be out in the middle of a night like this dressed only in his shirtsleeves.

"Yes, thanks," he called back. "I'm fine. What are you doing out here?"

"Lost my stupid cousin," said Tom. "Haven't seen him, have you? Eleven-year-old kid?"

"No, sorry." The man took a few steps off the path and came to shelter under the oak tree next to Tom. Close up, he had a friendly face. His voice was gentle and low, but despite the wailing treetops around them, Tom didn't have to strain to hear him. "What's an eleven-year-old kid doing out here in the middle of the night?"

Tom grinned. "Don't ask. Between you and me and the horse, I reckon he's gone bananas. But he's got these ideas in his head and he won't let them go."

"So you've come out after him?"

"I came with him! Thought it best not to let him out on his own, and he wasn't going to stay at home no matter what, so I stuck him on my ancient pony. Reckoned he wouldn't get anywhere very fast on her back. My mum'll skin me alive if I've lost him."

"Was it a piebald pony?" said the man. "Maybe I have seen him. I did see a flash of something out on the hilltop. Could that have been them?"

"Yeah, maybe," said Tom. "Okay, I'll get back up there once this wind drops a bit. Idiot kid. What a night to choose for it."

The man inclined his head in a neutral gesture. "It's the wild at heart who lead us into the places we'd never think to go. If I hadn't spent the last three hours following a badger, I wouldn't be here either."

"Badgers!" Tom said. "I know there used to be badgers in these woods, I remember seeing some when I was a kid. They're still here, then?"

"They are indeed," said the man, his voice taking on the tone of a smile. "In fact, there are quite a few setts around here. Are you interested in badgers too?"

"Yeah, definitely. Badgers, foxes, deer—I like all that kind of thing."

"Oh, yes? Me too, although it's badgers, mostly. What is it you like about them?"

Tom looked once more at the man's face. Although he couldn't quite make it out, it seemed familiar and comfortable.

"I don't know . . ." he tried.

The tree's branches creaked above them. And somehow, in the sound, Tom found his answer.

"I guess I just love the wild bits of the world," he said. "I just like . . . I like the way things go on, whether you're there or not. I don't like towns, where the buildings look like they make up the whole world. I prefer places where you can see that what people have built is just sitting on top of this massive, living land. I love birds, too—I'm trying to learn all the different bird calls at the moment. I live on a farm, so I hear them all round the place, and even the same birds don't always sing the same way. It'd be cool to know which birds were singing when you heard them, don't you reckon?"

"Well, yes," said the man. "Actually, I have to confess that I *do* know."

"You know bird calls? Which ones?" Tom's broad face swung round to fix on the man's narrow, still one.

"All of them," the man said. "It's a bit of a hobby of mine, actually."

"That's amazing!" Tom's voice couldn't hide its hope; he forgot about the rain and the wind and his horse. Apple was perfectly calm anyway. Something about the stranger had seemed to settle her; she was gazing at him with longing on her face.

"Oh, I've studied all sorts of things. I spend most of my time looking at nature," said the man. "It's fascinating."

"It is!" said Tom. How could he befriend this man without seeming weird? It was so hard to learn bird calls from recorded samples—what Tom needed was someone to go walking with who'd be able to say, "Hear that? That's a jay" or "a goldfinch," or whatever. This man would be perfect. Soon it would be Tom and not Danny who had swallows clinging to his sweater, called there by a perfect imitation of a swallow's song. That was how things should be.

"Are you a farmer?" Tom asked. "D'you live round here?"

"Oh, hereabouts," said the man. "All over the place, really."

He was obviously some kind of wild man of the woods, an itinerant tramp, the kind you got in old-fashioned storybooks who roasted hedgehogs and wandered the highways and byways, never looking for a home.

"Well, maybe if you're around for a while we could take a walk sometime? You could teach me some bird calls, maybe?" Tom asked hopefully.

"I can do better than that," said the man. "I've written a book that describes them all perfectly. Here."

He reached down into his boot and pulled out a thin paperback. It was slightly crumpled and bent in a half-pipe from having been wrapped around the side of his leg.

Tom's excitement faded. The man was plainly also a bit simple, and he'd probably been making it up when he said how much he knew. You couldn't learn bird calls from a book.

"Oh, you can," said the man. "Try it."

Tom started. He must have spoken his thoughts aloud without realizing. He took the book out of politeness and opened it, knowing full well it was too dark to read a word anyway. But the pages seemed to emit a light all their own—he could see the printed words quite clearly.

BIRD CALLS, it read, across the top of a page, AND THEIR USES.

That was an odd title for a start. What uses did bird calls have, other than to talk to other birds? Maybe that was just what it meant.

He read on.

SPARROWS, the page said. And then there was a space. Nothing written at all. Yes, the strange man was mad.

Tom closed the book and handed it back. "Thanks," he said, smiling. "Great book."

"How do you know, when you haven't read it?" said the man.

"Well . . ." How to placate him without having to spend ages staring at a blank book? More important, how could Tom extricate himself and go back up through the woods to find Danny? The winds were dying down now, and Apple would soon be happy to move.

He decided to be gentle but honest. Who knew, but he might even be doing this man a favor if he pointed out that he was delusional. "It doesn't really . . . say a lot, does it?"

"Of course it does," said the man. He opened the book again and held it out to Tom on the Sparrows page. "Read it."

Tom looked. Nothing.

"It's blank," he said. "It really is blank."

"Oh, to your *eyes*, of course," said the man. "Put your hand on it. Read it properly."

He must mean that there was something written in Braille. Tom couldn't read Braille, but he'd feel it if it was there. He put his fingertips on the page, just next to the printed words.

It wasn't Braille. Under his fingers he felt the soft contours of a sparrow's tiny, feathery throat. He traced it as gently as he could, and it began to sing. One sound, a single twitter. Tom was sure it hadn't broken the air around his ears—he hadn't exactly heard it, as such, but it had entered his head as if he'd seen the sound written on a page.

It was the call of a dominant sparrow shrieking that it had seen the wings of a sparrow hawk.

What was this book? He stroked the page a little farther down and another sound, a different kind of tweet, stuttered out. A female's chirruping that she was in a tree, quite lonely, and was there any company around?

The man took the book away. "Good, isn't it?" he said. "It tells you all kinds of things. Not just about birds, about other animals too—it's got the full range of their languages. Why, you could use it to learn the language of badgers, if you wished."

Talking to badgers? Was that really possible? But Danny had talked to animals somehow, hadn't he? Or he'd found a way to communicate with them, at least. Had he also met this man, gotten his own copy of this book, and not wanted to share it with Tom?

"You *wrote* this?" asked Tom. "How?"

"Well, that's a long story, and it did take me a long time to learn how to do it. I should introduce myself. I didn't, did I?"

Tom found himself staring at the thin white hand held out for a handshake. The fingers were long and deft. When he put his own hand up to it, the man's skin was rough and warm.

"Sammael," said the man.

A touch of blood leapt in Tom's heart. Sammael? But that was the name Danny had talked about. The name of the creature he'd been running from and toward at the same time. He'd talked about something fearsome, terrifying—unreal, even. Not this tall, warm man who loved nature and knew about bird calls.

And Tom understood it all. Danny had been terrified of this man because Danny was scared of the world. Danny didn't want to know about badgers and birds and the wild, whispering woods in the dead of night. Danny wanted to be safely tucked away indoors, protected from whatever he couldn't control. Danny didn't love freedom or adventure—it was Tom who loved those things, Tom who wanted to feel other life around him, untameable and glorious. And Sammael was just like him, only further along the path, closer to the wilderness.

"I've heard of you!" Tom said, eagerly. "You've met my cousin, the one I'm looking for! Or he knows you, at least. But he's scared of you. He's just a kid." He laughed, feeling his body flush with excitement. "He's made up this wild story all about you. I wondered what on earth he was talking about!"

"Wild?" Sammael's voice had a dry humor about it. "Well, he wouldn't be the first."

"Go on, then, tell me about the book," urged Tom.

"You've got some kind of"—he searched for the word—"*way* with nature, haven't you? Something . . . special?"

"You could say that," said Sammael. "It's more to do with impossibility, actually. For example—we all imagine things. Some we feel sure about—we see them around us or watch videos of them, and so we call them reality. Others we don't see evidence of, or they seem fantastical and dreamlike, so we dismiss them under the name of impossible. But when I wrote that book, I chose to think in a different way about birds and animals. I thought, What if the impossible was in fact reality? What if *everything* I heard was just another form of word? Well, I'd be able to write them all down, wouldn't I? So how? Well, that's even simpler. Everything you hear is just vibrations in your ear, isn't it? So everything you hear is actually movement. And everything you touch is the same—a movement of the nerves in your fingers that tells you what's underneath them. So what if you could touch the same movement that you hear? You'd be able to hear sounds through your fingertips. And so I pulled that feeling of hearing and that feeling of touching closer and closer together, until they came into contact with each other, and here is the result. Not impossible at all. Humans might tell you otherwise, but most of them can't see farther than their own eyeballs."

"But . . . what did you use? I mean *how* did you do it? And they aren't just sounds, are they? Because I understand what they mean. . . ."

"I used sand. Your cousin knows about me, you say? Well, then he must have told you about sand. You think of sand as being souls, in your terms—it's the essence of life. Every living creature has sand inside it, which sustains its life and returns into the earth when it dies. But there's more to life than just living. There're all the things you *could* do—all those are in your sand as well. And the things you know you can never do—they're there. So I used sand. I took the impossible, the unfulfilled, and I made something beautiful out of it. That's my job."

Tom ran his hand over the page in front of him again. It felt as if it had been made only for him.

"I want this," he said. "I really want it. I'd make the most of it, I really would. It's everything I've ever wanted."

"Not everything, surely?" said Sammael. "If I believed that, I'd never have shown it to you."

"No. No, of course, not everything," said Tom. "But I could use it to learn how to call like birds, couldn't I? And to talk like animals. I could live together with them, not just have to be some stupid human, blind and deaf to them all. Please let me have it. Or at least borrow it for a while."

"Of course," said Sammael. "I made it to be used. But if you want to take it, you'll have to understand one thing."

"Anything," said Tom, turning over a page and bringing up another sound, the gentle mewing of a kite.

"You can't read a book like that without becoming a part of it. It will change your fingertips, your ears, your blood and heart. The sand in the book will become mixed with your own sand. *Your* sand will belong to the book. One day, when you reach the end of your own adventures in the world, your sand won't go back into the earth like all the rest. It'll go with the book, wherever the book goes. If you take the book, you are stepping out of the normal run of the world, forever. You have to do that willingly, with your eyes open. Do you understand?"

Tom frowned. "Are you saying that when I die, I'll . . . what? Become a *book*? That's daft."

"No," said Sammael. "I'm saying you won't become worm food like everybody else. Not every bit of you, anyway."

"Well, that's fine," said Tom. "I don't think I'll care much by then."

"It's yours, then," said Sammael. "Here. Sign for it."

He fished a slim black notebook out from inside his shirt. "Write 'I,' and then your name, 'give freely my sand in exchange for possession of the book Nature at Your

Fingertips,' and the book shall be mine for as long as I live."

Tom wrote it down on the offered page. "Tom Fletcher," he said. "That's my name. We live up at Sopper's Edge, the other side of the county. Drop by if you're ever up that way."

"Sign it," said the man.

Tom signed his name.

"The wind's pretty much gone," he said, handing the notebook back and pointing out at the path. "I'd better get on trying to hunt down this cousin of mine. Thanks for the book."

He clicked his tongue to Apple. She followed him out from the shelter of the tree and began plodding up the path, with one last backwards glance under the oak tree to where the man still stood.

When Tom had gone only a few steps, he couldn't resist taking the book from his pocket again. He turned to a page about owls and stroked his fingers over it.

The hoot of a tawny owl rang out in his head, soft and mellow. It was calling for its mate, telling her it had caught a field mouse.

Tom smiled to himself and put the book away. He cupped his hands to his mouth and blew gently into them, making a dry, echoing note. Then he clasped his hands more tightly together and blew slightly harder. A little more like it. Just a little, but with some practice, he'd get there.

Behind him, Sammael slipped away from under the oak tree. He was about to snap his fingers together when he stopped himself and set his cold, terrible jaw hard against the night.

CHAPTER 20

ENDGAME

"He might still be in the woods," said Danny. "We can't leave without Tom. We should wait here till he finds us." His teeth began to chatter. Even his bones were complaining of being soaked through.

Danny's mum took her coat off and draped it around his shoulders, but he didn't seem to have anything left in his body that might produce warmth. Heat would have to come from somewhere else—a fire or a radiator or a hot bath.

"We need to get you home, my love," said his mum. "You're freezing. We'll go down to the nearest road. Where did you say we are?"

"S-S-S-Sentry Hill," stuttered Danny through his rattling teeth. "Near Great Butford. But . . . Tom? And Shimny?"

"Shimny?"

"Tom's pony. She fell down the edge of the quarry. . . ."

He stumbled over to the quarry fence and yelled for her through the darkness. His voice ran into the air and leapt away, down into the black, rocky cutting. Nothing else stirred: no noise, no hoofbeats, no snorting whinny as the pony trotted her way up the quarry path.

"We won't find her now, son," Danny's dad said, coming to take hold of him. "We'll come back tomorrow and look, I promise. First thing, we'll all come back. You'll be able to show us the way, won't you?"

"She saved me," said Danny. "She brought me all this way, and I wouldn't have found you otherwise. You'd be dead. . . ."

"We're not dead," said his dad. "But unless we all get warm and dry soon, we might have to rethink that. Come on, we'll go down. And we'll call out for Tom. If he's anywhere about, he'll hear us."

Together they stumbled down the hillside, skirting the woods, yelling for Tom. It would have been quicker to go through them, but Danny saw Sammael in every shadow. He refused all suggestions of cutting through the trees.

And then dawn was breaking, just as they reached the bottom of the hill and came out onto the Great Butford road. Dawn, painting the sky with promise, streaming royal blue across the horizon. A whole night—how had it been a whole night since Danny and Tom had stood outside the old barn and watched the swallows dive? It seemed like minutes.

He raised his voice again, although his throat was sore from shouting. "Tom! Tom!"

There was an answering shout. He'd grown so used to everything going wrong that he didn't believe it, almost didn't hear it. But then it came again.

"Danny! Hie! Danny!"

From far away behind them came the thundering sound of hooves, and then Tom appeared through a break in the trees. In two minutes he was galloping down the trail behind them and bursting out onto Great Butford village green like a raiding cowboy.

He slid to a halt, dropped off Apple's back, and came to stand beside them. Tall, cheerful Tom, as normal and as solid as ever.

Danny looked up at him. He wouldn't quite meet

Danny's eye—maybe he was still embarrassed about Apple having run off with him.

"What happened to you guys?" Tom asked. "Danny was saying all this weird stuff—I thought he'd gone properly bonkers!"

Danny's parents looked at Danny. He looked at them. But even if they didn't understand yet, they wouldn't betray him.

"We got trapped," said Danny's dad. "In the old quarry. We couldn't get out."

"So how did he find you?"

Danny's dad shrugged. "Lucky guess, I suppose. We'd mentioned about going there before. But we've lost your pony, I'm afraid. Danny says she ran over the side of the quarry."

"Oh." Tom, who had been about to ask more questions, was suddenly quiet. He stared down at his feet for a long moment and didn't say anything else.

"It's been a bad couple of days," said Danny's mum gently, reaching out to touch his shoulder. "For everyone. I'm so sorry, Tom. But thanks for looking after Danny. You obviously did a wonderful job. We really owe you."

"We owe you several," said Danny's dad. "Can you leave your horse somewhere here and come back with us?"

Tom shook his head. "Mum's coming here—I phoned

her. She's bringing the lorry. There's room for all of you in there. I'm sure she'll take you back. Although she might want to look a bit for the piebald. . . ."

And then, behind them, a shrill neigh flew out from halfway up the hillside. Through the half-light, a white, patchy shape was racketing down the trail, its ancient, unshod hooves thudding over the trodden earth. Its back was as dipped as a bowl, but its head was high and its black nostrils flared.

"Shimny!" yelled Danny.

But it was to Tom she went: to the boy she'd known all his life, who'd learned to ride on her swaying back and who'd never bothered to give her a name because he knew exactly who she was. Death had turned her back on Shimny, but Tom had always looked after her.

She scrambled to a halt in front of him and put her head down, panting heavily. Tom reached out a hand to pull at her ear and winked at Danny. "You did good, kid," he said. "You're a braver man than most of us. We all thought it was time to go home ages ago."

Danny watched as Tom loaded Shimny and Apple into the horse trailer. Aunt Kathleen was standing by the ramp, talking to his mum and dad. She looked entirely normal, dressed in tattered jeans and her shredded old farm coat. And she wasn't holding an axe. Of course she wasn't holding an axe.

His parents were talking slowly. His mum's hair was tangled, and both of them had scratches across their faces. He hadn't noticed the scratches earlier.

Three adults, two ponies, and one Tom. But there was someone missing, still. Did there always have to be someone missing?

They got into the back seat of the horse-trailer cab. It was dark and cozy, and the seat was full of springs. Danny's mum put her arm around his shoulders and he leant against her.

"Mum . . ." he said.

"Yes?"

"About Emma . . ."

"Yes." She hugged him a little tighter.

"Will you tell me about her?"

His mum was silent for a moment, then Aunt Kathleen turned the key and the horse-trailer engine shook itself awake.

"Please," said Danny. "I really want to know."

"Oh, Danny . . ." said his mum. "Oh . . . Emma. It still

hurts too much, even to think about her. . . . After she died, it wasn't— You can't know about that sort of thing. You're still too young."

"I'm not," said Danny, shaking his head. "I'm really not. You think I'm just a kid and I don't understand anything, but I always knew something had happened. It feels like you've got two families and I'm not in one of them."

"Love, you can't think that. We wanted you to just be yourself. One day—but I hope beyond hope you'll never have to know what it's like to lose a child. That's the best thing I can wish for you, really it is."

"But she's always there, isn't she? She always will be. She's been hanging over everything, *always*. It's just that, before, I didn't know what the hanging thing was, that's all. And now I do know. There's no point in pretending."

He wanted to say, I know a lot more than you think, and I always have. But she wouldn't believe it.

"Oh—we'll tell you about everything," said his mum. "Just . . . let's get home first. And you can tell us exactly how you managed to find us too. It must have been some journey."

Danny put his hand in his pocket. The stick was still there. When had he last used it? To talk to that tornado, and then he'd been so overwhelmed by finding his parents again that he'd thought of nothing else.

He still had it, though. He could use it for fun things now, like talking to Mitz, who was probably finding her own way home, like those cats you read about in the papers. He'd explain everything to her, apologize for taking her into the river, and they'd be friends again. And he could talk to the horses when he next went to visit the farm. But he could see quite well that if he told his parents about the stick, they might want him to go back to talking to storms. Which was, frankly, scary.

Then again, when he thought about what he'd done, most of it involved the stick. Or Sammael. Or the Book of Storms—and he certainly wasn't going after *that* again. All of those things were best forgotten. Especially Sammael's last words to him: *There are always other ways.* Whatever he'd been referring to, Danny wasn't going to think about Sammael any more than he had to, ever again.

But what would he tell his parents?

It was time to make up a story.

He settled back into the crook of his mum's elbow. I'll begin with the storm, he thought. Because that's when they went. And after that—after that, I'll go anywhere. I'll go wherever my wildest dreams take me. It doesn't matter if no one believes me—it'll be *my* story. And I'll stick to it.

They drove through the morning, back to the places they called home. Tom put his hand on his pocket, feeling the shape of the little book. The moment he was alone, he would take it out and begin reading it properly. What a find!

Danny closed his eyes and let his imagination wander. When it began to flag, and tiredness threatened to overtake him, he gave in to sleep with a grateful sigh. Maybe he'd find a better story in his dreams.

On the top of Sentry Hill, a tall figure in a white shirt stood over a patch of scorched earth. He waited for an uncountable time in the hope of seeing the earth re-form and rise up into the shape of the great gray dog he had loved, but there was nothing there. Never again would she come bounding toward him on her narrow purple feet.

He tipped back his head and turned his face up to the sky.

"You can't steal from me," he said, quietly. "No one steals from me and gets away with it. Not even Death."

And then he crouched over the scorched earth and began to gather up the ashes.

Don't miss the next book in
The Book of Storms trilogy

THE COLOR OF DARKNESS

Coming soon...